I0662248

Copyrighted Material

The Shadows of Blackbriar Academy copyright © 2019 by Olivia Ash.
Covert art commissioned and owned by Wispvine Publishing
LLC.
Book design and layout copyright © 2019 by Wispvine Publishing
LLC.

www.wispvine.com

978-1-939997-91-3

1st Edition

Wars of the Underworld

Sentinel Saga

By Dahlia Leigh and Olivia Ash

The Shadow Shifter

STAY CONNECTED

Join the exclusive group where all the cool kids hang out… Olivia's secret club for cool ladies! Consider this your formal invitation to a world of hot guys, fun people, and your fellow book lovers. Olivia hangs out in this group all the time. She made the group specifically for readers like you to come together and share their lives and interests, especially regarding the hot guys from her novels.

Check it out! Everyone in there is amazing, and you'll fit right in.

https://www.facebook.com/groups/LilaJeanOliviaAsh/

Sign up for email alerts of new releases AND an exclusive bonus novella from the Nighthelm Guardian series, *City of the Rebel Runes*, the prequel to *City of Sleeping Gods* only available to subscribers.

https://wispvine.com/newsletter/olivia-ash-email-signup/

Enjoying the series? Awesome! Help others discover Blackbriar Academy by leaving a review at Amazon.

THE SHADOWS OF BLACKBRIAR ACADEMY

BOOK TWO OF THE BLACKBRIAR ACADEMY SERIES

OLIVIA ASH

I made it through the trials, but now the real test begins.

Year One classes have begun in the enchanted halls of Blackbriar Academy, and they're more challenging than anything I've ever faced in my life. Surviving the Academy means brutal training, advanced magic, and a bloodthirsty student who is developing a dangerous hunger for my power.

Worst of all, it's clear someone knows my secret. And they have my father locked away.

Deep in the rubble of an ancient ruin, we find evidence of a ritual. One we don't fully understand, but one which most definitely involves me in some way. And as time runs out, we have to find out who's behind this before they kill everyone I love.

The traps are set. The clock is ticking. And I absolutely must save my father before he's slaughtered.

God help whoever dares hurt him. I'm not the weak, naive little girl I was when I came to Blackbriar.

My magic has never been stronger, and I've never had more control. I don't care if I risk going dark— I'll do whatever it takes to save the only family I have left.

Or die trying.

CONTENTS

CHAPTER ONE

S weat drips down my brow, despite the early
morning's chill.

The sunlight barely creeps over the ocean's horizon, filtering through the trees on the island as I stand
across from Soren in a fighting stance. Drawing on my
magic, I feel the hot flowing energy pool in my hands,
forming a bright white ball of power that crackles
with blue and purple light. I let out a deep breath
through my pursed lips. Soren prepares to launch an
attack, and I'm already shifting my magic, forming a
shield to block the blast he will certainly send at me.

Today, I'm going to show him that I'm ready, and I
can take care of myself. I have to. If I want to save my
father.

He releases his magic, filling our private training

area with bright blue light.

I lean into my shield as the blast rockets into me. The impact feels like a punch to the gut. I grunt, but I manage to hold my ground. My feet slide along the soft dirt a few inches, but I manage not to lose my balance.

"Good, now—"

He doesn't finish because I'm already sending a ball of white light toward him. He expertly blocks the attack with his own magical shield.

"That was a good one," he says.

I smile. "Thanks."

It's an intense training session before my first official class as a first-year student, and my nerves are all over the place. It's exciting. I'm anxious to absorb every morsel of knowledge I can. The idea keeps me a little distracted, but so far, I haven't nearly taken off Soren's head.

Yet.

We've been training as often as we could to help me control my powers. Always coming to our little secluded spot in the restricted section of the woods near the coast, giving a great view of the ever-brightening sky and ocean below.

I've learned so much about my magic and myself in such a short amount of time. My progress has been phenomenal. I'm stronger than I ever thought I could be. And as I dip low and dodge another attack from Soren, I can't deny how *powerful* I feel. I'm physically stronger too. I'm no longer sore after each training session, and my muscles are gaining definition along my arms, legs, and torso. My stamina has increased as well, since it seems to take even longer for me to get winded or tired. I can use fire and light to attack, sometimes even lightning.

The incident with Professor Lawrence made Soren up his game during our training sessions. Which, in turn, is pushing me to up my own game. I tap into my magic, reaching into its deepest recesses to access most of my power and strength.

Arms straining against the latest blow, I grunt against the force and peek around my shield. I hurl a beam of light at him. It soars toward him. Naturally, again, he manages to avoid getting hit. Not that I'm *trying* to hit him, but it would be nice to best him just once.

"Not bad." He shifts and sends a blast of fire toward me.

Thinking of the incident with Professor Lawrence raises my anxiety. My heart flutters in my chest as goosebumps crop up along my arms, and a chill trickles down my spine as my breaths hitch. His last words to me were my father was as good as dead. Soren's contact had mentioned a location where my father was last seen. As far as we know, he's still alive.

But there is a chance he isn't. With that possibility, I falter. The blast hits my shield, knocking me back. My feet slip on the dirt, and the world spins into a blur of colors. I end up on my back, crashing to the ground in a painful thud. My head slams against the ground, filling my vision with bursts of color. Dirt clouds puff up around me and the dusty taste of earth fills my mouth.

"Damn it, Wren!" Soren shouts as he rushes to my side and helps me into a sitting position. "What the hell happened?"

His voice is commanding and full of anger. Almost like he's pissed off at *me* for messing up.

The asshole.

"I was distracted," I snap back, rubbing the back of my head.

He huffs and checks the back of my head, being gentle with the pressure of his fingertips as he touches the area that hit the ground and then moves his eyes over my arms, lifting them and examining every inch of me for injuries. The worry in his eyes softens the anger in me.

I sigh. "I'm sorry."

He looks at me, and his amber eyes search mine for something I can only guess at. "Don't be. I was pushing you pretty hard."

His tone is soft, genuine, and the anger that was there only a moment ago seems to have dissolved.

He helps me to my feet, quickly hoisting me from the ground. Once I'm standing firmly, and the dizziness from the motion has passed, I dust off the back of my pants.

"What's distracting you today?" he asks.

I shrug. "Let's continue."

He shakes his head and returns to his spot. We reclaim our stances. "Are you going to tell me?"

I form my shield and wait for his attack. When none comes, I send out a blast of fire toward him.

He blocks it. Of course.

"I was thinking about the progress I made," I say as he sends a smaller ball of fire at me. Leaning into my stance, ducking behind my shield, I thrust forward with it, knocking away the flaming attack with ease.

"And?"

"And if you take it easy on me, I'm going to get angry."

He smiles. "Suit yourself." A harder blast of fire hits my shield, causing me to skid backward.

Now that's more like it.

I attack with a ball of white light. "About Professor Lawrence, and my father, and my classes."

His shield absorbs the hit, and he stands straighter. "Wren, after this weekend, you won't have to worry about him anymore."

I nod and bite the corner of my lower lip. "I want to go. I need to."

He pinches the bridge of his nose. "We've been through this."

"We have, but it's not fair." I stand tall, straightening my back, ready to take on this argument. And win.

"It's best if Gideon and I go alone."

"And risk your lives for my father?"

He stares out over the ocean. The sun has fully risen now, and the warmth rushes through with the breeze, pushing away the chill from earlier.

"Is that any different than you risking your life?"

"Yes. He's *my* father. He's in this mess because of me." I walk toward him, keeping a safe distance in case he decides to attack.

"You don't know that, Wren. Not for sure."

I shrug. "Well that's the only theory we have."

"Gideon and I have been in worse situations before. Believe me. We will get through this one just fine."

I shake my head. "We are a team, Soren. I can help, and you know it. I get that I'm not as experienced as you and Gideon. But I've proved my worth during the fight with Professor Lawrence. So did Milo and Jesse. We are stronger together. Besides, I want to see my father safe."

"That fight wasn't something you chose to do. It was forced on you. On all of us. If there was another way, I would have made sure you didn't have to be involved."

"And as valiant as that notion would be, I still don't like the idea of you two getting hurt on a mission on my behalf."

Soren shakes his head.

"Look, you've said it yourself. I've improved. I'm stronger than I was then. I'll be safe because I have you, Gideon, Milo, and Jesse to help keep me safe. No harm will come to me while I'm with all of you. And as sweet as it is that you don't want to see me get hurt, I know I can do this. We will make it through. Together."

"You're not going to give up, are you?"

I shake my head. "I just want to reach a compromise."

"You want a compromise?" He steps closer, never wavering from the hold his gaze has on me.

I nod. My breaths quicken, and my knees go a little weak as he approaches and stands in front of me. He tucks a strand of hair behind my ear and runs his fingers down my neck and arm, sliding both behind my back and pulling me close.

"The first sign of trouble, you have to get back here. No ifs, ands, or buts. No fighting. No arguing. Fair enough?"

Breathless, I nod. But I don't plan for anything to happen that would force me back here without them. We'll cross that bridge if and when we get there. For now, I count this as a win. "Thank you."

He smiles softly. In the private way that he shares only with me. I smile back and he kisses me. It's quick. Over just as soon as it started. He backs away and takes a stance. I quickly lower into mine. As soon as I put my shield up, a beam of light hits me, pushing me back. I strain against the force of it. When my shield fully dissolves the magic, I retaliate.

"What about your classes has you distracted?" He blocks my attack.

"I spent the last six years of my life with forest trolls. They don't exactly have classrooms."

He nods and closes the space between us. "Spar."

I nod. And prepare. He throws a punch aimed for my torso. I spin out of the way, grab his left wrist and forearm with both of mine, bending his arm back behind him. I kick the back of his knees, sending him to the ground with a grunt. He flips me over his back, the world spinning in my view again, and I land a lot gentler on the ground than earlier. He tries to lock me in an arm bar, but I roll out of the way.

"You're going to love the classes. They are hands-on a lot of the time. Not much book work, but you will have to study hard. Each term will have finals, and you will have to demonstrate your knowledge to pass."

I tackle him, wrapping my arms around his waist and as soon as his back hits the ground, I twist my body and straddle him. He bucks. I fall forward, just above his head. I roll and lift up on my feet, spinning to face him as a fist launches toward my face.

Twisting out of the way, I hook my arm over his, pulling it tight to my body and land a knee to his gut. As he leans forward, he grabs my thigh and pulls up.

For a breathless moment, I'm weightless. Then I start to fall toward the ground.

But Soren is *fast*.

He breaks my descent, pulling my bent leg to his side as he slides his arm free and wraps it around me. Our foreheads rest together, our breaths mixing together as we pant.

"Not bad," he says with a hint of a chuckle. "You should have seen your face."

I roll my eyes and playfully smack him on his shoulder as he holds me to him. "Yeah well, the ground isn't exactly forgiving."

"True." He sets me down but doesn't release me. Instead, we stand there for a few blissful moments.

This is the softer side of Soren that I absolutely love.

He brushes my cheek with the backs of his fingers as he stares into my eyes. Being near Soren makes my magic burn. But with his soft touches, and the way his amber eyes take in mine, my magic flows hotter through my veins, burning me from the inside out in a delicious, pleasant sensation.

The sheer level of bonding that has happened between us in such a short amount of time still amazes me.

He used to be leery of me, because of my power and some painful event in his past. He still hasn't told me the details of that.

A pinch forms in the center of my forehead.

"What's wrong?" he asks.

I pull away slightly and wring my fingers together. If we are going to rely on each other, we need to start being open—with both the good and the bad. "I've told you about my past with the trolls, how hard it was, and I just want to support you the same way you've supported me. I can tell whatever happened still affects you."

"And you think now is the time to talk about it?" His expression carries a touch of pain.

I shrug. "It was just a thought."

"I don't like talking about it." He turns away from me and looks out over the ocean.

I rest a hand on his arm. When he turns his sexy amber eyes on me, I say, "I know it's painful. But I want to help you through it. It will help me to better understand a part of your past, as well as the changes between us."

His eyebrows stitch themselves together. "You really think it's going to help?"

I nod. "I think so."

He sighs. "You're probably right."

"Of course, I am." I smile.

"I suppose you are going to find out eventually." He runs his hands through his hair. I can tell he's mentally preparing himself for the emotional blood-letting.

"True. Best to treat this like a band-aid and just rip it off."

He nods. "We better take a seat."

CHAPTER TWO

W e sit on the edge of the cliff overlooking the ocean as the sun rises above the trees. Soren has a knee propped up with an arm draped over it, and for a while, he is silent. I watch birds dive and swerve over the water while mermaids poke their heads above the surface, their shimmering, beady eyes staring curiously back at us. They remain at a distance. Thankfully.

I'm a bit leery of them since my interaction with them during my fourth trial.

"There was this girl Gideon and I grew up with," Soren begins. "We were close. Even loved her. Her name was Nadia. She was the youngest of the three of us."

I turn my attention to him. His amber eyes are

focused on a single point in front of him, somewhere in the ocean, but they are distant. Almost like he is reliving the memory as he speaks.

"For the most part, we were inseparable."

"What happened?" I ask.

"I came here. We lost touch, weren't as close as we used to be. Gideon was off doing his own thing, becoming the headmaster of the school. He was older than Nadia and me. And he attended here at a younger age than most."

"Ah, that explains things a bit more."

He nods. "Nadia didn't want to come to the academy, even though I desperately wanted her to. She didn't have a lot of formal training. Her parents weren't very wealthy. They were well-off, but not enough to afford the education she needed. They instead hired my family to tutor her once a week."

He swallows hard as he digs into his story, reliving the pain as his eyes start to gloss over with tears. I reach over, grab his hand, and give it a loving squeeze.

"I went home on break and wanted to visit her. But when I saw her, something was off about her. Different. Almost like she wasn't the fun, spunky tomboy I knew and loved. I tried to reach out to her, but that's when I saw the signs of her uncontrolled power. It was like being near her sucked the life out of me. I hated that feeling. Hated the change between us. We had always thought it was going to be us versus the world."

I lean against him, wrapping my arm around his, hoping he would take the gesture as me letting him know he was safe. He flexes his bicep as he takes my hand into his.

"Things got worse with her each time I came back home. Until she killed her family."

I gasped. "What? How?"

He shrugged. "No one really knows. Just that she lost control of herself."

"That's horrible. You know she killed her family for sure?"

"Yes. And that's not the worst of it," he says, shifting his pain-filled eyes to me.

What could be worse than killing your own family? I purse my eyebrows and shake my head.

"At the time, my family believed there was a gas leak in her house. One spark, and it set the house aflame. But I knew there was more behind it. But, like me, my family loved her. They loved her so blindly that they didn't see the things I did. I tried to warn them, but they insisted she come and live with them." He shakes his head, hands formed into fists. "They wouldn't listen to me."

He goes silent for a while. I can tell he's warring

with himself, reliving the painful past that initially put a wedge between us. I wonder if he will tell me more. Or is it too painful? I open my mouth to tell him that we can stop, but I can't force the words from my mouth. I want to reassure him, but don't know how. I'm stuck in a place of loss with him. All I want to do is hold him close. Make it all go away.

"They said I was just paranoid. Kept saying nothing would happen. She just lost her family and we were the only ones she had left. Thought it would make me happy."

"But it didn't?"

He shakes his head.

"Did you tell Gideon?" I ask.

"As soon as I got back. We planned to go back the following weekend just so he could see for himself. Even he had a hard time believing that our old friend was as dark as I saw her. But he was called in to work, and I had to go alone."

"What did you find out?" I ask, voice soft as a whisper.

"I was too late." His voice cracks. He sucks in a deep breath as he tries to fight back tears.

Tears sting my eyes as I feel the pain of his loss stab through me. His loss. I wrap my arms around him tightly as his body shakes from the memory.

"My family was gone. Half the block was gone. The news painted it as a gas line explosion. But I knew better. And as soon as I saw her, I knew beyond a doubt she had gone dark and became a shadow mage."

"My God, Soren. I'm so sorry. What did you do?"

"I killed her."

That was it. It was flat, blunt, and emotionless. A stone-cold fact.

"Oh, Soren. I'm so very sorry. I had no idea."

"How could you?" He stares at me with his pained expression.

I finally realize why he had a problem with me and my powers when we first met. "I promise things are different with me."

He cups my cheek. "I know they are." His voice is soft, tender.

Clearing his throat, he looks away. "We need to practice honing your magic."

I want to comfort him, but I also know when to leave things alone and let him process his feelings. He told me his story. Now that I know, he can heal from it again.

He stands and returns to our training circle. Magic pulses in his hands and he creates small targets of purple light that hover in the air. I feel my own magic coursing through my body, ready for me to call on it.

He nods toward the target. "Try to use one finger and shoot through the center."

"Okay." I point a finger and take a calming breath as warm pressure builds in my wrist, thrumming with my heartbeat. Focusing on the center of the target, I shoot out a stream of white light, obliterating the target.

"Not bad." Soren steps forward and draws a new one. "Try again. But this time, really focus. Control it."

I do. My shot hits dead center.

We repeat the process using smaller targets each time. Some I obliterate, others I don't. Before long, Soren dissolves the targets and faces me with a devious smile. "Time to get ready for school, little girl."

"Don't make me hurt you." I narrow my eyes on him, even though I can't help the smile tugging on my lips.

He chuckles and shakes his head. "Never gonna happen." He gestures toward the path leading out of our little area.

As we walk, we enjoy a peaceful, comforting quiet. We hold hands until we get to the stone path that leads up toward the castle. A figure leans against the stone wall at the base of the stairs. Within moments, I know who it is.

Jesse.

He turns his attention to us. "So this is where you run off to in the mornings."

Soren growls.

I cross my arms. "Sneaking around, are we?"

He shrugs. "I might be."

Soren steps forward. "Apparently, you have nothing better to do than spy on people. That can change really quick."

If Jesse was fazed by that not-so-subtle threat, he doesn't show it. "Just curious on what our girl here can do."

He's feeding Soren's anger. I really don't want to see the mess Jesse makes, so I step in. "You really shouldn't sneak around like that. Those woods are forbidden without special permission. Come on Jesse, I don't want to see you hurt."

He covers his heart with a hand and smiles in the way that makes my toes curl. "I'm touched by your concern."

"What she means is, stay away. That is for her *training*. You'll only get in the way, and I won't be held responsible for any injuries you acquire breaking the rules."

Jesse winks at Soren. "I never had you pegged for a guy to worry about my bodily harm. I really am beautiful, thank you for noticing. Though a few scars would be neat." He bobs his eyebrows and I have to force back a chuckle.

Soren steps forward, fire igniting over his hands and crawling up his arms. "That can be arranged."

"Oh. Promise?"

I clearly need to set some guidelines for these men. Though I know better than to believe that any set of guidelines will ever prevent Jesse from breaking them. He sees rules as challenges to overcome, and he makes it a personal goal to bend every single one with loopholes and clever wit. Still, I need to stop this little interaction from getting further out of hand.

"All right now, look. As much as I would love to see you two wrestle it out right here, I am going to be late. I still need a shower before class. So, can we just wave the white flag of surrender for now?"

Jesse shrugs. Soren huffs out a sigh and shakes out his hands. The fire dissipates.

"Thank you." I start climbing the stairs. Jesse and Soren follow closely behind.

"You know, I could walk Wren to her room."

"No," Soren says.

"Seriously, I didn't get the chance to check it out yet."

I look over my shoulder. It's true. Not since I got it all set up anyway.

"No."

"Come on! Pretty please with a cherry on top?"

"You're not going to leave this alone, are you?" Soren's voice is deep and sharp.

"You know me so well," Jesse says.

Soren sighs. "Fine. I have another stop I need to make anyway."

I turn and face him. He pulls me in and lays a deep kiss on me. "See you later."

"Uh-huh." I'm breathless, and my head feels like it's covered in fog.

He steps around me and walks off. I stare at Jesse as the fog clears. He smiles. "Bout time I got a turn to play, don't you think?"

I shake my head. "Pushing your luck with him, don't you think?"

He waves the thought off. "Nah, I just like to get a small rise out of him."

I quirk an eyebrow. "You're such a dork."

He chuckles. "I prefer the term *joker*. But, perhaps, I can be a dork, just for you though. Gotta protect my reputation. Care for a demonstration?" He steps closer and brushes the backs of his fingers along my cheek. He sniffs. "You stink."

I laugh and try to playfully smack his arm, but he

rushes out of my reach. "I already told you I need a shower."

"Fair enough. Shall we?" He gestures toward the main gate of the castle.

I turn and continue toward my room. As I move, I catch a glimpse of Anderson, watching from the side of the castle, hidden in shadows. He knows I see him. He smirks at me, just before disappearing from my view. I let out a deep breath. At least he didn't see me train. That would be problematic. Though one thing is for certain, he is turning out to be more trouble for me. Hopefully, I can make it through the year without too much nonsense from him. Otherwise, I will have to hurt him. Of course, I would rather avoid conflict at Blackbriar, but if I get backed into a corner... powers that be, help him.

But the more I see him, the more I realize that thought may just be wishful thinking.

"Come on slow poke," Jesse calls from over his shoulder. "Thought you were in a hurry?"

"Yeah, yeah, yeah." I step after him.

CHAPTER THREE

M y first official class is Introduction to Magical Runes.

The room is in a traditional setting, with a dozen tables sitting four to one, and they line the grey stone floor of the room, all filled with students idly chatting about their schedules. The cream toned walls are a stark contrast to the dark cherry finish of the tables. Windows line the back wall, and paintings of various magical creatures litter the spaces between the panes. The professor's desk displays an intricate design and reminds me of ivies growing up the trees back in the troll village. But this one is more beautiful. The dark stained wood reflects the light shining through the windows. A box sits on the top of the desk. The whiteboard that covers the wall on the other side of the desk is pristine, giving it a brand-new, shiny look.

Jesse, Milo, Savannah, and I all sit next to each other as we wait for the professor to arrive. The class is full of students chatting. Every single face holds an air of a lifetime of knowledge. More knowledge than I was given. Things passed down from generation to generation. Family secrets. I only see one other person who looks like a deer caught in headlights, and he's a thin, short little guy. He huddles in the corner of the room. I don't know his name, and I'm not sure I ever will. But one thing is for certain, I'm nervous about this first class and really want to put my best foot forward. However, Jesse won't stop making jokes. I have a feeling we're going to be separated if he doesn't learn to focus.

"The smell was just awful. I thought girls were supposed to smell like flowers."

I smack him on the arm. "Girls sweat too, you know."

"Yeah, well, I'm just glad you showered. Because the smell was worse than a men's locker room. I feel sorry for everyone who smelled you on the way in."

I have a mind to demonstrate a few moves I learned earlier today with Soren.

"Men can be immature," Savannah says, shaking her head. "No offense, Milo. You're pretty mature."

He grins. "No offense taken. I tend to agree with the sentiment."

He and I share a glance, and I smile. He smiles back, shoving his glasses up the bridge of his nose as he leans back in his seat.

A flash of golden light enters the room, and when it fades, a beautiful woman stands at the head of the room, looking over all of us. She's tall with skin that glows with a soft silver aura, almond-shaped brilliant green eyes, and pointed ears decorated in golden leaves and ivy. Her white hair is pulled back from her face and fastened with strips of gold. She's dressed in a white, loose-fitting gown with golden lace down her arms and a golden belt.

Whoa.

Savannah leans in close. "She's a woodland elf, a fae race. Isn't she beautiful?"

I can't seem to take my eyes off her, a real fae standing just feet away from me. "Very."

"My name is Lady Nimue. You may call me Lady or Lady Nimue. Never Nimue. And certainly, don't call me professor." Her voice, despite its sharpness, carries a melodic edge with a touch of enchantment in it. The hairs on my arms raise in response to the latent magical energy in her voice.

"Good morning, Lady Nimue," everyone in the class says.

She nods regally. "I will be teaching you the basics of runes, an earth magic."

Jesse leans back in his seat. "Teach me how to plant herbs for smoking so we can all mellow out. That's the earth magic *I* want to learn."

I stare wide-eyed at him as the room erupts in a cacophony of laughter.

He winks at me.

Oh. He's just joking.

Lady Nimue sets her glowing green eyes on Jesse. "Perhaps Mr. Taylor would like to demonstrate his knowledge of runes to the class?" She makes a sweeping gesture with her hand.

"If I had anything to demonstrate, Lady, I wouldn't need this class."

"How unfortunate. I thought with your wit and apparent intelligence, that you would be able to show us what you could do. Since that is clearly not the case, perhaps you should pay attention."

Both Milo and I shake our heads.

"Making friends everywhere you go," I whisper.

"It's my magnetic charm. No one can resist me." He gives me a smoldering look.

I giggle. "You're impossible."

He shrugs. "I'm not hearing any complaints."

"Let's get started," Lady Nimue says.

With a wave of her hand, several stacks of books piled in a corner of the room lift and hover, setting down in front of everyone. "You will not lose these books. Do not mark in them or deface them in any way, or it will result in a deficit in your scores."

The box that rests on the desk in front of her opens with another wave of her hand. Small black pouches rise from the box and drift toward us, setting themselves down in front of each student. "In addition, you are each given a set of runes. These are yours to keep. Don't lose them, as they are required for every assignment in this class and will be a necessity during your studies in the future."

A notebook bound in soft, light brown leather materializes out of thin air in front of us. "Use these notebooks to keep track of important concepts in this class as well as your experiments. Your assignments will also be done in your notebooks, which will be turned in at the end of each class."

I flip through the first few pages of the book and

browse the detailed illustrations of various runes and their descriptions. It's not very thick, but the information in it seems complex. Two runes that look similar in shape and design could actually mean completely different things, and a slight change to one could ruin a spell.

"Can anyone tell me what runes can be used for?" Lady Nimue asks.

Savannah raises her hand.

The lady nods at her. "Miss Fey."

"Runes are used for many different things depending on the skill of the mage, the intention of the spell, and ingredients needed."

"Very good, Miss Fey." Lady moves through the room as though she glides on air. It's mesmerizing to watch. I wonder if all fae races are so elegant and enchanting.

"Thank you, Lady Nimue."

Savannah and I share a look. I give her a thumbs up. She smiles.

"Runes can be as powerful as a hurricane…" she moves over to the white board and draws a rune that looks like a slanted, lowercase "N" and rests her hand over the symbol. A soft, silvery blue light glows from under her hand as she imbues it with magic. Wind fills the classroom, loud and roaring. Rain mixes in with it, and though I can feel the water pelt down and hit my skin, I don't get wet. Murmurs rise from the rest of the students in the room, mixing in with the foray of thunder and lightning strikes in the dark clouds that formed beneath the ceiling.

Within seconds, the storm ends.

"Or as gentle as a soft spring breeze..." She draws a symbol that is a cross between an "H" and a capital "N," placing it to the right of the first one and imbuing it with magic again. A warm breeze gently floats through the room.

She faces the room again. "Runes are also handy in enhancing traps, location or map spells, enhancing protection items, growth of plants, divination, and so on. The uses are great and varied. However, for the purpose of this class, we will only cover the most basic uses."

She takes a moment to meet the eyes of each student in the room. "Take out your runes. Familiarize yourselves with them."

Savannah lays her runes out in front of her in neat rows. As she flips some over to reveal their symbol, I dump mine out in front of me and organize mine in rows as well. There are twenty-four of them. But one of mine doesn't have a symbol on it. I raise my hand.

"Yes, Miss Blackwood."

This is the third time she's called a student by

name. I figured she had met Savannah and Jesse before. But I know this is my first time meeting her. Yet, she knows me. That is either really good or really bad. Either way, I'm pleasantly surprised.

"One of mine is blank."

"As it should be. All of you have one that holds no symbol. It is the symbol for eternity. Time out of time."

I nod. Well, all right then.

I look over at Milo as he takes each rune, one-by-one, and sketches them in his book. He's focused on every minute detail as he scribbles away.

Jesse leaves his scattered along the surface in front of him, leaning back in his chair with his arm draped over the back of my seat. I shake my head and return my focus to the runes in front of me. Each seems basic in design. Boxy, with straight lines and no curves.

Savannah stares at her runes. "These are said to be the language of the gods. When used properly, they can speak to you."

"Interesting," I say, fingering one that looks like an arrow.

"There are a lot of healing spells that use runes too," Savannah adds.

"Really?" That explains her devotion to the runes. "Do you know any of the runes already?"

"I know all of them." She breaks into a proud smile.

I nod, impressed. "That's a cool advantage to have. Maybe you can help me study them later?"

She leans in close and playfully nudges me with her elbow. "Of course!"

Jesse sits forward and yawns. "This is boring. I want to get to the real stuff."

"Maybe if you familiarized yourself with the runes, you wouldn't be so bored." I nod toward his runes.

Milo snorts as he scribbles furiously in his notebook, moving on to the descriptions from the book.

"I need to be entertained," Jesse says. "Engaged. So far, this class is far from those two requirements."

"Language of the gods," I mutter.

He sits forward. "Really?"

I point to Savannah who nods in my periphery.

"Why didn't Lady Nimue start with that? That's much more exciting."

I shake my head as I spin another rune in my hand, this one looking like a sideways hourglass. As I move to set it on the table, a bright blue and purple electric bolt of light shoots into my finger from the rune. The sharp sensation makes me jump.

"Are you okay?" Savannah asks.

I nod.

Lady Nimue's gaze turns toward us. "Be mindful of

your thoughts when working with your runes. They are very powerful. Almost like conduits. Intention is everything. Too much intent may result in unexpected outcomes."

I really wasn't thinking of anything, to be honest. I was just focused on wondering what the meaning was. That's all. Looking at the page for the rune in the book, the description I find is cryptic at best. It symbolizes a sword. Nothing referring to electricity or lightning.

"And here," Jesse says, elbowing me, "I thought I was the one with the shocking personality."

I chuckle. "You wish."

I thumb my way through a few more pages, trying to figure out how or why a rune would react to me like that. If I'm going to control my magic and prove myself, I'm going to need a lot more than mere personality.

CHAPTER FOUR

After a short time, Lady Nimue gathers our attention. "Now it is time to demonstrate your understanding of runes by performing a small experiment. Everyone is allowed to pick their partners."

"I pick you," Savannah says to me.

"What if I say you can't have her?" Jesse asks.

"Your loss for not acting quick enough."

I chuckle. "Good one."

"I know, right?" She grins at me.

"Very well, I'll share her," Jesse says, feigning disappointment. "Just this once."

"You're insufferable," I say.

He winks. "Milo and I could use some bonding."

"If you insist, however I would rather not get touchy feely," Milo retorts.

"I'm wounded. Deeply." Jesse mimes a knife in his chest. "Touchy feely is my forte."

"You'll live."

I try my best to stifle a giggle. Milo has some spunk. I like it.

We share a look. A proud smile stretches Milo's lips. Even being smug suits him. Everything looks amazing on him. It's impossible for him not to be hot as hell. My magic reacts to both him and Jesse, but it almost feels like it's responding more to him. They both flow through me, but his is more like rapids and currents whereas Jesse's is cool, free flowing, and almost icy at times.

"For this experiment," Lady Nimue continues, "You'll be combining runes to create an enchanted item. There are a variety of items you may chose from here." She gestures to a shelf next to the door.

"Please make sure your intentions are clear and you control the amount of energy you infuse into your enchantment, or you may get more than just a tiny zap, like Miss Blackwood."

I lift my gaze to Lady Nimue. She nods once.

Oh good. I'm an example.

Fun.

"So, what do you want to do?" Savannah asks.

I shrug. "I'm open to ideas. I'm completely new to runes."

"Really?" She seems genuinely surprised.

"Well, if I had learned anything about them, it was too long ago to really remember." Being a captive of trolls left little room for leisurely rune studies. In fact, little room for leisurely anything.

"Huh."

"So, do you have any ideas?" I ask with a smile.

"Let's go pick something out." She stands and approaches the bookshelf.

I join her, hoping she'll pick something that won't end up zapping me again.

A handful of crystals of various colors line one shelf. Another shelf has stones, twigs, and leaves stored on it. The third shelf holds various colors of string.

"We could enchant a crystal and make it glow," Savannah suggests. "Or, we could use a twig with some string and see if we can't get it to grow. The leaves are different. We could use them and a stone and make it a boat that will float in water or something..."

"All of them sound like really good ideas. I think we should try something with the twigs."

Honestly, I have no idea what to do, but I'm

anxious to get started, and though the glowing crystal sounded neat, I wanted to try something a little more intricate.

"I like your thinking." She grabs a couple twigs, green string, and heads back to our seats.

The first rune associated with growth is one that looks like two sideways "V's" facing and opening toward each other, with their top lines running parallel to each other. The other rune is one that looks like a "B." We place the runes on the twigs and wrap the green strings around them until it's a tight bundle.

Once we finish, Lady Nimue approaches us. "Let's see how your creation works."

Both Savannah and I nod to each other and lay a hand on the twigs. Our goal is to just make it come to life and grow a little.

Warmth enters my hand and radiates outward. I look to Savannah. Her focus is entirely on the twigs. Her face wears a smooth mask of calm.

White light glows beneath our hands, shining on the twigs that begin vibrating under our hands. They stretch out, turning green, and buds of dark green leaves grow in various intervals along their lengths. We remove our hands as the twigs take on a mind of their own, swelling until they conjoin to form a wide trunk of large oak. Roots curl and curve along the table, hanging over the edge, reaching for the ground.

Pretty damn cool if I do say so myself.

Everyone at my table stands up and moves back as we crane our heads toward the top of the tree that continues stretching up toward the ceiling. Large branches split off in every direction, sprouting leaves as the table creaks and groans under the weight of a nearly full-grown tree.

"Oops…" I take in a deep breath. The look on Lady Nimue's face tells me this isn't as cool as I thought.

Murmurs and chaotic chatter take over the silence in the room as the tree finally comes to a halt. Well, at least its little growth spurt is done.

I gawk at the giant tree taking residence in the room. Savannah shifts, and I look to her. We exchange wide-eyed glances. The Lady walks around the tree, her face a picture of utter shock as she states, "This… this is…" She shakes her head. "What was the intention?"

"Just to make it grow a little," I say.

"Yeah," Savannah agrees. "Nowhere *near* this much."

"How many runes did you use?" Lady Nimue asks, weaving her fingers together in front of her.

Savannah clears her throat. "Two—*Jera* and *Berkana*."

Lady Nimue's astonished expression switches between us and the oak. "Your intention was to make it grow only a little?"

I nod. "Just like an inch or two, with maybe a couple of leaves."

"You must have put too much energy into the growth. Also, next time, pulse your magic into the enchantment, and when you start to see an effect, remove your hands."

I nod.

Our attention is pulled away by tapping coming from the other side of the classroom door. Lady Nimue waves her hand. The door opens, and a large black and maroon megaphone floats into the room, hovering in the air. The charm of enchanted items usually intrigues me but looking at the massive tree sitting in the middle of the class, my excitement is dampened.

The megaphone bobs in the air as the message is given. "Wren Blackwood is expected in Headmaster Storm's office immediately."

With its job done, it floats back out of the room. The door closes behind it.

Great. Now I'm in trouble.

The babbling of students doesn't help matters either. My nerves turn erratic as a cold lump of weight settles in my stomach. I wonder if I just did the unthinkable.

I nervously look to Milo and Jesse. Milo shrugs as Jesse smiles and mouths the word "troublemaker" to me.

I roll my eyes.

Savannah pulls my attention to her with a hand around my arm. "Go, I'll take care of this."

My shoulders slump. "Thanks."

I stand and make my way to the door. Before I walk through, I turn and face Lady Nimue. "I'm sorry."

"All is well, Miss Blackwood." She gives me a soft smile. "We are all still learning."

And with that, I head to Gideon's office.

CHAPTER FIVE

A s soon as I turn down the hall that leads to Gideon's office, I see the large portrait change. The images that hide Gideon's office never cease to amaze me. They are different each time I visit and seem to correlate with a season or event happening at the academy. The current image is a school-like setting.

Students dressed in all black are gathered in a straight line, standing shoulder to shoulder, with their hands outstretched toward something I can't see. The room they're standing in reminds me of the arena here at Blackbriar. Their hands glow at the instruction of the professor pacing the line behind them, and all at once, beams of colorful light leave their hands. The glow expands through the entire wall, swallowing all the shapes. The image stills and dissolves away, leaving behind a bright, colorful forest with leaves in shades of autumn. A light fog hovers over the ground, moving through the trees in an eerie motion. Shadows of unicorns move through the trees. One looks at me with glowing red eyes. Its black mane moves with a breeze that dances through the trees, sending the colorful leaves falling to the ground.

I gasp.

I know this place. It's an ancient long-lost forest called Blackbriar Forest. It was home to unicorns at one point. Very magical. I don't recall the entire legend, but from what I do remember, the forest was said to be the birthplace of all magic, and unicorns were said to be its great protectors.

It's also the academy's namesake.

The unicorn continues on its way through the trees until it fades away into the shadows.

As the image dissolves, the door to Gideon's office appears. I approach and tap on the door. Seconds later, the sound of chairs scraping against the hardwood floor seeps through to me. The handle turns, and Gideon appears in the doorway. He smiles warmly at me.

My cheeks burn as I smile back. The man has a

killer, make me weak in the knees smile. I think he flashes it just to get to me.

I love it.

"Miss Blackwood," he says, opening the door wider and gesturing for me to enter. "Please, come in."

As I enter, my eyes settle on a thin woman, standing tall with flowing silver hair that glitters in the sunlight filtering in from a nearby window.

"You have a visitor," Gideon says.

But this woman needs no introduction. Her lips stretch, never parting enough to reveal teeth and never wide enough to reach her eyes. But within her brown eyes is recognition.

"Aunt Patricia." I rush to her, nearly knocking her over as I wrap my arms around the woman I haven't seen since I was taken by the trolls. It's good to see her, after all this time.

"Hello, my dear." She grabs my shoulders and gently pushes me back, holding me at arm's length. She studies me for a moment. "You look well. I was so worried about you. Thank goodness you are here at Blackbriar."

Gideon adds, "I've taken the liberty of explaining to your aunt the progress you have shown here so far."

Gideon takes a seat at his desk. He's official, distant, acting as the headmaster that he is. He doesn't share any glances, despite my magic still reacting to being so close to him. I figure it's to keep up appearances. He has a way with making sure I know exactly how he feels about me when no one else is around, and for the time being, I'm okay with that.

"Your adjustment to being here has been quite impressive, I am told." Aunt Patricia smiles. "And so quickly, too."

I nod. "Thank you." My mind instantly races to the tree in the class I just left. "I have a long way to go though."

"You will get there, I am sure. Oh, and do not fret about tuition, it has already been handled." She gives Gideon a matter of fact nod and takes a seat in front of his desk.

"Thank you," I say with a grateful grin. I had been wondering about that aspect, especially after Soren shared how some mages didn't attend Blackbriar because of money.

Aunt Patricia shifts in her seat. "You are quite welcome. As soon as I learned you were here, I knew you would need the assistance."

"When did you arrive?" I take the other seat in front of Gideon's desk.

"Just before you were called here," Gideon responds.

"Thank you," I say. "For allowing me to miss out on the last few minutes of class to say hello."

He nods with a smirk. There's a glint in his eyes that makes heat rush down my neck. I force myself to look away from his gorgeous face.

"Despite it being her first day, she's showing significant promise to become a great and powerful mage." Gideon nods toward me. "I'm sure this will make the Blackwood family proud."

"Yes. Quite interesting, considering the circumstances of her birth," Patricia adds. She seems lost in thought. Her eyes cloud over with a memory that replays in her mind. She blinks it away.

Gideon adds, "It's not common for a half-mage to have such skill, that's true. But I have seen reports of it. She's a rare delight, indeed."

Right. Half-mages don't typically have powers. I do. Because of the meteorite I fused with when I was a little girl. "I'm just as surprised as everyone else. How long are you planning on staying?"

"Only a few days. Enough to catch up and spend some time with you."

I'm elated to have my aunt back. I almost don't catch the nearly imperceptive way her lips curl downward at the corners. Her brown eyes, like my father's, seem perceptive, catching onto more than what they let on. It makes me question why she isn't as excited as I am over our reunion, but then I remember that my aunt is a very proud woman. High class, and rich. She had been raised to have strict control over her emotions and reactions, and when I lived with her, she tried to instill the same in me. She seems rigid, but maybe she's just tired from the trip. She was half-way across the world not too long ago.

"I am looking forward to it." I smile.

"Your classes are going well so far then?" Aunt Patricia's tone softens, and I suppose that's her way of talking in a friendly manner. At least she's trying.

I nod. "I've only had the one so far, but yes. It's Introduction to Runes. Fascinating. What was your favorite class?"

"It's been so long that I can hardly remember." Patricia gently bats at the air.

"Yes, speaking of," Gideon says, "Wren has another class coming up. Since it is her first day, I would prefer her to miss as little as possible. I can escort you to your room and make arrangements for you and your niece to have time tonight. Maybe have a private meal."

"That would be lovely, Headmaster Storm," Aunt Patricia says. "However, I don't need an escort. I can find my way on my own. I do remember the halls quite well."

"I'm sure." Gideon rises from his seat. He reaches into a drawer and pulls out a key. "Here is the key to your room. Normally we wouldn't allow students in the faculty wing, but this is a special occasion, so I will allow Wren to visit you there for sake of privacy."

I nod. "I appreciate it."

Aunt Patricia and I stand from our seats as well. We follow him to the door. She moves with such grace that it's almost demeaning. I feel like a troll walking next to her. However, she seems oblivious to the difference in our gaits. Either that, or she doesn't outrightly draw attention to it.

Gideon opens the door and escorts us out. He steps out with us, and the door becomes hidden once more by a moving image of a wolf howling at a large full moon. It hangs in a midnight blue sky sprinkled with a dusting of glittering silver.

Gideon's voice draws me back into the present. "It was a pleasure meeting you, Miss Blackwood. If you need anything at all to make your stay here more comfortable, don't hesitate to ask."

She inclines her head in acknowledgement. "I am sure everything will be just fine. Wren, dear, I will see you this evening."

"Yes, I can't wait." I watch her turn and walk off.

Gideon faces me, pulling my attention to him. "My... *sources* told me about the mishap in your runes class."

I drop my gaze to the floor. Of course, he'd have a way of knowing when magic got out of hand in his school. Using a bent finger, he lifts my chin so that I meet his amazing blue-green eyes. "I'll have to share with you some of my more embarrassing mishaps when I was a student here." He chuckles.

"The great Gideon Storm made mistakes? Say it isn't so." I smile.

He smirks. "Oh yes. But that is, sometimes, one of the best ways to learn."

I nod. "Thank you again for letting me see her before class was out."

He shrugs. "You probably needed a way out of there anyway."

I laugh. "I really did."

After looking down the hall, which is now empty, he rests his hand on my upper arm, warming my skin with his touch. He levels his gaze on me, and I can already tell what he is about to say next is important.

"I'm glad you are happy about reconnecting with your aunt, but I would appreciate if you didn't tell Patricia about your father."

My eyebrows knit together. "Why? He's her brother. Wouldn't she have a right to know?"

"Yes, but it could put her in danger. And the less people who know about Michael, the better."

I narrow my eyes. "What aren't you telling me?"

"Nothing, yet." He slides his hand from my arm down my side and along my waist, and I nearly melt into a puddle. Every nerve is on high alert, and I'm quickly starting to imagine doing very naughty things with him. His green eyes take hold of mine and I almost become lost in his gaze. "Something else that's bothering me is that I can't get a good read on her. She's protecting herself with wards or enchanted rings."

"You read my aunt?" I try to quell the irritation in my voice, but it's hard to. She's my blood. My father's sister. Why would Gideon be suspicious of her?

He must've detected the unspoken question by looking at me. "Wren, all guests of Blackbriar know they are safe, and their privacy is respected when they step onto the island. If she's still warding herself, that's going to raise an eyebrow or two."

"Well she just came from the outside world, maybe she forgot to… turn it off."

He gives me a thoughtful look and nods. "She did arrive in a hurry to meet you. Perhaps I'm just being overly cautious. You'll have to forgive my need to protect you. We can tell her once we're certain it's safe to. Please. Do this as a favor to me." His eyes shift toward my mouth, and he steps a little closer.

I chuckle. "You're devious. You know that?"

He laughs under his breath. "I'll make it up to you. Promise."

"Oh, you had better. I'm gonna hold you to that promise too."

"I wouldn't have it any other way." He kisses my forehead. "Better get to class, Miss Blackwood. Tardiness is frowned upon in this establishment."

"Mm hmm." I pull away from him despite everything inside me screaming at me not to let go. Like he said, I have class.

I make my way down the hall, mind buzzing with thoughts of us wrapped in each other. Once I turn the corner, a bell chimes through the halls, signaling the end of the first class. I take a deep breath to clear my head.

That man is going to make me implode with lust someday.

CHAPTER SIX

Dressed in a conservative outfit consisting of a navy-blue pencil skirt and silver silk blouse, I head to my aunt's room for dinner. My hair is pulled into a tight bun, and my makeup is natural looking and makes my brown eyes stand out more. I tuck a lose strand of hair behind my ear as I take a deep breath, letting out slowly.

My nerves are a mess of excitement and anxiety. My heart is pounding so hard that it feels like it is about to flutter right out of my chest. I tug on my pencil skirt as I walk down the hallway leading to the faculty suites. I barely glance at the magical paintings dotting the walls or the scenery outside the windows as I nervously move toward the only family I have here. The heels of my black shoes clack against the stone floors as I move, echoing down the hall and likely announcing my arrival before I even make it to the door.

The faculty section of the castle is like an apartment building with old stone walls on the bottom half and deep burgundy paint on the upper half. Domed glass ceilings top the walls, allowing for the ambience of the setting sun to cast shadows along the wide hall and make the statues that stand guard ever so often, feel like they move.

The statues are probably moving to watch me. But I don't waste time on trying to figure the ins and outs of it all. I'm more concerned with making a good impression. I want my time with my aunt to go well, and after going so long without seeing her, except for the short time earlier today, I don't know what to expect.

I wipe my sweaty palms on my skirt and adjust my blouse. It's uncomfortable being so dressed up after years of wearing tattered rags. Savannah helped me with my hair and makeup, which made me realize how much I've missed out on. But she made it a fun, girly experience. We laughed and talked about cute guys at the school as she brushed on a bit of blush, and I made sure to stay still when she applied lipstick. I refused to plop on false lashes and settled for mascara, and beamed with pride when she told me I looked stunning. It feels good to have a friend to bond with like that.

I dressed like this at my aunt's request, per the note that was left on my bed when I got back from my last class. Though I prefer a t-shirt and jeans to even the school's uniform, I'm dealing. I figure making a few concessions, even if it's uncomfortable and doesn't fit who I am, probably wouldn't hurt. Especially if it will help my aunt reconnect with me. Besides my father, she's the only family I have. And that means something to me.

I finally make it to the door and tap my knuckles on the hard, mahogany wood. Moments later, the door opens, revealing an opulent sitting room with lavish furnishings and expensive, ivory satin curtains covering the windows that are open to allow the cool fall breeze through the room. A small fire pops in the fireplace from the far-left wall. Two doors stand on either side of the fire, and to my right is an open kitchen with a hall that ends at another door.

I walk toward the beige and white striped sofa, accompanied by a matching love seat and two ivory high-back chairs. I take a seat, sinking into the cushions. But I don't have to wait long before my aunt enters the room with a long black trumpet skirt, matching blouse, and red shawl draped over her shoulders.

"You have arrived on time." Aunt Patricia's eyes study my appearance. "I see you got my note."

"Yes. Is this okay?"

She softly sighs. "It will do. Come, let's sit at the table."

I stand from the couch and make my way to the ornate dining table. Its fabric-covered ivory seats shine like satin in the low candlelight that fills the area. It all looks very cozy and intimate, and I can't help but wonder if my aunt isn't trying too hard to keep up appearances. Like a show. I get that she's rich, but this feels a bit forced.

I take the seat directly across from her, and within moments place settings appear before us along with plates of delicious food. A roast with seasoned potatoes, carrots, onions, and celery are all situated in the center of the table. I breathe in deep all of the mouthwatering aromas.

"Tell me, now that your first day is behind you, what do you think of your courses so far?" Aunt Patricia spoons lumps of vegetables onto her plate followed by a chunk of roast.

I watch her move with grace and confidence. She's

such a conundrum. Figuring her out is a difficult task. "It's interesting and challenging."

"Are you enjoying yourself here?" she asks as I start to serve myself, picking up the extravagant silver serving spoon, lumping a few vegetables onto my own plate.

"Yes. Very much so." Good grief this conversation is stiff and uncomfortable. The statues in the hall have more personality and warmth than this.

"That is good."

I study my aunt for a moment. Her silver-white hair is pulled back into a fancy bun. Extravagant crystal earrings catch the light around her, creating prisms of reds and gold, yet her brown eyes are cold and her face is stern.

"I'm very happy for the opportunity to attend here. It's more than I ever hoped for."

"I'm sure it is, given your history and situation."

I narrow my eyes and clench my jaw. Sure, I'm a half-breed, and I spent years as a captive of trolls, but I managed to escape. Now I'm here, and I'm ready to become a full member of this community. Why can't she see that? I wonder if my past bothers her that much and if she is ashamed. I recall a few conversations with my aunt when I was in her care. One that sticks out the most is a formal list of expectations and rules that I was to abide by while living in her home. It looks like she hasn't changed.

I clear my throat and reach for my drink. "True."

"I'm sure you have questions about what happened?"

It came off like a question, but with the way she looked at me with a stone-like stare, I don't believe it was an invitation to start asking them. "A few."

"Ask away." She cuts a chunk of potato and pops it into her mouth in an elegant, smooth motion.

I feel so out of place right now. Everything about this woman is so posh and high class. After living with trolls for the past six years of my life, eating as delicately as my aunt is probably not going to happen. I'm probably going to dribble gravy down my blouse before the night is over.

I push that thought to the side and dig into my questions. "How long did you look for me before giving up?"

She sets her stone-like gaze on me as she finishes chewing. Once she swallows, she takes a sip of her wine. "I never really stopped looking for you, my dear."

"Never?" My heart skips a beat at that. From what I knew, which isn't much, no one searched for me. At least nowhere close to the troll village.

"No. I always hoped that if I did not find you first, that you would someday come looking for me. I always knew you were alive. I felt it deep down." Her brown eyes hold mine as she speaks. When she is finished, she spears a carrot and places it in her mouth.

"What do you remember from that night?"

She chews on the carrot for a moment. "I was curious about that very thing."

I wait for her to continue as she cuts into her meat, but as she pierces me with her eyes and very slightly raises her eyebrows, I realize she wants me to answer the question first.

"Oh. Um… not much, really. Just going to sleep in my bed and waking up in the troll village. I was dizzy, groggy, and I couldn't focus on much for a few hours after I woke up."

She frowns. "It sounds like you had a bit of a concussion. Trolls are vicious, but they are awfully stupid. No doubt that gave you an advantage. Things turned out well enough though, right?"

I shrug. "I guess so. I mean, now things are better. A lot better."

She taps a finger on her chin. "Let's see. What do I remember about that night? Ah, yes. Well, after we said our goodnights, I went to bed. Didn't hear a sound the whole night. When I woke up, I went to wake you up for breakfast. But you were gone."

"You really had no idea where I was that whole time?"

"Why in the world would you ask that?" Her eyes widen, and the light within her eyes brightens the woodsy brown to a more honey color.

I gape at my aunt, no words coming to mind. I snap my mouth closed with an almost audible crack.

"If I had known, I would have brought you back without a moment's hesitation." She trails off for a moment. "I suppose I should admit that part of me wondered if you were just unhappy with coming to live with me. I had assumed, incorrectly, you ran away. Yet, as the weeks passed, I began to suspect that what happened to your parents happened to you. But I never stopped looking. Not once. I always felt in my heart you were alive and well." She sits back and narrows her brown eyes on me. "Or as well as you could be, considering your plight with the trolls."

I nod. Partly because I don't know what to say in response to that and partly because this conversation feels... cold, rehearsed. Not what I would think a warm, genuine conversation would be like. Nothing compared to what I expected from the only family I have left besides my father. But until we have confirmation that he is still alive, I can't get my hopes up. And after living with the trolls for so long, this is my best shot at having some semblance of family back.

"What do you know about my parents? In terms of what happened with them, I mean." Right now, I have forgotten all about the delicious food sitting on my plate. I'm too curious to finally have my questions answered and having a *real* conversation with Aunt Patricia.

"I don't know more than you do, I'm sure." She glances at my plate and points at it with her fork. "Eat your food."

Figures I wouldn't be able to pry any information on my parents from my dinner-by- the-rules aunt. Sighing, I dig in. My stomach growls in thanks, and I realize I hadn't eaten much of anything all day long. I cram the food in as fast as I can, without choking to death or breaking any of the table rules I recall from my life before the trolls, which strikes me as some-thing that would upset my aunt.

I can satisfy her request to eat now and leave the rest of the conversation for after dinner.

Once we finish eating, we move to the sitting room. Surprisingly, I didn't dribble gravy on my blouse. Not a drop of food stains the sleek silver cloth.

I check that off as a mark under victory and take up the loveseat while my aunt sits on the sofa.

"What is it you do?" I clutch a beige, crocheted throw pillow to my chest and lean back into the corner, facing my aunt.

"For work?"

I nod.

"I am an ambassador. I pretty much go and mediate conflicts between mages that hold office in various governments."

I nod. "That sounds like an interesting position."

"It's a necessary evil. I daresay some of the mages are as savage as trolls." She heaves a heavy sigh as she shakes her head. "Especially during mediations."

I giggle at the thought of her regal figure, with outstretched hands, trying to separate seething mages on the brink of conflict. "Oh, I can imagine."

Trolls' egos are as big as the Earth is round. Needless to say, when one feels wronged, it's a showdown. Literally. Sometimes, they even fight to the death just to prove themselves right. I often wondered, during my time with them, just how much damage a forest could withstand during the many disputes I've witnessed.

I'm glad I get to see this side of my aunt. I feel like

it's a rare glimpse beyond the hardened shell she usually shows anyone.

She adjusts her shawl around her shoulders and repositions on the sofa, seeming much more at ease. "Have you thought about what you would like to do when you leave here?"

I pick at a loose string on the throw pillow in my lap as I shake my head. "I haven't thought much about anything other than passing the trials. And now, all I can concentrate on are my classes. The future after Blackbriar hasn't really crossed my mind." I shrug my shoulders.

"You should think about it and have a plan. This way, when you graduate, you are prepared."

I nod.

"What do you plan to do on breaks?"

"Can I come and stay with you?" I meet her gaze.

There's that half-hearted smile again. It's too fake. Not a single grin she has flashed me has made it to her eyes. Her actions are starting to unsettle me. Maybe my memory of my aunt was contrived through many sleepless nights, lying on the cold hard ground, painting pictures in my head that were better than the life I actually lived. I thought for a moment I broke through the icy interior of my aunt. Now, it seems like we are back at square one.

"That would be lovely," she finally says. "Of course, you realize that I am not home all the time, so your visits will have to coincide with my schedule."

"Of course." I'm not sure what to think of her answer. Is that a yes, a no, or a maybe? She gives me no idea of what she means with that answer. I'm clueless, seriously, clueless.

Then again, Aunt Patricia has seemed overly guarded since I first met with her in Gideon's office and then again tonight during our dinner. Her answers to my questions all seem rehearsed. My memories of my aunt are clouded and faint, though I dig deep and try to recall if there had ever been any tender moments between us. Or, maybe there were those loving times and I just can't remember specific instances?

Silence settles between us, and soon, Aunt Patricia yawns. It's the most human and normal action I've seen from her thus far, and I smile at the sight.

"My dear, I believe that is the sign that it's my bedtime. It was lovely to see you though. I'll see you tomorrow, unless you are busy."

I stand and nod. "Sounds good."

Aunt Patricia stands and walks me to the door. I wrap my arms around her in a hug, but there isn't any real reciprocation. No love. No joy. No comfort. It is more like a hug you offer to a stranger.

Unfeeling and cold.

Empty.

Her lack of emotion stings, but I remind myself that she had just flown half-way across the world to see me. That has to count for something. And, we haven't seen each other in over six years. Things are new, tense, and somewhat awkward. Maybe it's too optimistic of me to expect an aunt who has never really been "hands on" to suddenly be all hugs and smiles with me. It'll probably take time for her to warm up to me. We are, in a sense, strangers.

Still, it creates a small seed of doubt.

It'll take time to relinquish the idea I had of her in my head—a loving, caring, doting aunt—to the cold-hearted woman who I spent the evening with. I'll try to work with what I'm given. She's my blood, after all. My family.

With a final goodnight, I step back into the hall. The door clicks shut behind me and my attention is caught by the resident gnomes that flit in and out of view, carrying miniature lamps and tools I can only guess at. Such interesting creatures.

I really need to learn more about them.

As I walk, I feel more at peace, more whole, now

that a piece of my past is filled in. Although nothing will ever replace the hole my mom left, with luck, soon, my father will be back, and I will feel even more complete.

That thought brings a smile to my face. One that doesn't stop as I entertain visions of being reunited with my father and what that will feel like. I continue smiling to myself as I move through the halls. Suddenly a weight presses on my shoulders in the way that it does when someone is watching me. I don't need to look to know who it is.

Fucking Anderson.

My intuition flares when it's him. The air I breathe turns sticky and stale. I can actually feel his eyes caress my body in ways that will never, ever happen. It's a sensation that twists my stomach and covers me in an everlasting chill.

Whatever. I can't sacrifice this small bit of happiness to reprimand him. I refuse to let him take this joy away from me.

CHAPTER SEVEN

I'm so caught up in my thoughts that I move on autopilot through the halls. That is, until a hard body suddenly stops me. It takes a moment to shake the jarring halt from my senses, but as I stare into his deep brown eyes, I smile. My magic rushes through me, strong, powerful, cooling and calming.

"Milo," I say.

"I was looking for you."

"You were?" I cock my head to the side.

He nods.

Aww, he missed me.

"Well don't you know how to make a girl feel special."

"I haven't seen you all day, wanted to see how

things with Gideon went." He pushes his glasses up on his nose.

I chuckle under my breath. He will never know how adorable that little move of his is and the places that tingle when he does it.

"Everything went well. I reconnected with my aunt today. That's why he called me to his office. She had just arrived."

His eyes widen and he grabs my shoulders. "That's… that's so wonderful!"

"Thanks, Milo. I love that you are happy for me." I gently grip his arms, unable to wipe the smile off my face. He just seems to know exactly what to say.

"Well, yeah." He shrugs. "Why wouldn't I be?"

"I don't know. I suppose it isn't that you wouldn't be happy, but rather unaffected, I guess." He seems much happier than I am. It's cute.

"Are you kidding me? This is huge! You haven't seen your aunt in what? Six years?"

"A little over that, but who's counting?" I wave a dismissive hand through the air and slip my arm into his. "Walk me back?"

The muscles under the sleeve of his shirt flex, and I bite the corner of my lower lip as I picture his arms wrapped around me, pinning me against his chest as we grind against each other in the most tantalizing ways.

Holy hell. I've been corrupted by these men. I can't seem to get through a single moment with them around without my mind going to naughty places.

"Absolutely. But tell me everything." He gives me an expectant look.

I chuckle as we start down the hall together, explaining the dinner, the questions, generalizing the whole visit because I am not sure I want to share my worries about my aunt's dismissive ways just yet. I'm not convinced I should suspect anything, to be perfectly honest. Not only that, but it's still *new*.

But damn it all if Milo doesn't absorb every single word I say.

"What are you not telling me?"

I look him in the eyes, questioning him just as he does me.

Hell, he probably even hears the hesitation in my voice.

"You seem disappointed with the time."

Yeah, he does.

I shrug. "It's still new and not exactly how I expected it to be."

"What did you expect?"

More warmth, more depth, more meaningful

exchanges… the list probably could go on forever. "I dunno, really. Maybe it's just gonna take more time than I thought it would."

"You wanted her to jump right in and act like the gap in time, the significant events you probably both went through, didn't happen?"

Damn. He's got a point.

I hadn't thought about what she may have gone through. She's probably just as nervous about seeing me as I am of her. That explains things a little more.

I smile. "You're right. It probably is hard for her. She doesn't know about my father yet. So, it's probably painful and nerve-wracking with everything that happened. She just needs a little more time to adjust to things."

He lifts his shoulders up, raising his hands to his sides, palms facing the ceiling. "Makes sense to me."

I realize we hadn't talked like this for a couple weeks. It's refreshing.

The tension in my shoulders ease. I didn't realize I was so wound up as I ease deeper into our talk. I don't even mind that we're walking in a very wide circle back to the House of Phoenix. I sort of miss having our chats like this. We hadn't had much time alone since the trials started.

And that bothers me.

"We haven't had a lot of time together recently, have we? Feels like it's been forever since we've talked like this." I stop in the hall and face him. The dim light casts dancing shadows that play on his features. I take it all in, the angle of his chin, the point of his nose, the angle of his eyebrows. Even the shade of his beautiful brown eyes. I have to lift my head a little to look him in the eyes as he steps closer to me.

He shrugs and rubs the back of his head while he shoves his other in his pocket. "Yeah, it has been a while. But, I get it. I've been working on a few projects, and you've been busy training. Plus, you have a lot on your plate right now. Besides, we're making up for some of that lost time now, right?"

"I guess so. What do you say to making this time last a little longer?" I nod toward the corridor that leads to the garden.

He smiles, and I'm dazzled by the sight. "I would love to."

We make our way to my favorite garden, finding a bench to sit on. The rush of the ocean below whispers toward us as sprites fly around, blinking their lights as they dance in the air. I lean into the back of the bench and curl up next to Milo.

"Are you excited about seeing your father?" Milo asks.

My anxieties flare through me as I ponder the question. I suck in a deep breath through my nose and let it slowly slip between my lips. "I'm nervously excited."

"I get the excited, but why nervous?" He sits forward and twists to face me.

I sit up and shift to face him, tucking my foot underneath my right knee and draping my arm over the back of the bench. "I don't know what to expect."

And really, I don't. It's an unknown. I haven't seen my father in years. He disappeared a few days before I went to stay with my aunt. When I saw him in the mirror in Professor Lawrence's secret room, he looked so frail, weakened by years of what seemed like abuse. I had a rough time with the trolls, but he looked like he had it far worse than I did.

To be honest, I don't know how much of my father will be left when we finally see him.

"That's understandable." He covers my hand with his. "It'll all work out just fine, I'm sure."

"I know it will." I realize that I've never thanked him for helping find my father. After all, if it wasn't for him, I wouldn't even know my father was alive. "I appreciate your help with that spell. It made a huge difference, and soon I'm finally going to see my dad."

He nods once. "I'm glad I was able to help."

"Well," I say with a heavy sigh, "tell me about your day. I'm curious."

He shrugs. "It was just like any other day except full of classes. I had hoped to have more with you than Jesse. He never stops joking. I wonder if he even has a serious bone in his body."

I chuckle. "It's buried somewhere deep inside him and might take a microscope to find it."

"Microscopic in size," he adds with a chuckle.

"Soren carries enough seriousness for all of us," I say.

"No kidding. I should make him a chillax potion." He looks out to the side, somewhere in the shadows.

"You... You're not actually thinking about it, are you?" I ask.

He shifts his gaze to me and flashes a devious grin. "No. That would be no different than drugging him. But I'm entertaining the thought."

I laugh. "It's a rather tempting idea sometimes, huh?"

"Yup."

I shake my head as more laughter bubbles out of me. We need to change this conversation before it gets further out of hand. "Jesse may be a bad influence on you. But he can never know of this idea. He'll never leave it alone."

"He would probably take over the idea and drink the potion himself."

"Possible." I weave my fingers through his. The touch of his skin against mine is smooth, soft. The simple gesture ignites my nerves. Heat rushes between my thighs.

I'm so thankful to have him with me tonight. I can be myself without worry. He teaches me much more than he will ever know. He's so smart and kind. Hot as hell. And he's quickly becoming a cornerstone of my life. I never thought I would be surrounded by him or the others when I came here. But I'm glad I am.

Of course, I would be even more grateful if I could break through that wall Aunt Patricia keeps up. I really want her to be a part of my life. I think I'm gonna have to do something especially extravagant. But what? Hmm… this is all so new. I really don't know what families are expected to do together. It's been so long since I've had one.

"Going back to the family thing… Have you heard from your family? Are they stoked you're in?"

He snorts. "The letters don't stop arriving." He shakes his head. "I told them about you. They want to meet you eventually."

And just like that, it's hard to breathe. "What did

you tell them? You know what? Never mind. I'd love to meet your family someday."

He smiles. "Really?"

"Hell yes."

Shuffling footsteps whisper toward us, and we both snap our heads in the direction of the sound as Lady Alene steps into view. Her every movement is smooth, fluid, and commands attention with the grace she holds. The fact that she's a living statue made of stone makes her even more enchanting.

"Good evening Milo, Wren."

"Good evening, Lady Alene," we take turns saying.

"I'm just giving you a friendly reminder that curfew is rapidly approaching. You two best be off to your houses." She gestures with a nod toward the castle.

"Okay." I really want to reach out and stroke a strand of her hair, because it looks so flowy. But, I know better.

"Thank you for the reminder, Lady," Milo says.

She softly smiles and returns deep into the garden.

We stand, and as we start on our way back, Milo possessively grabs my hand and weaves his fingers through mine. And I can't hide the smile on my face if I tried. Before I realize it, I'm back at the House of Phoenix.

I face him and smile. "Thanks for bumping into me."

"You bumped into me. But I'm glad. I enjoyed myself." He tucks a strand of hair behind my ear and trails the tip of his finger along my jaw to my chin. A pleasant, thrilling chill rushes through me.

Lifting up on my toes, I kiss his cheek. "Have a good night, Milo. See you tomorrow."

His eyes darken as his gaze falls to my lips, but I pull away and turn toward the door. No sooner than I set my hand on the doorknob, he turns me around and pulls me into his arms. He slides a gentle hand behind my head and presses his soft, warm lips into mine. He deepens the fiery kiss and I breathlessly melt into him. I don't want him to stop, but Milo being tardy for curfew isn't an option.

Talk about your catch twenty-twos.

He breaks from the kiss, resting his forehead against mine. His voice is low and deep as he says, "Goodnight, Wren."

He gently pulls away and quickly walks down the hall, shoving his hands into his pockets as he moves toward the House of Drakon. As soon as he disappears around a corner, I head to my room for a cold shower and much needed rest.

CHAPTER EIGHT

The rest of the week passes in a blur. And now, I sit with the rest of the House of Phoenix in the arena set up in honor of Professor Lawrence's *unfortunate* death.

Two tapestries hang from the expanse of the ceiling, depicting his image outlined in gold. The face he showed everyone in the academy. The one that hid his true nature. The Blackbriar emblem covers the far wall as a backdrop to a podium that stands in front of it, decorated with a wreath of glowing flowers. A few oak trees stand guard on either side of that with sprites flitting in and out of view.

If I didn't have to be here to keep up appearances, I wouldn't be. It's uncomfortable honoring a man who tried to not only kill my men, but my father as well. He may have tried to kill me, but I think we all know how that one ended. The point is, no one messes with the ones I care about.

Mess with the bull. Get the horns.

Soren nudges me. I turn my attention to him and take in his concerned expression. It's a silent question asking me what's wrong. I shake my head. He grabs my hand under the table and gives it a small squeeze. I smile at him, thankful for the kind and reassuring gesture. But I'm really okay. Just... uncomfortable with the show.

The *lie*.

But no one can know the truth. To know the truth would destroy everything. My life would end. I would be labeled as a shadow mage. My men's lives would be turned upside down. And I just can't let that happen.

Someday the truth may come out. Someday in the future. Just not right now.

So, I'll grin and bear it for now.

Gideon takes his place at a podium. "Tonight, we gather to honor the memory of one of our most accomplished professors here at Blackbriar. While off the island for a business matter, Professor Deacon Lawrence was killed by a basilisk while protecting a group of young mages. He sacrificed himself, knowing that basilisks spew deadly venom. He did this for the sake of others. Strangers that had never met him before. The unfortunate and untimely death has affected all of us. He will be missed."

Soren leans in and talks low into my ear. "What do you think?"

I shrug and lift my lips to his ear. "It's still a lie, but I understand why we have to do it this way."

"It won't be like this forever."

"I know."

Gideon's voice reclaims my attention. "I'll open the podium for anyone who wishes to say a few words in honor of Professor Lawrence's memory."

"Do you want to go up there?" Soren asks.

I shake my head. Mind you, I'm still incredibly grateful to Professor Lawrence for the invitation. I'll at least give him credit for that. I wouldn't be here if it weren't for him. But that's where my gratitude stops. "I doubt anyone wants to hear what I have to say, especially since ninety-nine percent of it isn't nice."

Gideon steps down from the podium and takes a spot on the wall. I stop paying attention at this point. Especially as a teary-eyed student approaches the podium and begins her heartfelt eulogy.

"Oh, that reminds me," I say. "Did you find out what happened during my fifth trial?"

He nods and leans in closer. "The trial was supposed to end as soon as you stepped through the mirror. But the professor had other plans. Lady Alene didn't know until it was too late, and once a trial starts, there can be no interference. She didn't know where you were taken because he somehow cloaked your location with a powerful spell. I've never seen anything like it, but Gideon is looking into how Deacon was able to use it the way he did."

"How was the professor able to use an unknown spell? I thought that's impossible." A pinch forms in the center of my forehead. The idea that a spell like this is untraceable doesn't make sense. Professor Lawrence was up to no good, for sure. But to use unknown and likely unsanctioned magic that even Gideon wasn't familiar with?

There's more behind this. I *feel* it.

"Not impossible." Soren's breath brushes against my ears, sending warmth down my neck. "Just difficult."

I nod. "Thank you for the update. I'm just happy we don't have to worry about him."

An overbearing sensation of being watched overcomes me, and I look around the room to find out where the person spying on me is hiding. I find him, lurking in the shadows. He dips out of view just as I catch sight of him.

I roll my eyes and groan. Anderson.

"Anderson, however, is another story. I keep seeing him lurking, watching me."

Sometimes, I don't see him. But I know it's him doing it. The feeling is always the same.

I shiver. Just the idea of him gives me the creeps.

I catch sight of him again, across the room, staring at me with the eyes of a predator.

Soren leans in further. "Anderson wouldn't dare make a move on Blackbriar grounds. To do so will actively go against the treaty set in place between the mages council, magusari, and zacars. It's almost an automatic expulsion."

"Treaty?" I ask.

"Only a handful of zacars and shadow wolves are allowed to attend because though they don't have magic in a traditional sense, like you and I, they have a magical nature and are granted traditional schooling for that purpose."

"That's confusing." I shake my head.

He shrugs. "Such is politics."

"Be that as it may, I have my own means of taking care of issues like Anderson. If I have to, I will take matters into my own hands. I refuse to walk on eggshells here, and I won't let anyone, especially Anderson, take away my peace."

I may be a first-year student here, but I spent six harsh years learning how to fight, how to defend myself, and how to thwart an enemy. If Anderson thinks he can stalk me without consequence, I'll show him exactly who he's dealing with.

"Don't do anything that could backfire on you," Soren warns. "If he becomes an issue, let me and Gideon know. We will handle it."

I shrug. "Avoiding him has been relatively easy so far. We are on a giant, enchanted island, after all."

Between classes and time with my men, I am busy. Throw in a dash of time with my aunt, there's even less time left for him to press his luck.

"Very true." Soren chuckles. "Makes playing hide and seek fun."

I quirk an eyebrow and narrow my eyes on him. "You play hide and seek?"

"Trust me, my version is a lot more fun than the child version. You're allowed to use your magic."

I nod. "Interesting."

"That could eat up time," Soren says and there is something about the tone of his voice that hints at much more than a simple game.

I chuckle under my breath. "Yes, and when my aunt visits, I'll also have her."

Aunt Patricia had to leave early to take care of an important business matter. She promised to visit as often as she could since I'm busy with school. She felt that it would be easier to make appearances rather than taking me from my studies. Especially since this is my first term.

The connection between my aunt and I never improved since that first dinner we shared. After that, we had lunch once. Our conversation went from the weather to my most recent class, and then centered on me and what I had done during the time I was missing. It seemed like she was putting the pieces of a puzzle together, and I couldn't figure out what exactly she was trying to solve.

She's continued to keep herself guarded and distant. The part of me desperate to have my family back together wants me to think it will take her time to warm back up, but I'm really starting to doubt that she will ever come around.

He nods. "All true."

"And after this weekend, I'll have my father back as well."

"Hopefully," Soren adds.

"True."

I skirt my eyes across the crowd and catch Gideon looking in our direction. He nods once. Soren nods in return. "I'll be back."

"Okay." I watch him as he walks off. I find Jesse, Milo, and Savannah sitting with their houses, looking bored out of their minds. For some reason, that makes me smile.

CHAPTER NINE

After about the fifth or sixth student that praised Professor Lawrence and mentioned how unfortunate his death was, I had to leave the eulogy part of the ceremony. Damn the consequences. I made an appearance and stayed as long as I could tolerate the nonsense, so they will have to forgive me.

I walk through the halls, enjoying the quiet. My feet whisper along the floor and the muted echo from the arena fades away as I walk farther away from it.

A heavy sigh escapes me. The tension in my shoulders ease, and I start to relax into the peacefulness that surrounds me as I make my way to one of the gardens. The beauty on this island is simply too great for words, but the gardens? They are one of my favorite spots to visit.

As soon as I find a bench a good distance away from the commotion, I take a seat and breathe in the salty air from the ocean mingling with the floral scents of late blooming flowers mixed with the chill of winter that will soon be here.

The moon is in the shape of a crescent, hanging down in such a way that I feel if I stretched myself enough, I could touch the bottom of it with the tips of my fingers. Wisps of thin clouds float past, and the stars stretch on for miles. The Milky Way shines in the distance in the south, and toward the north, colorful lights dance in waves.

Absolutely enchanting.

My magic pulsates, and I smile. "Hey, Jesse."

"I'm getting rusty if you knew it was me." His voice comes from a few feet behind me.

"Nah, I'm just that good."

"Hiding from the crowd?" he asks.

"Maybe."

He chuckles and walks into view from my right. He takes a seat next to me, wrapping his arm around my shoulders. "Why would you ever do a thing like that?"

"I would like to think it's obvious." I lean into him a little.

"The show a bit much for you?" He runs his thumb

over my arm. The sensation leaves a trail of goosebumps.

"Let's just say there's only so much flagrant lying I can stomach for one evening when it comes to Professor Lawrence. Hearing all those students' stories about how good he was ties my stomach in knots. How is it we are the only ones who knew his true colors?"

He shrugs. "All a part of the art of illusion, my darling."

"Well, he sucked at it."

"Naturally." He leans deeper into the back of the bench. "I still say we should've gone with my explanation of accidentally blowing himself up."

"So, come to check on me?" I ask, changing the subject.

"Well I did see an opportunity to get you alone for a bit. Too good to pass up." He smiles at me. The light of the moon reflects off his blue eyes, making them seem like they glow with silver. It's a bit mesmerizing.

"Satisfied with the outcome?" I ask, a little breathless. He does it to me. All of the men have a way with getting to me.

He shakes his head. "No complaints so far."

I shake my head and chuckle. He makes it so easy

to be around him. "Are you returning to the memorial after the eulogy is over?"

"Only if you are."

"I have to make an appearance. I was his last initiate. It would raise eyebrows if I didn't go."

"Then I guess I'm going. Can't let you have all the fun."

I snort. "That is the furthest thing from fun that I can get. It's more obligatory."

"That doesn't mean you can't have fun while doing it," he whispers in my ear. The warmth of his breath seeps into my skin. Heat builds between my thighs and I squeeze my legs together to keep the pressure from building any more.

I meet his gaze darkened with desire and mischief.

"How 'bout it, Wren? Wanna have some fun?" His voice is deep, heavy with unbridled desire.

I take in the shape of his lips and meet his gaze again. Narrowing my eyes, I ask, "What sort of mischief do you have in mind?"

"Oh, you'll see." He winks.

"That's not very reassuring," I say through a chuckle.

"That's the point." His devilish smile stretches his lips and there's a glint in his eyes that makes me question what he's up to.

"What devious plan are you hatching in that gorgeous head of yours?" I tap his forehead.

"So, when is your aunt supposed to be back?" he asks.

"Don't change the subject."

"I just did." He nods pointedly at me. "Now, answer the question."

I level my gaze on him. "Really? It's like that?"

He slides his hand along my cheek and says, "It could be like this."

Before I have a chance to respond, his mouth is on mine. And I'm working to keep up with the expert moves his mouth makes. I'm filled with a primal need to let him take me right here and now. And as much as that need really pushes aside my much more logical self, this is a very poor place to be exposed for all the world to see. I don't want to think about the repercussions if someone were to happen across our little session.

I reign in the desire as much as possible, as his tongue explores my mouth with delicious motions.

He pulls away, just before I lose all my self-control, and leans back against the bench. He settles his eyes on me with a devilish smirk.

I stare at him for a moment, still recovering from his kiss.

He smirks. "Now, about that question?"

I shake my head. To be perfectly honest, my head is empty of everything except the raging hormones still coursing through my veins from that amazing kiss.

He laughs under his breath. "Your aunt? When is she supposed to come back?"

I shrug. "I don't know. Why?"

"Curiosity killed the cat, but satisfaction brought him back."

"You realize you come up with some of the most ridiculous things to say?"

"Makes you smile, doesn't it?"

Though he's correct that I'm smiling right now, I often find myself wondering where he gets all these little sayings and if he is purposefully trying to confuse me. "Seriously, why?"

"I know it means a lot to you. And what you care about, I care about."

"Oh." Wow, that's actually kinda sweet.

"I love a woman of few words."

I smack him playfully and he chuckles. "Watch it, you."

"How about it, ready to make one last appearance?" He stands from the bench and holds his hand out for me.

I blow a raspberry. "Do we really have to?"

"You said it yourself. It's obligatory."

I take his hand and stand. "Fine. But no foolishness."

"Let's not get too ahead of ourselves, hmm."

I shake my head as a chuckle bubbles out of me. As we make our way toward the memorial, I silently thank whoever is out there looking over me for giving me Jesse. He makes me feel so relaxed and free. Helps me to see the lighter side of things. Without him, I probably would spend the rest of the night in solitude, mulling over how horrible this whole charade is.

Not to mention I love spending time with him. And kissing him too.

CHAPTER TEN

Once we arrive, most of the academy is already here mingling, and the reveal of the memorial plaque is complete.

The guy gets a freaking plaque immortalizing him as a great professor of Blackbriar Academy.

A plaque!

That's too much.

As I get closer, I see the poem dedicated to him, etched under his name, and that damn near makes me shoot it with a ball of fire. My magic pushes into my palms, asking to be freed.

Jesse squeezes my shoulder.

I turn my attention to him. He nods once and pulls me away so that other students can have a chance to look at it and place flowers and cards at its base. Just in time, too. It helped ease the anger boiling inside me enough to calm my magic. I have to remind myself that this is all for show. I have to keep what really happened under wraps. Showing my true feelings toward the man would only raise questions, and I don't need that right now.

Savannah catches up with me, sliding her arm through mine and whispering in my ear. "I know there's more behind this. Are you okay? With the show I mean."

I nod.

Of course, Savannah knows there's more behind everything. The girl is practically unstoppable with her uncanny knack to pick up on things most wouldn't. Though she's right in her deduction, I don't want to share the full truth just yet. I still need time to get comfortable with the idea of friendship. Though Savannah hasn't ever hinted at a reason not to trust her, I'm still hesitant on completely opening up so soon.

I suspect she already knows that, coupled with being new to friendships, and is respectful of my boundaries and willing to give me that time. She's not pushy. I appreciate that.

"Everything is fine. Just processing."

She levels her gaze on me as though she's waiting for me to go into more detail. I won't though.

"I really don't want to talk about it."

Savannah smiles. "That's okay. Just know that when you are ready, I'll be here. We can talk about *anything*." She wraps her arms around me. I breathe in the lavender scent of her hair. She pulls away as Milo, Soren, and Gideon join us.

"Wren," Gideon says. There's a serious look in his eyes and that sets my nerves on edge.

"Yes, Headmaster Storm?"

"We need to talk."

I nod. "Okay." I turn to Savannah who instantly waves me off.

"Go, have your talk with your men." She winks.

"Catch up with you later?" I ask.

"You know it." She waves me off again.

I face Gideon. "Lead the way, Headmaster."

His lips quirk a little, almost imperceptivity, as he turns and heads toward the castle.

Sitting with my men in Gideon's office, we discuss our plan for the morning.

"So, we are leaving early?" I ask from my perch at

the window. The sooner, the better. I'm finally going to see my father.

"The faster we get there," Soren says, "the sooner we can get back." He sits in a chair in front of Gideon's desk.

"And the less people will be suspicious of us leaving," Gideon adds from his seat.

Jesse leans against the farthest wall, playing with a small flame in his palm. Milo sits in the other seat in front of Gideon's desk, relaxing into the back, seemingly at ease.

"What if there is trouble?" I twist to face the room.

"You mean, if it's a trap?" Jesse asks. His eyes hold a devious glint in his eyes, and I can't be sure what to make of it. With him, it could be anything.

"As you and Soren have already agreed," Gideon continues, "you will leave with Jesse and Milo at the first sign of trouble. Soren and I will handle any problems that may arise."

"I know what I agreed to." I cross my arms over my chest. "I'm also aware that we need to walk into this fully prepared for it to be a trap."

Soren turns his attention to me. "Having second thoughts?"

"Absolutely not." The audacity. Honestly. I know full and well he's trying to get me to stay behind. I made my position on this matter clear. I approach Gideon's desk and rest my hands on it. "I just don't think it makes sense for three of us to leave if there is a fight."

"What do you propose?" Gideon sits back in his chair and tents his fingers with his elbows resting on the arms of his chair.

"We all get out at the first sign of trouble. We are all stronger together. There's strength in numbers. If it is a trap, we are either going to have no choice but to fight together, or we're all going to have to leave together. Not just Milo, Jesse, and me."

Soren sits forward in his seat. "If there is a fight, you won't be fighting."

"You may not have a choice in the matter." I set my gaze on his. "I refuse to sit back and let you go in and risk your lives for me. I realize you want to protect me —all of you—and I adore that. Truly. But I could never live with myself if something were to happen to any of you if I stayed behind twiddling my thumbs. I'm useful. I can hold my own. And besides, he is *my* father, and I have a right to be there."

"You agreed." Soren's voice is deep and full of warning.

Milo raises his hand, drawing our attention to him. "You guys have to admit that what Wren suggests is not only smart, but feasible. With all of us working together, we have a better chance of survival. Whether that be getting back at the first sign of trouble or staying and fighting once the trap has sprung."

Gideon nods. "Indeed. With a little more careful planning, we can be prepared for any outcome. It's a smart choice."

"You're agreeing with her?" Soren pinches the bridge of his nose.

"She's being smart about this," Gideon interjects.

"Oh, I'm not?" Soren stands from his chair to pace the floor behind it and Milo's.

"I didn't say that." Gideon rests his hands in his lap. "She's considering all angles and possibilities. She also deserves to be there for her father, providing things work out according to that plan."

"And if they don't?" Soren faces Gideon, hands clenched into fists at his sides.

"Then we will either disarm our adversaries long enough to get back, or we stand our ground. It will all depend on the direction things go, whether her father is there, taken somewhere else, or if it was all a hoax to get us there."

"You're going to allow her to risk her life?" Soren's voice raises in volume, bouncing off the walls with more anger in each word that leaves his lips.

"I would risk everything I have to protect those I care about," I snap. "How dare you assume I'm a helpless damsel. After everything we have been through so far? I may not be as skilled as you or Gideon, but I'll be damned if I let you risk your life rescuing my father on your own. Which, I might add, is precisely why I said we should all leave at the first sign of trouble."

"Gotta love our little firecracker," Jesse adds. "She's standing up for what she believes in."

Soren spins to face Jesse. He points a finger at him. "Not another word from you."

Jesse shrugs as if it was a casual comment and not a warning.

Gideon turns his attention to Milo. "Any input you want to add?"

He sits forward. "With our skills combined, we stand a chance to come out of this relatively unscathed. But, as Wren mentioned, only if we work together. Now's not the time to let our egos get in the way of our goal."

Soren growls. "I don't believe this."

I roll my eyes. "Look, we go into this prepared for a fight. If it turns out to be nothing, then all the better. Splitting up would be a mistake."

"So, we go in there," Jesse says, "at the butt-crack of dawn. What else?"

"We will portal to a location about one mile from the facility where we believe Michael is being held." Gideon leans forward in his seat. "We take our next steps, depending on what happens when we get there."

"Why can't we just portal straight there?" I ask.

"Because," Soren says, calmer now, "if it is a trap, we land right in the middle of it. It's best we give ourselves some distance. This way, we can scope the area for any signs of danger on the way."

I nod. I hadn't thought of it that way. But now that it was explained to me, I see that it makes perfect sense.

Milo nods. "Arriving a short distance away will also ensure we remain unseen. It's safer."

"Are we good on this now?" I take time to look at each of my men individually. They each respond with a nod, a smile, or a wink.

"Very well," Gideon says. "Now that it's settled, we need to discuss what we will do with Michael once we have him safely out of the hands of his captors."

I narrow my eyes on him. "What do you mean?"

He stands from his seat and approaches me and places his hands on my shoulders. "I received word earlier today that your father is a suspected criminal."

"That's horse shit."

"Wren, we have to consider this as a possible reason he disappeared." His voice is calm and gentle.

I shake my head and pull away from his grasp. "No. I refuse to believe it. What is he suspected of doing?"

"I don't know. Gaining information on your father's past is proving difficult." Gideon maintains his tone. "But if he *is* a criminal, he can't come here."

"Then where do you suppose we should take him?" I cover my face with my hands and take a few steadying breaths. I just can't allow the image of my father to be shattered by an accusation that can't possibly be true.

"I've secured a private safehouse on the East Coast. We'll take him there and make sure he's safe until there is proof of his innocence or guilt."

I shake my head. "So, we save him only to keep him at a distance from me?"

"Not necessarily." Gideon returns to his seat. "You will be able to visit him. We will do everything we can to make sure he remains safe and protected with wards and a few of my most trusted magusari friends."

I cross my arms as a pinch forms in the center of my forehead. "I don't like it, but fine. At least he will be safe."

"I'm sorry, Wren." There is something in Gideon's

voice that pulls my attention to him. And he, for all the world, looks truly apologetic.

"I understand."

For a moment, things are silent.

"Anything else we need to discuss?" Gideon asks.

"I have something." I step forward.

"What is it?"

"Savannah Fey. She's a friend of mine, but she hinted to me just before we came here that she knows the service for Professor Lawrence is all for show."

"Are you worried about this?"

"No," I say as Soren says, "Yes."

I narrow my eyes on him. "No. She's a friend. She's helped a lot, in fact. And she's never given me a reason not to trust her."

"Yet." He points at me.

"I agree with Wren on this," Gideon says.

"You do?" Soren's eyebrows knit together as he takes in his best friend sitting casually in his seat.

"I do. Until I see otherwise, I will stand by that. But I believe it is best for all of us if she's not involved."

"I agree," Soren and I speak at once. I snap my eyes to him and smile. He's too in shock to fully enjoy the rare occasion that we agree, much less at the same time.

"Aww, how cute, the lovers agree." Jesse approaches and pats Soren on the shoulder.

Soren huffs and shakes his head, but his lips quirk up at the sides and I smile a little wider at that.

In fact, I'm grateful for him. For all of my men. Hell, I'm even grateful for my friendship with Savannah.

Though all of this is still new to me, I can't see making it through any of this without all of them. As I take a moment to enjoy the sight of my men in the room with me, working together to help me save my father, I realize that my adoration is quickly becoming something deeper for each of them.

And as far as Savannah goes... I'm starting to adore her too. It's nice having a girl to talk to.

Lady Alene appears in the room. "Good evening, everyone."

I approach her, and there's an expression on her stony face that reminds me of regret and guilt. I smile. "I don't blame you for what happened during my fifth trial. I hope you know that. In fact, I wanted to thank you. Your help meant a lot to me while I was going through the trials."

The stony façade shifts into one of relief and joy, and she smiles as she rubs the length of my arm with her hand. It's such a tender and warm touch for her being made of stone. "That brings me such relief. I'm grateful for your kindness."

"Of course."

"I do hope you will continue to visit while you are attending."

"I promise." I turn to face the rest of the group. "If we're leaving as early as Gideon suggested, we should probably get some sleep."

"What?" Jesse feigns shock. "But the night is still young."

I chuckle. "You'll get over it."

Gideon stands from his desk once more. "I agree. You all need to get sleep. I'll catch Lady Alene up on the plan and head to bed myself. Goodnight."

"Goodnight everyone." I leave the office and head straight for my room. Though I doubt I'll be able to sleep well, I know I at least need the rest enough to *try*.

I'm hours away from seeing my father again. That feeling creates a sensation of butterflies in my stomach along with an overwhelming sense of glee. I know anything can happen tomorrow, but for now, I allow myself this hope.

CHAPTER ELEVEN

The sun isn't even up yet. With hours before it is set to grace the world with its light, I stifle a yawn and stretch my arms over my head, bending back slightly.

I stare out the window in Gideon's office, my thoughts lost in the details of our rescue plan. If we succeed, I get my father back. If we fail... well, there is no room to fail. I won't let it come to that, and I know my men won't either. So far, it's just me, Soren, and Gideon waiting in the office. We're all lost in our own thoughts of the coming mission. Jesse and Milo have to walk farther than we do. Their houses are on the other side of the castle.

They'll be here in a few minutes.

Soren yawns and grumbles about waiting just as a tapping sound comes from the door. Seconds later, the door opens. Milo and Jesse enter with excited expressions on their faces. Jesse is so energized he's almost buzzing with enthusiastic vigor, and by the look on Milo's face, he's exhilarated by what the new day will bring. These men are impossible, and I love it.

"Good morning," Milo says.

"Morning," we all mutter.

"Time to go." Gideon moves toward a floor-to-ceiling framed piece of art made to appear as a real bookshelf. He pushes the frame in and steps back. The section opens and reveals a small set of stairs that lead upward.

One by one, each of us take the stairs. Soren leads, followed by Milo, Jesse, and me, with Gideon sealing the secret staircase and taking the rear. We arrive at the top of a tower. As soon as I take in the sight, my breath stills. I step closer to the short wall that separates me from the very long fall to the ground below. Up here, the wind blows stronger, colder. But the view...

Breathtaking.

The island below kisses the edge of the ocean that meets the sky which is just barely starting to brighten with the rising sun to the east. To the west, night still lingers. The last thin strip of silver light from the moon sinks under the water. Up here, I can almost touch the stars. Standing on the top of this tower, I feel as though I can fly.

Below us, mermaids swim toward the shore. The waning moonlight makes their colorful scales glisten as some of them rest on jagged rocks guarding one side of the island. In the woods, sprites sluggishly flash their lights. They're nocturnal, and they seem to be tired and readying themselves for bed after a long, chilly night of dancing among the stars. Some windows in the kitchen area are alight with busy staff, working to prep breakfast for the rest of the academy. And in the distance, small lights dot the horizon from the mainland.

The whole scene is simply serene. Peaceful. It's a breath of fresh air that brings me hope as we prepare to head into a dangerous situation to rescue my father.

"Beautiful," Jesse says, but he's looking at me and not the sight that makes me want to stay up here forever.

"Gather around." Gideon's voice pulls my attention to him as he moves his hands in a graceful and quick way. In one smooth motion he performs what looks like a ritualistic gesture, crossing his arms over his chest, palms facing his body, and thumbs interlocked.

Light fills the space in front of him as we all stand in a circle around a newly formed portal. It's a tall pillar of sky blue with sparkling specs of white glitter throughout, floating upward.

With a nod from Gideon, we step inside, and I feel as if I've been sucked into a vacuum. The sickening yet weightless feeling of being pulled and pressed overcomes every other sense. Before long, my feet settle on solid ground. It takes me a moment to gain my bearings. And, judging by the look of the others, they need a few seconds as well. Gideon and Soren seem to be the only ones not fazed by traveling through the portal, which makes me wonder how often they've done this.

As planned, we're one mile away from the location where my father is being held, somewhere deep in a forest in Arizona. The ground is sloped, and as my eyes regain focus, I stare at the pine tree covered mountains surrounding us. High above us must be the peaks of these massive mountains, but I can't see them from the little outcropping we're standing on. The change of salty, moist island air to the sudden warm dryness makes it hard to breathe, and I know it's only going to get hotter and harder to catch my breath as the sun continues to rise above us. Luckily, the trees will provide sweet relief from the overbearing rays.

We pause for a few moments, listening for the slightest sound of an alarm or a footfall nearby. I watch both Gideon and Soren turn their heads and scan the area, their faces screwed up in concentration as they reach out with their magic. Satisfied that our arrival remains undetected and that we haven't triggered any magical traps, we start our silent hike toward the facility.

A short while later, a tan colored building comes into view, surrounded by a twelve-foot fence topped with military-grade concertina wire. It strikes me as a building that's out of place with its surroundings. Though it's tucked away in a large national forest, it's definitely not open to visitors.

It's a compound with several smaller buildings resembling storage sheds, flanking the main building that are joined by a short, covered walkway. For all intents and purposes, it looks like a research facility in the middle of nowhere. I can't imagine what mundane studies would be conducted here, but what does catch my interest is the fact that no cars surround the building. No roads lead here, not even the barest hint of tire tracks mark the ground, making it seem like the only way to get here is by walking a long distance.

If I had happened upon this building during a hike, I would think this building is abandoned. There are no lights or sounds. No guard in site, much less a guard station. The compound appears hollow. Research long forgotten. Left to the elements. Simply there to bake in the hot desert sun.

But I know better.

I'm certain there are guards, mages, and who knows what else, set up somewhere out of sight. Getting in and out seems like it would be easy based on the misleading appearance. And getting in may very well be *easy*. Especially if this turns out to be a trap. Getting out? Well, we aren't going down without a damn good fight.

We follow the length of the fence and search for an opening in the chain link wall, or a gate that provides an entrance to the compound. After a short time and an anxiety-filled moment of thinking there may not be a way in, we find a gate, sitting open, not more than fifty feet away from us as we take huddle within the cover of trees.

Gideon and I exchange a determined glance. This is playing right into our plan.

He and Soren approach and enter first. After a moment of looking around for signs of unwanted guests, they wave for us to continue. I head in next, and then Milo and Jesse file in after me. Standing in the center of the compound, Soren and Gideon stand in front of me, I'm in the middle, and Milo and Jesse take up the rear. After a brief look around, keeping our ears peeled for the slightest sound that comes out of place from the woods surrounding us, we cross the large, empty, red-dirt yard to the main building. The double doors in the front blends into the rest of the building, only revealing itself as we approach. Like the gate, the doors are unlocked.

The muscles in Gideon's and Soren's shoulders tense as they prepare for an ambush as soon as they open the doors. My magic pools in my hands, glowing with the power rushing through me.

After a short pause, Soren pushes the doors in, revealing...

No one.

Either this will turn out to be one hell of a trap, or we're being toyed with. I push the uneasy thought to the side. I try to ignore the glance that Gideon gave Soren. Soren then immediately looks at me, making my nerves feel like they're on fire with apprehension.

It's still early. We still need to find the room my father is being kept in and get out of here.

The hairs on the back of my neck stand on end as we move inside and through the halls, opening doors to random rooms. One is filled with boxes, another is filled with desks and papers, and yet a different room is filled with filing cabinets. So far, it's a whole lot of nothing, but with my intuition flaring, I still keep my guard up.

One thing I've learned in my time with the trolls that's proved especially true in any circumstance, is not everything is as it seems. Appearances are deceiving. That's what my gut is telling me right now, and over the years, I've learned to trust it. My men seem to believe the same as their shoulders tighten with tension while we slowly move through the compound. Their expressions are of stony seriousness as they scan every nook and cranny we pass.

Just when I begin to think we were given faulty information, we approach the last room. Its door hangs off its hinges. The smell of smoke hangs heavy in the air as we step inside and scan the room. Torn pieces of paper litter the floor. Something has charred the white cinderblock walls. Up-ended chairs are scattered at opposite ends of the room, and splotches and puddles of blood add to the stomach-churning scene in front of me.

I hope beyond all hope that none of it belongs to my father, but I'm not convinced. I'm not sure if I should be grateful or worried that no bodies are strewn across the floor. Where is my dad, and how hurt is he? There's too much blood for no bodies to be present.

A note folded in half sits on the table, tented on an otherwise empty surface.

Gideon approaches the table and gingerly picks up the note, quickly scanning the words before setting a sad gaze on me. He holds out the paper toward me.

I swallow hard as I numbly take it and read it aloud. "Too late. Better luck next time." I look up from the letter and shift my attention between my men, each of them with somber, solemn expressions. "How the hell did they know we were coming?"

"Not sure," Soren says.

"From the look of this place, they left in a hurry. That means they've only recently found out and had to move quickly." Milo adds.

Gideon nods. "I agree. And by the look of things, there was a fight. Probably your father trying to get away, but with the amount of blood, I'm willing to bet several people lost their lives."

Though I agree with their assessment due to the lack of bodies, I shake my head, unwilling to lump my father in with that lot. "Nope. He's alive. I *feel* it."

"Wren." Soren's voice is soft as he takes a step toward me.

I hold my hand up, trying to defend myself from a

possibility I won't accept. "I'm not entertaining that idea. All right? I can't."

"Or, what if he's responsible for the damage here?" Jesse kicks at a sheet of paper on the floor.

"Next time..." I start to anxiously pace. "Whoever has him is already anticipating us coming for my father again?"

"Seems like they're a step ahead," Gideon says.

"But that means he's alive, right?" I look into Gideon's blue-green eyes.

"If it's not meant to bait you, yes."

I nod. Yes, I like that idea better. Although, we have to start from scratch to find him again.

"This is simply a hurdle. Not a complete road-block." Gideon's voice is full of promise. "We *will* find your father. It'll just take a little longer than we first thought it would."

"I was really looking forward to a fight." Jesse sighs wistfully.

We turn our attention toward him. He looks between us. "Did I say that out loud?"

"You're right," Gideon says. "I, too, was expecting some opposition here, but for some reason they saw it as more important to forcefully remove your father and jump ship. They obviously need something from him."

"Still, we need to keep our eyes open and remain vigilant." Soren's feet shuffle over the debris covering the floor as he makes his way to a small window sitting high at the opposite wall. The glass is shattered, leaving jagged shards sticking out of the frame and glass littering the sill and floor beneath it.

I stop pacing to face the headmaster. "I don't think we're done here yet."

"Anyone else as unsettled as I am?" Milo's voice is distant as his eyes focus on the puddle of congealing blood at his feet. His skin pales and I worry if he's about to throw up.

"Well, what are we waiting for?" Jesse spins, a gleeful glint in his eyes. "Let's finish checking out this place. Maybe we'll still run into someone?"

Though I agree, I also can't shake the feeling that there's more than what meets the eye here in this room.

"Let's look for clues. I want to make sure there's nothing here we can use." I gesture to the room. "Just in case."

Milo steps forward. "I'm on it." He scoops up tattered papers scattered along the floor, leaving the ones soaked in blood alone.

A pinch forms in the center of my forehead. "What is all that?"

"I don't know." He grunts as he continues to bend over and collect the pages. "Directions, blueprints. I'm not sure yet. We can piece these together later."

"Blueprints?" My voice sounds almost foreign, but my magic churns within me, and a dose of dread fills me.

"We need to hurry." Soren speaks from the corner, continuing to stare out the broken window.

Jesse starts to help Milo. I collect the pages surrounding me. Gideon pitches in as well. Once all the salvageable pages have been collected, we stack them in a haphazard pile and pass them all to Milo. He clutches them in his hands and holds them like they are the most precious gift in the world. Close to his heart. But there's a shadow that crosses his eyes and I wonder what it is about the pages that bothers him.

Before I can ask, we file out of the room. Now is probably not the best time, anyway. I trust him enough to tell me once he has a solid idea of whatever is hidden within the numerous pieces of paper.

We step through the dilapidated door of the bloodied and destroyed room as Gideon's words ring true within me. We'll find my father. Maybe not today, but someday *soon*. I won't give up on him. I *will* find my father, even if I have to overturn every rock on this earth.

Just as we step into the glaring hot sun again, a heavy weight falls upon my shoulders. Something dark and foreign. It's a magic I'm not familiar with.

Shit! There *is* someone here. And by the feel of this unknown presence, it's not good.

CHAPTER TWELVE

The uncomfortable sense of something incredibly imposing nearby doesn't let up as we make our way through the empty building, back toward the double doors at the front. We're all tense and unsettled because things hadn't gone the way we anticipated. My magic pulses through my wrists and into my hands, waiting for the chance to be freed.

We're not out of the woods yet.

Once we make it to the dirt outside the building, my eyes adjust to the brightness of the sun casting waves of heat down on us. And leaning against the gate is a man wearing skin-tight jeans and a leather belt buckle with silver spikes. His bare torso shows off his greyish skin. His long black hair cascades around his shoulders, and his black eyes narrow on me as his lips quirk into a grin.

"You must be Wren Blackwood." His voice is calm, even, and coated with a hint of enjoyment. There's a slight southern twang to his words and part of me believes his demeanor is being played on to distract us from his true purpose.

Call it gut instinct.

"Who wants to know?" I ask from between Gideon and Soren. This is it. This is what we were waiting for. It has to be.

He stands straighter and holds out his hand as though he wants me to approach and shake it. "Name's Jackson Cane."

"And what if I am Wren Blackwood?" While I stare him down, I take in the subtle way his body angles just slightly before shifting his weight in the same direction. His shoulders are a bit more tense than the casual tone he speaks with. His hands rest at his side, but they are partially closed. Like he could start throwing punches at any moment.

"Wren, what are you doing?" Milo asks behind me in a low whisper.

"Stalling." My word flows quietly from my mouth as my eyes search the surrounding areas. There's a trap here. I feel it. And this Jackson person's appearance confirms this. But he's not alone. I know this deep in my gut. I just can't see anyone else just yet.

But they *are* here.

Somewhere.

I search for a getaway route as well. I don't know enough about using portals to know whether doing it in the middle of a confrontation would allow unwanted guests to join.

Gideon and Soren angle their heads slightly toward me, but never turn their backs toward this Jackson character. Soren's amber eyes take in mine. It's a silent cue that he's going to join in on this stalling game we have going on. And it's an intense one at that. I nod, silently agreeing.

Soren steps forward. "What does it matter who she is?"

Jackson chuckles under his breath. "Let's just say I have something she wants."

"And what," Jesse says, "you're just helping out of the kindness of your heart?"

I stare into the shadows, deep into the trees for any movements, any signs of the trap we've anticipated during this mission.

Jackson takes a step forward. Gideon and Soren tense. He chuckles again. "Relax. I'm just trying to help."

"Prove it," Gideon says.

Yeah. That. He's not trying to help. He doesn't look like the helping type. Aside from the air of dark intentions this guy gives off, he's standing too casually. His words are too calm. This whole thing stinks of ulterior motives, like trash baking in the hot summer sun or trolls before their yearly baths. I adjust my feet just slightly, taking a fighting stance. My hands glowing with magic, prepared for the trouble I can feel brewing.

Jackson's gaze takes in my hands and meets my eyes. He clicks his tongue. "Is this how you react to everyone trying to help you?"

"What could you possibly help us with?" Milo asks. "And better yet, why?"

"I know where her," Jackson points at me, "father is." His eyes settle on mine. "Don't you want to see your father?" His voice is coated with honey. He's goading me. His pleasantness is too plastic. Too fake.

And I'm not going to buy into it.

"Tell us the real reason." Gideon steps forward, his voice full of warning. "Now."

Jackson smiles as he takes another few steps toward us. He's closer to closing the gap between us. He holds his hands out to the side as he struts forward. And suddenly, I'm aware of the possibility that it's him that's stalling more than us. And that lets me know that there is definitely backup coming to help him.

Time to get to the point of this little talk.

"That's far enough." I hold out my hand, full of magic, never averting my eyes from his. I refuse to give him the satisfaction. That would show that I'm afraid of him. And if it's one thing I am not, it's afraid of Jackson Cane. Showing him fear will give him power over me, which is *never* gonna happen. I refuse to give him any type of power. "Tell us the real reason you're here. Now."

He casually shrugs as though he doesn't know how close to death he really is. Because I know if a fight breaks out, that's the only way this can end. And I'll be damned if anyone but him dies.

"Very well, clever girl."

I arch an eyebrow.

"My…" he pauses to look up at the sky as if the right word is going to fall from the heavens, "boss wants to see you."

"Who is your boss?" Soren asks.

A scuffling sound hits my ears, alerting me to nearby movement. I search the area around us, peering into the shadows and blind corners of the buildings around us and behind us. As I turn around, I notice Jesse and Milo doing the same.

"She will find out soon enough."

Jackson strikes me as being cocky and too full of himself. I just may have to knock him off his imaginary pedestal. As a favor, of course. Since he's so willing to do the same for me.

Tit for tat, and all that.

"No, I won't. I'm not going anywhere with you."

"You'll never find him on your own." Jackson smiles, and it's threatening. "Give up the girl. All this can end peacefully. Otherwise, I'll be forced to take her." He sighs, shaking his head, a false expression of worry on his face. "I would rather not get dirty."

I snort.

Yeah, right. He wants a fight. And I'm willing to give it to him. Judging by the expressions on the faces of my men as I quickly glance toward each of them, they are too. I step forward, magic filling my hands and shooting him a daring glare of challenge.

Jackson's lips stretch into a dangerous grin. He chuckles.

"Challenge accepted." Jesse's voice is deep, full of dark warning. There is also a slight hint of anticipation.

Gods help Jackson. He's trudging a thin line and he doesn't even realize it.

"She's not going anywhere." Fire erupts over Soren's skin.

Gideon's hands ignite in magic. "You'll have to go through me first."

Jackson chuckles and shrugs as he takes another dangerous step forward. "Wren, I'm told to keep you alive. Well, as much as possible. But you," he gestures to my men, "you're all fair game."

Oh, hell no. He did not just threaten *my* men.

I step between Gideon and Soren. I'm done playing games and stalling. No one threatens my men. I fire a blast of magic at Jackson's feet. "Enough!"

He halts, staring at the area now scorched from my ball of fire. He slowly drags his black eyes up to mine, a silent threat flashing through his expression.

"No more games. Who do you work for?"

He shrugs nonchalantly. "The hard way, then."

Black smoke erupts along his body, condensing into his core. Growls and howls surround us as wolves made entirely of smoke and shadow emerge from where they were hiding. They stalk slowly toward us, enclosing me and my men in a circle. Their red flaming eyes narrow on us as they snap their jaws full of razor-sharp teeth at the air. There are a dozen of them, at least. And I'm not sure if there are more hidden in the trees, behind the buildings, or anywhere else not easily seen.

"Oh goody, shadow wolves." Jesse's voice pulls my attention to him. He's not smiling. Instead, he stares with a grim expression at the few wolves at his sides. "Let's dance then."

I turn my gaze back to Jackson. "Really?"

He smirks and charges. The wolves bark and rush in as well. I clench my fist and swing, connecting with Jackson's left cheek. His head snaps to the side as he stops mid-stride. I cast a quick glance over my shoulder to see how my men are faring. Shadow wolves look ethereal, but they are far from weak and harmless. They can cause serious physical damage. Incapacitating them is difficult, but not impossible.

Jesse kicks one in the head with a resounding thump. Milo blasts another one with purple light, setting it on fire. Soren shoots flames at two wolves who are trying to separate him from the group, and Gideon...

What the...?

Gideon is spinning a staff of light, creating a small shield in front of him, stopping three attacking wolves in their places, while he blasts a ball of bright white light at another.

Damn. Okay then.

Jackson kicks my feet out from under me. The world spins in my view, and I realize I had become distracted. Cursing myself, I blast a ball of fire at his smug face and stand, conjuring my shield at the same time.

This is what I've been training with Soren for.

I know this. It's familiar. Practiced.

He shoots a smoldering black, inky substance toward me. It barrels like a ball shot from a cannon toward me. I dig deep into my stance and brace for impact. It hits with more force than anything I've ever felt before. My shield cracks. My arms give out as the force becomes too much to hold back. My shield knocks into me, and I'm thrown backward. I fall against the ground, the world blurring in my sight as I land with a painful thud. I groan. Dots line my vision as I struggle to sit up. My vision teeters, the woods and compound twisting in a blur.

I must have hit my head harder than I thought.

I catch sight of my men, standing with their backs touching as they struggle to keep the wolves from overwhelming them.

Jackson steps into my view. He holds his hand out for me to take.

I slap his hand away, roll back to my knees, and settle my eyes on him, hoping he realizes the mistake he's made. I doubt he does. And I have no problems with delivering that little lesson.

I rise to my feet, keeping my gaze steady on his. Fire erupts over my skin.

Jackson's eyes widen a little. His lips barely part, but it's a motion that doesn't escape my notice.

"You'll regret that." My voice is low and full of warning.

His cocky façade returns as he chuckles darkly. "We'll see."

I fight him with all I have—magic, kicking, and punching. But he's there to block and deliver equally powerful blows. And before long, I am running out of steam. But I refuse to let Jackson see that.

"Where is he?" I kick him, landing the blow to his gut. "Tell me now!"

He catches my fist as I move in for my uppercut, and with his other, lands a crushing blow to my gut.

I fall to my knees and gasp for air.

A blinding light fills the area around us, and a loud boom thunders through the air, shaking the ground, the buildings, and everything surrounding us.

When the light dies down, my eyes struggle to focus, but when they do, I see a figure in a cloak fighting off the shadow wolves.

Soren joins my side and helps me to my feet. "Are you okay?"

I nod and look for Jackson. The shadow wolves are busy with the new arrival—whoever it is—as well as Jesse, Milo, and Gideon. But Jackson? He's nowhere to be seen.

Coward.

We rush into the fray, taking out the wolves one-by-one until they dissolve into black ash. As the final three are backed into a corner, they snap at the air to keep us back, but we don't stop advancing. As soon as they realize they are the last ones left, they tuck their tails and run off yelping.

As I pant for breath, pain rockets through me. My pulse drums through me and a dark rim encircles my vision. I nearly fall to my knees, but I fight against the growing pain and stay on my feet.

The cloaked stranger rushes to my side. The hood of her cloak falls from her head, revealing black hair with purple streaks.

"Savannah?" She presses her fingers against my diaphragm, and I flinch.

She speaks over my shoulder. "We need to get her back before we have more friends show up. She's good. Just bruised."

Yup. It's Savannah. But before I can say I'm not

going anywhere, I'm pulled into a portal. I shout, "No," but my voice is carried away by the gravitational force of the portal.

Within seconds, we land in a courtyard on Black-briar's grounds. I fall to the grass and scream in rage. Fire burns along my skin again.

We were so close to rescuing my father. We should be pursuing the remaining shadow wolves, not jumping through a portal back to Blackbriar. Now that Jackson didn't die, he's going to be a problem for us in the future. The fight wasn't over. Not for me.

The blades of grass around me singes and blackens. Little plumes of smoke float into the air.

I focus myself, taking in a few deep, albeit extremely painful breaths. Slowly, the power dissipates, and the flames sizzle out.

In my periphery is Soren, Milo, and Jesse. Behind me, I feel Gideon's presence. I vaguely hear Savannah saying that I need some time alone.

"What makes you think we are willing to leave her alone?" Soren's voice is livid. I peek over my shoulder and watch as he approaches Savannah. "Just because you helped us back there doesn't mean *you're* trustworthy."

Fire burns along his skin. It's sweet that he's protective over me. Sometimes a bit overprotective, but this is Savannah. Why would she risk her own life to help us if she had ulterior motives? It just doesn't make sense.

Just before I stand up to intervene, Gideon beats me to the punch.

"Soren." Gideon's voice comes from behind me, out of view. "Stop."

Soren snaps his attention in the direction Gideon is standing and his eyes nearly burn with rage. "What?" It comes out flat, and I wonder if Soren will snap and try to fight his best friend.

"I've seen her soul." His voice is soft and warm. "She's good."

Soren narrows his eyes on Savannah. "How did you find us?"

Savannah takes a cautious step back. Her eyes flit to me and I want to intervene. She saved us. Keeping my eyes locked on Savannah's and watching for the slightest flinch from Soren, I start to stand up.

Savannah holds out her hand to stop me and almost imperceptivity shakes her head. I nod. Something inside me recognizes that this is her way to prove herself a friend to me.

"She's..." Gideon's voice seems almost pensive. Like he's thinking out loud. "interesting. She has the ability to see glimpses of people's lives. She's a truth seeker. She sees events from a person's past and very near future. That's how she was able to find us and help with the fight. She's also a healer, using her magic to pinpoint ailments and provide relief."

Everything about Savannah, I already knew. Everything except the truth seeker part.

"Truth seeker?" I move to sit on the grass and take in Gideon as his gaze turns from that of almost looking through Savannah to seeing her directly. He blinks away the trance and settles his gaze on Soren who still stands like he's about to go to war.

"It's the technical term for people like me." Savannah's voice is still calm, even in the face of Soren's anger. I smile a little. She returns her attention to Soren. "Satisfied I won't hurt her now?"

It's a few long tense moments as the two stare each other down. Savannah refusing to show fear, and Soren desperately looking for the one miniscule sign that Gideon is wrong. Soon, the fire covering Soren's skin disappears as he takes in a deep breath. Letting it out, his shoulders relax, and his hands ease out of the tight fists.

The static-filled tension in the air fades.

Faint footsteps lead away from me. I sit there, forcing myself to calm down from everything that just happened, running the thought of losing my men to those wolves through my mind. Replaying how those last few moments in Arizona slipped through my fingers, along with my shot at saving my father. The more these thoughts run their course on a never-ending loop, the angrier I become.

My attention turns toward Gideon's office. We need to discuss what happened and come up with a plan to get my father back. I stare at the charred grass and feel a small lump of guilt. It's a sobering sight. I damaged a piece of my home in my anger. Maybe that's what they wanted? To throw me off balance while they get the upper hand.

Well played, Jackson Cane.

He may have won the battle. But he most definitely will *not* win the war.

I'll see to it personally.

Inside Gideon's office, Savannah forces a healing potion down my throat as the men are gathered around discussing what happened. I'll never get over what could be the worst possible taste ever. Bitter with an underlying sour taste mixed in with the sludge-like texture and smell of something putrid. I know it's meant to help heal me from the fight, but still. Does it have to be horrendous?

"Someone knows of her and her power, Gideon." Soren paces the room. He's going to create a worn-down path of wood in the floor if he doesn't stop pacing soon.

"I know, Soren." Gideon pinches his nose. His squares his stiff shoulders, and his expression is one that suggests one wrong word will send daggers shooting from his beautiful blue-green eyes.

Savannah pushes the potion to my mouth again. I growl.

"Take it like a woman," she says.

"I like her." Jesse points to Savannah. "She knows how to handle Wren."

I glare at Jesse, telling him with my eyes to keep his comments to himself, as Savannah chuckles. I gulp down the last of the potion and shiver as the bitterness holds onto the back of my throat. This stuff is awful. Still, the slight warmth starting in my stomach spreads through me, easing the tenderness in my ribs and torso.

"Good girl." She smiles and winks at me before taking the cup and putting it in her bag. She plops down in a chair at Gideon's desk.

I return to my favorite perch on Gideon's window sill.

"Could it be the Order? I don't recall shadow wolves being a part of any government not their own." Milo's voice speaks from the corner of the room, where a bookshelf stands filled with tomes of who knows what. Gideon is the headmaster, it could be expansive knowledge of higher levels of magic. After what he did back in Arizona, that's where my money is at.

Gideon shakes his head. "They've been known to exchange favors for some sort of gain. So, there is no telling who is behind this."

"Deacon Lawrence must've let knowledge of Wren slip to the others." Soren leaves his line of pacing to lean over Gideon's desk.

I roll my eyes as I continue to stare out the window. The setting sun casts golden rays over the changing autumn colors, creating a beautiful scene that I don't want to pull away from. "We all knew it was a risk. That's why we went in prepared."

Gideon nods. "We'll need to take each step more carefully than before. Especially with Wren."

I snap my head toward him. "What?" My voice comes out angry. Fire burns within my veins, and pressure builds in my wrists. My magic seems to be pissed with that thought too. I take a few deep breaths to calm myself a little.

Soren stands straighter. "It's too dangerous for you now."

I stand from my seat on the sill, shoulders back and chin in the air. "Then we'll just have to train harder and make it less dangerous. I already feel responsible for your involvement and injuries. Now that I'm in this deep, I can't stop now. I can't hide and let whoever Jackson Cane is working for think they've won. With you all by my side, I'll make it right. But I need your help."

"She has a point."

Every head turns toward Savannah.

She shrugs. "What? It wouldn't be fair to cut her out now."

"Nor you, you sneaky little vixen." Jesse takes the seat next to her.

"Indeed." Gideon nods in agreement. "Your involvement helped us at the moment we needed it most. It was dangerous." Gideon levels his gaze on her for a moment. Suddenly he's the headmaster again. And like a flash, my powerful teammate is back. "But thank you, nevertheless."

"I knew what I was getting into." Savannah turns her gaze to me. "With the vision I had, I couldn't sit back and wait."

I step in front of her and look into her eyes. "What did you see?"

Her eyes darken and gloss over. She squeezes her eyes shut and a crease forms between her eyebrows as they knit themselves together. Whatever she saw, it was painful.

"I saw glimpses. Still images, like pictures. It was bloody. And all of you were lying face down on the ground."

Gideon and Soren exchange shocked expressions. "Yes," Gideon says, "there is much more to you than meets the eye."

Gideon seems… impressed. If he senses anything negative about her, he doesn't show it. I highly doubt there is, though. This is Savannah. She just risked her life to save us and earned a great dose of respect not only from me, but my entire team. She's also earned my trust as well. For all intents and purposes, it seems like she found her niche in our group. The group that is rapidly becoming family to me. And that means more to me than anything.

Family.

"Thank you from all of us," Soren says. "We really couldn't have done it without you."

"I'd do it again if I was given a chance to." She tilts

her head from side to side. "I may need to make me one of those potions. My neck is tense."

"Let's hope you don't have to help again. I'm not in the business of letting any of my students jump into dangerous situations." Gideon sits back in his seat. "I'll call on some more of my connections. See what we can uncover. What movements are happening."

"I'll research tracking spells." I look at Milo.

He nods. "I'll help."

I smile gratefully. He does too.

"Jesse," Soren says, "see if any of your Winterwolf house members know anything about shadow wolves and their leader."

"Assuming he is the leader," Jesse adds.

Soren huffs. "Fine. Just whatever you can find."

Jesse nods. "Aye-aye, capytan."

Soren faces Gideon. "I'll reach out to my magusari connections. See if perhaps they heard any chatter of possible Order movements or members, as well as any other helpful information. After all, if Michael is a suspected criminal, they'll be looking for him too."

"Not. A. Freaking. Criminal." I huff and cross my arms over my chest.

Gideon holds up a quieting hand, drawing my attention to him. "We don't know that yet, Wren." He abruptly turns his attention to Soren. "I'll handle Wren's training while you are gone."

Soren nods in agreement.

"Well, if this is all done, I'd like to get to the infirmary myself." Jesse stands up and rubs his hands together.

I shake my head. "I'll go with him to make sure he stays out of mischief."

He smirks. "You know me so well."

"Yeah, yeah. Come on." I make my way across the room and push him out the door as soon as we reach it. Just before I step through, I look at Milo. "I'll meet you in the library after."

"You got it."

CHAPTER THIRTEEN

J esse is all bandaged and making the special potion he made for me during the trials. He sips the potion as I sit on a counter. He hands me some and I sip it slowly. The liquid is warm but does nothing to fight back the cooling sensation that Jesse's nearness puts my magic through.

"Bout time I get you all to myself for a while." He smiles, and there's a hint of something much more naughty flashing through his eyes that makes heat rush down my neck.

I chuckle. "You're impossible."

"Mm... but I'm charming." His steel blue eyes ensnare me, pulling me in. "I've been wanting to make good on the promise I made you back during our trials, for a few weeks now."

I chuckle. "Dare I ask?"

"I don't hear a question." He places himself between my legs, setting both hands on either side of my legs. His thumbs brush erotically against my thighs.

I shake my head. "What is that promise?"

"Now was that so hard?" He leans closer, eyes focused on my lips.

"Uh-huh."

His lips press into mine. His tongue enters my mouth, flicking expertly along mine as his hands move to my ass.

My hands move up his arms and to his long, wavy brown hair. My fingers weave into his soft locks and a moan escapes his mouth, prompting a rise out of me. He slides me closer to him, and I can feel his growing erection bulging against the restrictive fabric of his pants.

My shirt lifts from the waist of my pants, and his thumb gently brushes my exposed skin. Pressure and warmth fills the space between my legs. A small voice in the back of my mind whispers that we should stop before I become too consumed by him.

But my body doesn't listen.

I really don't mind. Jesse is a fantastic kisser.

A tugging pulls at my consciousness. I give in to that sensation, and to images of us wrapped together in the sheets, naked as he thrusts into me repeatedly, at first slowly and then faster. It shifts to me pressed against the wall as I cling to him, riding me into a full-on orgasm. Another picture enters my mind of him beneath the sheets and me clutching the pillow on both sides of my head.

When you're ready... rushes through my mind as soft as a whisper and as tender as the touch of a feather along my skin.

My body switches between the heat of passion and the cooling sensation my magic takes on with Jesse's presence.

Damn it all, I'm tempted to make him good on his sweet, erotic notions right here and now. But I'm sore, and the infirmary is hardly a romantic spot. Anyone could walk in on us at any moment.

He breaks the kiss at that thought, as though he heard me think it. He pulls away gently.

"Let's get you to the library." He holds out his hand toward me, a devilish smirk stretching his lips.

I nod, breathless, and take his hand.

Hopping from the counter, I follow him out of the door of the infirmary. Though I have to admit, a big part of me wants to stay and continue watching those delicious images play through my mind.

Before long, we stop outside of the door to the

library. Before walking through, he turns and faces me. His face is serious, which shocks me. "You know that whatever you decide, wherever you go, I will be by your side as long as you'll allow me? No matter what."

I smile. "Where is this coming from?"

He narrows his eyes in a manner that makes me weak in the knees. "I just want whatever will make you happy."

"I appreciate that Jesse. I'm kind of fond of you too."

He quirks an eyebrow. "Kind of?"

I smile, blushing. "You know what I mean."

"You are truly a force to reckon with. Never met a girl like you. Never want to. Not anymore. I'm yours. Until my last breath."

I chuckle. "You must've gotten hit in the head pretty hard." I kiss him on the lips and turn toward the library.

CHAPTER FOURTEEN

I arrive at the door to the library as Milo is walking out with a stack of books piled to his nose. He peers at me from over the stack. "Hey, you."

"Hey, you got a lot of books there. Taking them back to your room?"

"Yeah. I figured you could use the break. Savannah is already in there." He nods behind him. "She helped me get all of these gathered up."

I nod. "Oh. Okay."

I admit, part of me is disappointed. I really hoped he and I could spend some time together. But I appreciate the effort he's putting into it, and when Milo pours himself into his research, he goes all in. That's part of what I adore so much about him.

He uses a foot to keep the door open for me. "Go ahead. Enjoy your girl time."

I giggle. Ever the gentleman, even when his hands are full. "Thanks, Milo. Let me know if you want any help, okay? I don't want you doing it all on your own."

He shakes his head. "I'll let you know if I find anything. You go. Let me handle this."

As I walk in, I find Savannah sitting at my favorite table in the library. She looks up and smiles, tapping the side of the table across from her. I smile back at her and take the seat. "How goes the research?"

She frowns. "Slower than I would like. But that's the point of school, right?"

I nod. "You know that vision that caused you to show up to the fight?"

Her eyes darken a bit as she nods slowly.

"Thanks."

She smiles widely. "I've already been thanked."

"Not by me. Personally."

She reaches across the table and covers my hand with hers. "That's what friends do. They help each other out. Besides, who else is going to get you dolled up for dinner with your fancy aunt?"

I chuckle. "But really, I appreciate your friendship. I don't know many people that would risk their life for me or my men as well."

"Hey, it's a package deal, right?"

"Right." I laugh under my breath.

I want to tell her more. Open up to her completely. Especially about what happened with Professor Lawrence. But the library isn't the place.

"Wanna go hang out in my room?"

"I could use the break." She slams her book shut and we share another laugh.

As Savannah sits at the foot of my bed, I tell her everything that's happened up till now, and she absorbs every word as though I spoke the gospel. As soon as I finish, she shakes her head. "I knew he wasn't right. I saw some strange and disturbing things with him, but I couldn't make out most of them. They were all too blurry."

My head bobs in agreement. "You're taking this really well."

She shrugs. "Like I said, I knew he wasn't up to any good."

"That's true." A flash of memory burns through my mind. A picture of me exploding magic on him. I shudder.

"So, your father's rescue was a bust, huh?"

I sigh as I spin and plop down on my bed next to her. "Yep. Looks like it."

"Whatever I can do to help, I will. Even prove his innocence. It'll just take time." She falls back onto my bed and stares at the ceiling.

"That's the thing." I turn to face her. "My father may not have time. There has to be something we can do to find him. And soon."

She rolls to her side and props up her head with her arm. "Though the future isn't written in stone, I *know* we'll find him."

"But how?" Frustration rises in me, and I jump up from my bed and start pacing my room.

Savannah shakes her head. "I don't know. But, between the six of us, we'll find a way."

"I just hate… waiting."

"Well, at least you have one family member you can talk to, right?"

"Sort of." I face Savannah. "She's distant. It just doesn't feel right sometimes."

"It's been a while since y'all have spent time together."

"True. That's what I keep telling myself too."

"But…"

I wait for her to continue. When she doesn't, I bite the bullet. "But what?"

"Just be careful. I can't get a good read on her. It's not often I come across people like that. So, with that in mind, just be extra cautious, okay?"

"What do you mean?"

She sighs. "Often, experience has shown that whoever I can't see clearly is going to great lengths to hide something. Or, it could mean they're warded and harder to read than the average mage."

"She is a very proud woman and keeps herself protected. It's not surprising that she sets up a few wards around herself." I bite the corner of my bottom lip.

"Like I said," she smacks the bed, "I don't experience it often."

"Like trees growing from runes?" I ask with a laugh.

"Right?" she joins in the laughter.

We spend the rest of our time talking about our runes class and joking about making a tree grow or something just as shocking... into a weekly deal.

CHAPTER FIFTEEN

The night before Soren leaves, I'm sitting in his room, staring at the fire burning under a stone mantel. Holding a steaming cup of sweet-smelling hot chocolate out to me, he smiles and gestures for me to take it. I smile up at him from the chair and take the warm cup.

"You certainly know your way to a girl's heart."

"Shut up and drink your damn cocoa."

I giggle. "Thanks."

"You know I wouldn't be leaving if I didn't think it was necessary." It wasn't a question but a statement.

I look at him from over the rim of my cup as I blow away a bit of the steam. I take a sip and let the hot, creamy liquid settle in my mouth, savoring the sweet chocolatey flavor. I swallow it down and enjoy the sensation of heat filling my core and spreading outward. "Getting sappy on me?"

He growls, and I can't help but chuckle. He's too easy to rile up sometimes.

"I know you're doing what you think is right." I stand from the chair and set my cocoa on the mantel as I approach him. I look into his amber eyes and slide my hands around his torso. "I also know you wouldn't leave if you didn't feel like you absolutely had to."

"I'll be back as soon as I can." His eyes search mine and drop to my lips.

"You better." I smile.

His lips lower to mine, and I give in. To everything. To him, to the night. To the very fact that I won't see him around for who knows how long.

I give in, completely.

Our cocoas are forgotten as we become lost in exploring each other.

Before long, our clothes and the comforter from his bed are tossed to the floor in a discarded heap of fabric. And shortly after that, my body is sent to brand new heights of ecstasy. I ride wave after wave of pleasure that he takes me through. Once I feel like I've given him enough of a chance to have his fun, I flip him over and straddle him. Slowly, making sure to take my time and enjoy our time together, I ease him into his own climax. Another climax pours through me as our eyes meet and I'm lost in the pleasure and light of ecstasy in them.

At some point just before dawn, our bodies are spent. We collapse under the sheets, wrapped in each other's arms. Spending the final hours of our last night together for a short while, we sleep blissfully.

Tonight is for us. Just Soren and me. Tomorrow morning, we'll say our goodbyes. However short the time apart will be, I will miss him like crazy.

Although no one knows for sure how long Soren will be away from Blackbriar, I know that he'll return to me as soon as he possibly can. His absence will affect not only me, but Jesse, Milo, Gideon, and Savannah too. No matter what the others say about Soren, they all care deeply for him.

The last fleeting thought that rushes through me as my eyes are pulled shut by a well-earned need for sleep is this... Family. Because that's what my team is to me now.

My family.

CHAPTER SIXTEEN

My mind races with all kinds of possibilities as I sit in my Introduction to Alchemy class. I spot silver daggers, and mortars and pestles on a table in the far-left corner. A collection of herbs and potions sit invitingly on a shelf behind the professor's desk, and I wonder if we're going to practice making youth elixirs, healing salves, or even something I can use in pursuit of finding my father.

My gaze settles on the board where some information in a scrawling script, rich with curves and flourish, has been written down for us. I'm hoping this class turns out better than runes, though there is one thing I've already noticed.

Houses sit with Houses.

Bummer. It would've been nice to sit with Savannah.

I look over my shoulder at the corner designated for House of Kraken. The wall is painted navy blue with an orb of teal that darkens and fades into the navy blue. A large Kraken silhouette is centered in the middle of the teal orb. Savannah is smiling and chatting it up with her classmates. She seems happy. That's good.

House of Drakon's corner is sky blue with silver-lined white clouds. A silhouette of a dragon with wings spread and mouth opened in a silent scream takes up the corner behind me. Milo isn't here. He's in another class. I miss him. It would've been nice to have alchemy with him since it's his thing.

House of Winterwolf's corner is similar with a midnight blue backdrop and silver moon with a shadowy cliff and silhouette of a wolf in the middle of a silent howl. Jesse is also in a different class, and I wonder what he would say right now to sitting with his own house instead of with me. However, Anderson is here, and I can't help but wonder what the hell he is up to. My shoulders tense, a painful pinch entering them, and my hands form into fists so tight my nails bite into the palms of my hands. He's not a first year, but he's in a first-year class. It doesn't make sense.

He keeps showing up where he's not wanted.

Like a bad penny.

Looks like, for this class at least, I'm stuck with him. Maybe Gideon will take pity on me and let me switch my class to a different time. Though, I doubt that would do much good since Anderson has a habit of being a bit of an annoyance. Like a pebble in my shoe.

I blow out a raspberry.

Sooner, rather than later, I'm gonna have to put my foot down again. Forcefully. My focus needs to be on my coursework, training, and finding my father. Not dealing with a man who seems to be nurturing an obsession with me.

I roll my eyes and then steer my gaze elsewhere.

Finally, my corner, and probably the most vibrantly colored of all, is painted in the colors of a fire with vibrant reds, yellows, and oranges which make the dark silhouette of the phoenix stand out in contrast. My classmates are busy chatting it up, but I don't join in. Soren couldn't share this class with me since this is his last year and this class is beneath his abilities, which makes my house corner feel empty.

The door at the opposite end of the room opens, and a man struts in. His dark brown hair is cut close to his head, with the sides shaved. His almond-shaped brown eyes flit toward me as he moves through the classroom. He then reaches the front of the class, where a table set up for some sort of experiment stands between the lines of blocked off desks and the white board.

He stares out over the students who slowly stop talking as they realize the professor is waiting for them to shut up.

His expression is stony, cold, and he gives off an air of superiority. Neither a smile nor a word of welcome crosses his lips. I wonder if he hates teaching.

The last of the voices quietly hush as the professor drags his eyes over the thirty or so students.

"I sincerely hope you got all of your ridiculous chatter out of the way. If not, too bad. From now on, there will be no talking before class. You are to use the time you have to brush up on the reading or finalize your assignments. Pointless gossiping has no place in this classroom. Understood?"

Yeah. He's going to be super fun to learn from.

"I'm Professor Remo. For the next quarter, you will learn the basics of alchemy, including transmutation circles and the correct way to write the symbols. My goal is to teach you well enough so that you fools don't blow yourselves up—or take me along with you. Now, turn to page twenty-eight."

I look down, and a dated book of alchemy instruction is already on the desk. I didn't even see it appear.

Man, I love magic.

I flip to the correct page, and I quickly become enthralled with the different transmutation circles, their purposes, and the symbols of elements. Instantly, my eyes are drawn to a symbol of fire. It's a simple triangle, but when infused with energy, it becomes a powerful, destructive weapon.

"Practice individually. Work on your form. Trace the symbols twenty times before you draw them on your pages."

A short stack of parchment paper materializes in front of me, along with a pencil with no eraser.

A student raises his hand. The professor huffs as he pointedly stares at the student. "Well, what is it?"

I spin in my seat to see who the student is. He sits with House of Drakon and mumbles out, "What if we make a mistake?"

"There's a stack of pages on your desk for a reason. I suggest you use them." His voice carries an edge of annoyance.

This guy needs to get laid. Might improve his mood and make him a fraction more tolerant of his students.

I shake my head and start to trace the first transmutation circle for earth. A circle within a circle, and a diamond within a square. It takes my complete concentration, and I immerse myself in the simple strokes of my pencil. I forget that I'm in close proximity to Anderson.

I'm too focused to care about him.

With the first transmutation circle complete, I sit back and study my work, comparing it to the one in the book.

Looks close enough.

I don't dare infuse energy into the symbol, given what happened in my rune class at the beginning of the year. Knowing me, I'd probably open the wrong portal and who knows what could come through. That, or the entire class could end up in an unpleasant spot.

I nod, satisfied with my work.

Professor Remo snatches the page from my desk and analyzes it with a sour expression.

"Partners. House with House. Now."

He hands the page back and he can't even bring himself to look at me properly. Instead, he makes it seem like it's too much work to do more than just shift his eyes.

"Mr. Stone, kindly show Miss Blackwood the

proper way to form a transmutation circle beyond simply drawing what her eyes see."

Anderson stands up. "Gladly, Professor Remo."

Oh no. *Anyone* but him.

Where's Milo when I need him...

"Profe—"

"Enough. Assuming you didn't flunk math as a child, you'll notice that you don't have an even number of members in your house. Therefore, I designated him to pair with you. Problem?"

I stare at him blankly. What the hell happened to him to make him so callous?

"No? Good."

I groan as Anderson slides a chair to the other side of my desk and plops into his seat. I lean away from him to create more distance between us. He smiles. My eyes narrow on every single minute movement. I shake my head and groan.

"What a surprise having a class with you. Good thing I failed this class last year. Spent the summer studying under him. Great guy. Spending time partnered up with you is an unexpected but welcomed bonus." He reaches out with his hand.

I lean back farther into my chair. "If you so much as act like you're going to touch me, I'll break your hands off and gouge out your eyes with your own fingers. Got it?"

He hangs on to his smile as he hides his hands in his lap. "Now, now, Wren... no need to be hostile. We can take things as slow as you want."

I give him the dirtiest look possible. "We're not taking anything at *any* pace. I don't like you."

He chuckles under his breath. "Though a man like Soren gets to have every inch of you."

I quirk an eyebrow. "You don't know what you're talking about."

"Yes, I do. I know of your... extracurricular activities." He leans forward slightly and lowers his voice to barely above a whisper. "If a guy like him has a shot with you, so do I. I won't accept anything other than you agreeing to a date with me."

I reward him with a look that would stop a mermaid's heart. His knowing about me and Soren could be dangerous. He could use it against me, and somehow manipulate my relationship into something twisted, dark, and entangled versus the beautiful, powerful and amazing thing that it is now. And there is no way in hell I'm going to let that happen. He's pushing all the wrong buttons with me. Unless his intention is to piss me off, then he's pushing the right ones.

Either way, I can't show him that what he's saying is bothering me as much as it is. Not a teeny, tiny bit. I know him well enough to understand he's manipulative and will do and say anything to get what he wants. I have half a mind to ask if he paid his way into this class. Of all the classes he could join to "make up," he chooses this one.

He knows more than he's letting on as well, which not only puts my relationship with Soren at risk, but my relationship with all my men. That is not something I will let slide. But now isn't the time to retaliate.

But if he thinks throwing my relationship with Soren in my face is going to get me to cave into him, he's got a rude awakening waiting for him.

"How 'bout it, Wren?" His eyes take in mine and I'm overcome with a serious bout of nausea.

"No." I shift once more in my seat, turning my attention to the assignment. But that doesn't stop Anderson from continuing.

"I promise I'll make it worthwhile."

I sigh. "Why? So you can steal more of my energy?"

"Steal? Oh, no." He chuckles. "That's not what happened. You allowed me to take some, I most definitely didn't steal anything."

The hell I did. My magic burns through me as strong and swift as my anger, pushing against my hands, begging to come out. My eyes return to the text, focusing on reverse circles, and I desperately want to reverse this class. But I can't.

Right now, I have a choice. I can either give in to my magic's need to be released and burn Anderson to a crisp right now, or I can take the higher ground and remove myself from this situation before I cause damage to the other students and the classroom.

The choice wars within me for a few precious, agonizing moments. Finally, I settle on the latter. I stand, bringing Professor Remo's attention to me. His scowl settles on me and I suck in a deep breath. "I'm not feeling well. I need to be excused."

He checks the time on his watch covering his left wrist. "You can wait for the last few minutes left in class."

Crap.

Anderson smiles triumphantly, and the restraint that's keeping me from ripping him into shreds is rapidly diminishing.

The moments tick by as slow as molasses in winter. I clench my hands under the desk and bounce my knee as I focus all my attention and energy on not killing Anderson. When the bell chime rips through the air, I let out the breath that I had been holding and quickly rush to Savannah's side before I wring Anderson's neck.

The smile that stretches her lips is not one of joy but of an apology. I shrug. "I'm going to switch classes. Don't worry."

"Good."

As we walk out of the classroom, I look over my shoulder, finding Anderson smirking at me. He winks. I turn around and look forward, walking away from him a little faster now. But not fast enough for him to pick up on just how much he really rubs me the wrong way.

CHAPTER SEVENTEEN

I think of Soren as I make my way to Gideon's office. It's been a week since he's left, and the night before his departure was so blissful. I bite the corner of my lower lip as I replay some of my more favorite, erotic moments. Though I don't know when he'll be back, I know it will be soon. I didn't think being separated from him would affect me like this. It's almost like a part of myself is missing.

With that, I realize I'm quickly becoming irrevocably attached to him.

I hope he's keeping himself safe.

I turn a corner toward the headmaster's office and nearly bump into him. He greets me with a smile. "Good afternoon, Miss Blackwood."

I chuckle under my breath. "Good afternoon, Headmaster Storm."

"Ready for your training?"

"Yes." It just may be what I need to release the pent-up tension from my unwanted but forced interaction with Anderson.

With a nod, he escorts me to a room within his office. It's a magical room, expanding as we enter. I stare in awe as the walls stretch and move, spreading into a massive, open area.

"Whoa."

Gideon twists to look at me. "Like it?"

"Yes. I love it."

He nods. "This is where we will be training. You'll be facing dangerous scenarios to better hone your magic outside of running drills one-on-one." He beckons me closer.

As I walk closer to him, my magic buzzes through me, growing stronger with each moment I'm in his presence. I simply *adore* the feeling.

I step through the threshold, gaping in awe at the expanse of the room that was no bigger than a closet only moments ago.

Gideon shuts the door, pushes me against the wall, and kisses me deeply and passionately. Delicious fire creeps through my body in ways that make me want to melt into him.

He rests his forehead on mine, panting to catch his breath.

"I was wondering if you were ever going to kiss me again, Headmaster Storm."

He chuckles. "Damn pretenses and propriety, not lack of want, have kept me from giving into that desire."

"Pesky rules."

"You'll never realize how often I want to do that, and I will take advantage of every chance I get." His eyes darken a bit as he takes in my lips once more. "But we have to be careful."

"I know." I kiss him again. The tips of my fingers brush along the back of his head as the kiss deepens. His arms wrap around my waist as his lips move along my neck. He nibbles a sensitive spot at the base of my neck before returning to my lips. I moan against his mouth as my knees want to give out and pressure builds between my legs.

Just when I'm about to give in and start ripping off his clothes, he pulls away and takes a step back. His voice is dark, heavy with desire. "We should get to your training."

I work to catch my breath as I nod. "What did you have in mind?"

He presses his hand against the wall. Magic pours from beneath his palm, rippling outward, spreading throughout the room. The walls sink beneath the floor, replaced by a forest with tall evergreens, pines, and aspens sprouting from the floor and stretching to where the ceiling should be. Soft light resembling a setting moon floods in through the back of the room. A dense fog rolls in, soaking what used to be the wooden planks of the floor in a murky mist.

I stare as small hills and boulders rise up to create natural terrain. All of it is mesmerizing. The imagery reminds me of the woods from the troll village, and I'm suddenly alert and ready for anything.

Gideon's voice comes from behind me, somewhere in the shadows. "We're going to focus on using your powers against the shadow wolves. Keep a cool head and don't let your magic overwhelm you. You must use it to your advantage without losing control."

I search the shadows looking for signs of the wolves.

"I must warn you," Gideon adds, "they will be just like the real thing."

"Oh, great."

"Be careful…"

I look over my shoulder. "Right."

Shadows low to the ground start to move. Growls reach my ears, and I conjure my shield to ward off any sudden attacks.

"Any word yet if they are involved with the Order?"

"It's possible, but we don't know for sure. However, we should err on the side of caution and believe they are, for now."

Shadow wolves emerge from the darkness and mist, eyes glowing like lava, snarling as they approach. They move as one toward me. Though there are only four shadow wolves, the challenge will still be enormous. Especially considering how powerful they were when my men and I faced off with Jackson Cane. I know better than to underestimate what these creatures can do. Illusion or not.

Fire burns in my hand and I throw a bursting ball of it toward them. It knocks two of them back, sending them sliding across the ground. Their whines fill the air, but my focus changes to the other two shadow wolves charging me. My arms tense as they lunge at me from a few feet away. I use my shield to knock one back, but the other manages to claw at my upper arm, leaving gashes. I cry out in pain. A burning sensation fills my injured biceps, and I know I can't take another hit there because it will be rendered useless. Fighting with one arm isn't my idea of fun.

I falter for a moment. My numbing arm draws my attention away from the fight. The other three have recovered and are charging me again. I strike out at them using lightning. A loud boom vibrates throughout the room. The flash of my magic nearly blinds me, as it hits two of the wolves.

When my eyes are able to focus again, I notice the two that were hit are on the ground, lying still. They dissolve into ashes and blend into the scenery as though they never existed in the first place.

Trembling with the buildup of pressure, my magic burns almost uncontrollably in my hands. I'm distracted by the sensation. I can't lose control of my magic like I did with the lamia and Professor Lawrence. I couldn't live with myself if I hurt Gideon in the process.

Digging deep into myself, I reach for focus and calm. I know it's here within me, somewhere. Breathing in deep, I soothe my magic, like the way my mother would calm me on nights when a storm scared me and I refused to go back to sleep. The sensation pulls me deeper, and I know I can't let myself withdraw completely. These wolves are serious, and they do have a mean strike with their claws.

Slowly, like a small trickle of a leaky faucet, my magic subsides.

My arm stings and blood drips from the wounds as I face the last two wolves. Sweat drips down my face as I dodge their attempts at trapping me in their sharp teeth. Dodging attack after attack, delivering kicks to knock the creatures back. They only keep coming at me, with more ferocity than before.

I can't keep up with the pace the wolves are setting. I'll soon be exhausted and won't be able to defend myself from another injury.

"Focus, Wren." Gideon's voice echoes to me, and I take a deep breath.

The shield isn't serving me in this fight. I need to get rid of it. I shake out my arm, and it disappears. Magic light with purple and pink electrical currents fills my left hand, and fire fills my right.

I settle my gaze on the two remaining shadow wolves. They bow their heads low and hunch their backs as black, ink-like smoke rises from them. My body ignites in flame.

"Keep calm, Wren." Gideon's even tone reaches my ears from somewhere behind me.

"Oh, I'm calm." Even I hear the dangerous promise in my words. Because what I said is true. I am calm, but I'm also determined. The light of my form reflects in their glowing red eyes as I step forward and the magic builds in my hands.

The wolves separate, trying to flank me on both sides. I move backward and keep both of them within my sight. I hurl the fireball at the one to my right while I shoot my ball of light at the one to the left, launching the shots simultaneously across my body and surprising the wolves.

The one to the left falls to the ground, dissolving into ash that eventually fades into the dirt.

"Good."

The little bit of encouragement I get from Gideon lets me know I'm on the right track. Lightning. Powerful and dangerous. It damages them. But if that's the case, why didn't the men just do that?

Now isn't the time for that question. I still have one more shadow wolf to defeat.

But I can't help but wonder if it's perhaps not a coincidence.

Focusing myself, I concentrate on the pulsing electricity inside me. I pull on that, urging it to cover me instead of the flame. And when it does, I'm almost shocked.

Almost.

But the buzzing nips at the surface of my skin, sometimes sharp and sometimes not. It's distracting. A sharp nip causes my focus to falter, and an arc shoots out from me.

"Careful. Focus." Gideon's voice comes from the opposite end of the room this time.

"I'm trying." I speak through clenched teeth as I search for the shadow wolf.

Movement in my periphery draws my attention to the left. The creature is hiding in the shadows between two trees.

Poor bastard. That won't save him.

I let loose a bolt of energy. It shoots toward the tree, shattering the bark with a loud snap thundering against the walls of the room. The shadow moves.

Shit. I missed.

Hitting a hovering target? Sure. No problem.

Hitting a moving target? That's a bigger challenge.

I find the shadow wolf again, hiding along the base of more trees. I smirk. Firing off another loud bolt of energy, I miss, again.

Again, and again, the shadow wolf scurries and hides. The more trees I disintegrate with my magic, the more frustrated I become, knowing that I missed. After the fifth time of missing, I stomp my foot and growl.

"Easy, Wren. Calm. Control."

"Yeah, I got that. The damn thing won't stand still."

"Nor will they in a real battle. It's always life or death. Lose control, and you could die. Keep yourself calm, and you will live. Remember that."

I search my surroundings for Gideon, so I could send him an annoyed glare. But he remains hidden somewhere in the room. Probably watching from a perch in the shadows. He's likely staying a safe distance back, so I don't accidentally hit him with my magic.

My heart sinks into my chest a little, slowing in beats before quickly returning to normal. Worry fills me. In my anger, I lost sight of the purpose of this training. And in that, I could have accidentally blasted Gideon with fire or lightning, which would have seriously hurt him.

And that's just not something I can live with.

I draw in a deep breath of air that tastes like earth, rain, and moss. On the exhale, I gain a little more control over myself. The electrical magic covering my skin ebbs to the point that it's only covering my arms.

"That's my girl." The pride in Gideon's voice forces a smile on my face.

I step into the woods, searching for the shadow wolf. It doesn't take me long to find him. When I do, I aim a single finger at him. The creature blinks once, and I sense that he is accepting his fate. No more hiding. No more cowering.

Time to die.

I shoot a string of lightning from my finger. It hits the center of the creature's chest. Ashes fall to the ground, disappearing like the others had.

All at once the trees disappear and Gideon approaches me with a proud smirk. His hands are clasped behind his back. I meet his gaze and my lips curve upward, parting in a wide grin as I take him in.

"You did well there at the end. Very well." He angles himself to get a better look at my arm. He shakes his head. "How does it feel?"

I look at my arm. The gashes no longer bleed, and they don't look as deep as I originally thought. I shrug. "Fine. Barely notice it."

He nods. "We will train here as often as possible until Soren returns."

"When will that be?" My heart skips a few beats at the sound of his name.

"Soon." He gestures for the door leading back to his office. "It all depends on what he can find and where the leads take him."

I take in his words as the feeling of something missing nearly overwhelms me. My heart aches a little, and I have to take a deep breath to calm the sensations coursing through me. It's like an empty space inside me.

A thought comes to mind. Each of these men have found a place not only in my life but in my heart. They each make my magic react in different ways. Thrilling ways. I want to mention this to Gideon. He may have some clever insight that would explain the feelings, but I really don't know if now is the right time.

We step into his office, and I turn and watch the room shift back into a closet. Magic just may never cease to amaze me.

And I'm okay with that.

I return to my thoughts as Gideon walks toward his office door. I ponder telling him about my magic. As soon as I work up the courage and open my mouth, he checks his watch. "Training is done for the day. You're going to be late to your class."

Okay then, later it is.

"I'll walk you to your next class and excuse you personally."

"I appreciate that." I'm reminded of the last class and I speak up. "Is there anything you can do about switching my alchemy class time to Milo's?"

He gives me a sideways glance, and hmms. "Is there a reason why? Professor Remo is our only alchemy teacher for first year students."

"No, no. It's not the professor, although he could have a bit more finesse."

"Oh? Then what is it?"

I take a deep breath, and on the exhale dive into it. "Anderson."

I also tell him about catching the creep spying on me in the halls. Gideon's hands clench into fists so tight his knuckles crack. "I understand."

There's something in his voice that is dark and dangerous, and I realize it's never good to see Gideon pissed off.

"Not only will I switch your class, but I will have a word with him as well. As headmaster, of course." He winks at me.

A giggle bubbles out of me. Pity the soul. He won't know what hit him. "Thank you."

"Of course."

We reach the door to my class and he opens it and pokes his head in. "Pardon her tardiness," he says in a cordial tone to the professor.

"Absolutely, Headmaster Storm."

He winks at me one last time before walking down the hall. I chew on the corner of my lower lip. I know beyond a doubt this man will undo me in ways I can't possibly imagine.

And I can't wait to find out.

CHAPTER EIGHTEEN

I take the vacant seat next to Savannah at the first table in the room. Smiling at her, I silently thank her for saving it for me.

She smiles and nods once.

"Miss Blackwood, I was just doing my introduction. To catch you up, I'm Professor Brindle."

"Nice to meet you, sir."

"Indeed."

His voice has a deep growl which makes him sound like he's older than he looks, despite his salt-and-pepper hair and wrinkles at the corners of his eyes and mouth. He stands tall with his shoulders back, showing off the fact that for an older gentleman, he's in great physical condition. I would probably say he appears to be around fifty years old, but the wrinkles around his eyes and his voice gives me a hint that he may be a little older. His skin holds a constant summer tan, far from showing the paper-thin skin that pales as age sets in.

The professor turns his clouded eyes to the classroom, shifting over every student. "I'm a master herbalist. In this class, you will learn that herbs have a wide array of uses, from healing the slightest sniffle of a cold, to deadly potions that are so toxic, a drop will take down a full-grown man in seconds."

I chuckle to myself. I know one potion already. The birth control potion.

"You will gain a basic understanding of herbs, although those of you with some home-based herbology education may find this to be more of a review."

He shifts toward the greenhouse attached to the classroom. "You will learn about using herbs in combination with runes and alchemy, bringing all of your classes into a full circle of knowledge. However, you will not practice these uses until your advanced courses here at the academy."

Professor Brindle waves his hand toward the bookshelf. "Each student will partner up and share the texts."

Savannah nudges me and I smile. She slides her

arm through mine and we share in a giggle. Oh, the trouble we can get ourselves into with this class.

"Turn to page—yes, what is it?" The professor looks at someone sitting somewhere behind me.

I turn my attention in the direction the professor is focused on. A student, blond with blue eyes, and looking rather cocky with the way he sits in his seat like he can't be bothered with posture.

"What about telling us what herbs have done for you, personally?"

Professor Brindle nods. "As you can see, I'm an old man. But herbs have enhanced my cognition and physical strength. At ninety years old, I still have the strength I gained in my teens."

Oh, he's much older than I thought.

Amazing.

He lifts the desk in front of him, which I know can't be light. He nods as gasps ripple through the room. Once they end, he sets the desk down. "I will not disclose the ingredients in this class, so if that is your next question, Mr. Rowe, put your hand down."

I glance over my shoulder to see that he does. I shake my head. Male pride. I'll never understand it.

"The purpose of this class is solely an introduction," he heavily emphasizes that word, even going as far as to write it upon the board, "to herbology with more basic," he underlines that word, "applications."

He turns and faces the class and claps his hands together. "Any questions?"

After a few moments of no one responding, he checks his watch. "Oh my." Lifting his gaze to the room, he takes a moment to, I assume, mentally count the number of students in the room. "First half, head toward the greenhouse. Second half, read pages ten through twenty-four."

A chorus of groans echo through the room as Savannah and I stand up and fall in line behind Milo and Jesse, which makes me realize why my magic has been tingling, two of my favorite men are in this class. Professor Brindle weaves through the rows of desks with grace as he heads for the greenhouse door. He enters and waves those of us standing in line into the room.

"Feel free to spend time familiarizing yourselves with these herbs. You will be quizzed on them at random times throughout the term."

Milo is in nerd heaven as he stops by the most unique plants, doodling a sketch of them in his notebook and then jotting down the information written on the little tags sticking out from the soil.

"Such a nerd," I say in his ear and wink at him as I wrap my arm around him.

He chuckles and adjusts his glasses. "These are going to be pivotal in my alchemy projects."

I cock my head to the side, curiosity getting the better of me. And I can't resist a chance to know more about Milo. "Oh yeah?"

He beams proudly. "This one here." He points to a green plant that is short and stalky with spiky leaves tipped in red. "This is commonly known as dragon's breath."

"Interesting." I finger the tip of a leaf.

"It's a useful plant to ward off digging pests as well as for making a sleeping potion. Depending on the use, it could be a poison."

I snap my hand back. "How do you know all this stuff?"

He shrugs. "I just find this fascinating."

"And you keep all that information straight in your head?" I playfully narrow my eyes at him.

"Mostly."

"Uh-huh." I nudge him. "Keep going. I know you'll be a great alchemist."

He smiles. "Thanks, Wren."

"No problem." I turn my attention to Jesse as he meanders through the aisles with relative disinterest. I carefully make my way around the other students until I'm standing behind him. "What's up?"

"Wishing my parents didn't spend all that time drilling this stuff in my head."

"You already know all of them?" I take in the rows of colors and various shades of green. There's so much here, I know I'm going to struggle with remembering them. Besides that, it's hard to think Jesse takes anything seriously, much less his studies long enough to memorize plants and their functions.

"Nearly every single one." He taps his temple. "It's all in here."

He pauses at one and narrows his eyes on the tag as he gently brushes his fingers across the leaves. "I'll be. Here's number three."

He pulls out his notebook and jots down a few notes on the plant. Once finished, he snaps it shut and tucks it back under his arm, sliding the pencil behind his ear. "This one," he points to a bluish-green, vine-like plant. "This one is a great aphrodisiac." He winks at me.

I shake my head. "There's the Jesse I know and love."

"Love? Kiss got ya that bad, huh?"

I playfully shove him. "Says the man who confessed his undying devotion to me outside of the library."

He points out several more plants that are "great aphrodisiacs."

"Just tell me which ones you want to try first. There's no reason to try them all at once."

I smack his arm. "Focus."

"Okay."

A pull enters my mind and I have a feeling I know what it is. I smile as I surrender to the sensation. It's a vision of Jesse feeding me the aphrodisiacs as hands of a clock constantly spin with a faint outline of two lovers, entangled between the sheets, moving in erotic ways.

I shake my head and try to put my mind on other less naughty things as I fan myself to cool the heat burning my cheeks.

Jesse peeks over his shoulder at me with a devious smirk.

Savannah comes up behind me. "There are so many herbs here. Many of them I'm familiar with, so it will help me recognize the attributes in the ones that have healing properties. I've been researching unusual and rare magic in the library in hopes of finding a way to help heal my sister."

I reach over, covering her hand with mine and giving it a gentle, reassuring squeeze. "I really hope it works out for you. If anyone can do it, it's you."

She smiles. "Thanks for the vote of confidence."

"Just giving credit where it's due."

"Hey, so... we should hang out sometime. It's been a while."

I stop and turn to face her as I realize she's right. "You know what? It has. Let's do it."

"Great. I need some girl time." She turns her attention to the herbs and nods once. "How are you doing, absorbing all of this?"

I shrug. "I'll get it. Eventually."

"If you need a study buddy for when Milo and Jesse are busy, come to me. I've got your back."

"Thanks." I chuckle.

I turn my focus to my own notes and jot down everything I think will be useful, but I have to admit it's a bit overwhelming with the sheer number of herbs in the greenhouse. Not to mention, many of them seem to have both healing and injuring capabilities, depending on what they are blended with. It's going to be a lot to pin down.

But I'll do it.

I have to.

Besides, I never know when this knowledge may come in handy someday.

The bell chimes through the air, signaling another

class time coming to an end. Some of the students near me groan.

On the way out, Savannah stops me. "I forgot something. I'll be right back."

"Okay. I'll catch up with you later."

She twists as she walks to wave bye at me, a smile stretching her lips and brightening her violet eyes.

That girl is something else. Always so bubbly and happy. It's contagious.

CHAPTER NINETEEN

I move along the halls, avoiding the crowds and idle chatter that rings in my ears. Once I turn a corner, it's empty. I sigh in relief and quickly move along the hall as I try to make it to my next class. I'm not paying attention to where I'm going when a figure steps in front of me. He grabs my attention just before I slam into his body. I stop as realization dawns on me. I frown as Anderson smiles, seemingly rather proud of himself. Of course, he would corner me when no one else is around. But one thing stands out more than the fact that he's smiling like a madman. He looks… sick.

His skin is unusually pale, and his eyes are sunken in and his lips chapped as if dehydrated. Sweat beads down his face, and he has an odd, desperate expression that I've never seen him display before. It actually takes me by surprise, because he seemed fine when I saw him in alchemy class. Well, whatever it is, it's not my problem. And an energy-stealing creep like him probably had it coming.

I stare him down. "Not you. Not now. Not ever. Leave me alone."

"I need to talk to you."

I groan. "Really? No. What is so hard to accept about that?"

I step around him and start to walk off.

Jesse and Milo approach with confused expressions. Jesse's eyes focus on Anderson.

"Hey guys!" I say loud enough to let Anderson know that I have backup.

"What's going on?" Jesse asks.

"Anderson won't leave me alone." I look over my shoulder at him. His eyes are wide and wild. His shoulders rise and fall with each breath which he takes in an exaggerated motion.

He reaches toward me, stepping nearer to close the gap between us. As he moves, my energy starts to seep away as his hand gets closer to me. I take a sluggish step backward. Jesse and Milo approach. Both of them push him back. I barely hear the echoes of what they say as words seem like they are coming from underwater. My whole head feels buzzy, and a lump forms in my throat.

As the sensation passes, anger burns through me.

That's the final straw.

Anderson breaks free, twisting out of their grips and taking a few steps back as he adjusts his clothes, smoothing out the wrinkles from his shirt. Milo shrugs and shakes out his arms, scowling at Anderson with a look that makes me want to cower. I'm not used to seeing that expression on such a beautiful face. He returns to my side, a look of concern twisting his features as he glances me over.

"I'm fine." I give Milo a confident nod before glancing back over at Jesse, who's still positioned between me and Anderson.

Jesse looks like he's seconds from destroying Anderson in the halls as he acts as a barrier between me and Milo and Anderson. "I *dare* you to take another step forward."

Anderson only stands there and glares at Jesse. His eyes shift toward me. Jesse steps in the way. "If you ever come near her again, I'll end you." Jesse shoves a finger into Anderson's chest.

His darkened glare settles on Jesse, and I want to jump in and stop whatever is forming in Anderson's twisted mind. "Try and stop me." Spittle shoots from his lips. "She belongs to me!"

The hell I do. I belong to no one.

Time to end this.

I step forward. "I will never belong to you. And after I get done speaking with the headmaster, you will be lucky to step foot anywhere near this island again."

Jesse smirks at me with pride. He knows I've got this, and I know that he'll always have my back. I try to ignore the pull in my lips... I let them quirk a little.

"Come on," I say to Milo and Jesse. "Let's get this over with."

Without waiting for them to follow, I head straight to Gideon's office.

CHAPTER TWENTY

We file through Gideon's office door and I'm surprised to find Soren standing there. He has a look of concern as I storm through, stop, and take in his gorgeous form.

"Soren!" I rush to him.

"What's going on?" Gideon shuts the door behind us.

I face him as Jesse answers. "Anderson."

Gideon's brows knit together as a frown pulls down the corners of his lips.

I shrug. "He tried to steal more of my energy. He looked... sick."

Milo steps forward. "I think he's obsessed with Wren's power. He's got a taste for it, and now it's like a drug for him."

"He also said I belong to him." I cross my arms over my chest as I take a calming breath. Repeating those words angers me.

The nerve.

"He did what?" Soren stomps forward. "Let me handle it."

Gideon shakes his head. "No. I will. As headmaster of the school, I'm in charge of delegating punishments. And considering the sensitive nature of this one, I think there is only one thing I can do."

"And that is?" I ask.

"Suspend him for the remainder of the semester. It'll be like detoxing from Wren. It may be enough for him to wise up. Especially if it's anything like Milo suggests and it's Wren's power he's attracted to. This is all still new territory, so it's possible the meteorite is what's drawing him in. Being confined to his room for the rest of the semester will give him the chance to make the right decisions."

Honestly? I don't like it. I want him expelled so there's no chance for him to try again. "And if it's not enough to make better decisions?"

Gideon sets his gaze on me. "Then he will be expelled."

"Oh, so we just leave Wren out there on a silver platter with an engraved invitation? Please, come and steal my power." Jesse shifts and leans against the wall. His arms cross over his chest as his steel blue eyes settle on Gideon with a dangerous glint.

Soren growls. "I can't believe I'm saying this, but Jesse is right."

"I can't just expel him. He has to be suspended first. According to the treaty that allows him to attend here, there are steps I must follow. For all involved." Gideon rubs a hand through his hair. "Trust and believe, I don't like the fact that he remains at Blackbriar anymore than any of you."

Soren shakes his head. A sarcastic laugh leaves his mouth. "He's grown cocky of his place here. More needs to be done."

Gideon holds up a hand to stop the onslaught of arguments. "I understand and agree with each of you. Believe me, I do. But even I have rules I have to abide by. Per the council, I have to give students a chance to prove themselves here. I hate him just as much as everyone else. He won't be an issue for the remainder of the semester. If he steps out of line just once," he holds up a finger, "after he's back, his ass will be thrown out of here fast enough to make his head spin."

Milo steps forward. "We can't risk him finding out about her powers. It's bad enough he won't leave her alone, but to have him siphoning her power whenever he pleases is unacceptable."

Gideon nods. "You're right. However, it's possible he's already aware and has become possessive over it. Thus, his comment about her belonging to him."

"That's great and all," I step forward. "But that doesn't fully explain my power's effects."

They all shrug.

"Which reminds me…" I take a deep breath. This seems like as good a time as any to bring up my magic. "My magic responds to each of you in a different way. Only you four. No one else."

They all stare at me with a mix of surprised expressions and raised eyebrows.

"Well that explains so much." Milo shoves his glasses up his nose and smiles.

"Huh?" I stare at him as if he's grown a second head.

"You feel it too?" Soren asks.

"Wait. You all feel the same thing?" I shift my gaze between the four of them. "And none of you decided to bring that up?"

"Pot calling the kettle black, darlin'." Jesse smirks.

I glare at him. "Oh, don't *you* start with me."

"Just calling it as it is." He shrugs, arms still crossed over his chest.

I shake my head.

"I feel it too." Gideon faces me. "I just didn't know how to bring it up. But it is an interesting development."

Milo steps forward, brows furrowed in concentration. "If we all feel something near Wren, then it's possible that the meteorite has more of a story behind it. If it's able to choose us and not others, perhaps she fused with something sentient. Or, maybe, there is a deeper explanation. I can do more research once I'm done with my current project. However, if my suspicions are correct, that's exactly what's going on here based on what I've already learned about magic and its history in the world."

"Oh good. I'm invaded by an alien life-form."

"Well," Jesse says from his perch, "I always felt there was something otherworldly about you." He smirks.

I shake my head, but damn it all, I can't help but smile.

Still, even I can't deny the feeling inside me. It feels right. My magic churns through me even now, prompting me toward some purpose that I have yet to fulfill. I know, deep down, that he's right. Although it wouldn't hurt to have some sort of proof.

With proof, and my men backing me, I can do

anything. Maybe my purpose is to change the world. Right the wrongs and create a lasting peace.

But I'm getting ahead of myself.

For now, we'll dig deeper into this. It'll take time and patience on my part.

Besides, my father is still out there somewhere. I'll also need to deal with the Order.

"It makes sense." Gideon's voice pulls me from my thoughts. "And if that's the case, this changes everything. Wren could usher in a new age. New magic." He shakes his head as he falls into his own thoughts.

"I suppose that explains Anderson's persistence." Soren paces at a slow canter. His gaze catches mine, and I'm frozen in place with the intensity of his stare. "What does this mean for the Order though? What could they possibly want with her?"

"Isn't it obvious?" Jesse joins the rest of us in the middle of the room. "Power. And she has a lot of it."

I shake my head. "No. That's not it. It's deeper than that. I just don't know exactly what it is, yet."

"Either way," Milo says, "it's nothing good."

"Speaking of..." I shift toward Soren. "What did you learn on your trip?"

"There is some unexplained movement. But there's no confirmation of who or why. However, it is a considerable group, and it appears they are on high alert."

"That's it?" I ask, dumbfounded. There has to be more.

"That's it. Basically." He shifts and faces Gideon. "I have suspicions they are moving throughout the country to all of their compounds in an effort to throw off the magusari. Especially now. They're covering up something."

"Where my father is being kept."

He shrugs. "We don't know that, however it is possible. And that leads me to the next thing on the list." He takes a deep breath. I almost want to shake the words out of him. "I couldn't find anything on your father's supposed criminal activity."

"Really?" Joy fills me and I almost jump with excitement—until Soren holds up his hands.

"Magusari don't have official criminal reports or warrants, and they are usually the ones who deliver those. Because there is none, it means your father isn't a wanted man in the mage community."

Still, I'm relieved.

"For now, this is a good sign. But please don't get your hopes up. Just because there isn't anything now doesn't mean that there won't be later, especially since a search was conducted."

I nod. "Thank you."

"He still can't come here. We have to be sure beyond a doubt. For now, the safehouse is best until things settle down." Gideon's attention settles on me and I nod in agreement.

Well, that's disappointing.

"We need a plan to keep Wren safe. Knowing now what we do, anyone could be after her. Especially the Order."

I shake my head. "If that's the case, why don't they just come here and take me?"

Gideon's blue-green eyes ensnare me again. "Because of the special protections and provisions this island has that covers the students and faculty."

"Meaning?" I ask.

"Meaning, no individual or group may come onto the grounds without express permission from the council and myself. This is a Switzerland of sorts. So long as you are here, you are protected by these regulations."

Soren pulls my attention to him as he speaks. "Which also means, the Order, as vast and powerful as they may be, would never go against the protections here. It'd come across as an act of war, and expose their existence to the world."

"I don't like where this is going." I shake my head and start to pace the floor myself.

"Think of it as a sanctuary." Soren stops my pacing to gaze deep into my eyes. "You're always going to be safe here."

I nod. "But what about when I'm not?"

"For now," Gideon says, "you won't leave the island."

I shake my head. "That's not fair, and you know it."

He sighs and pinches the bridge of his nose.

My mind goes full tilt as I think of my father and our quest to rescue him. They're not going to kick me off the team that easily. "What if I had some sort of protection charm? Savannah mentioned she can't see my aunt well because of one. That may be useful. So, when I'm off the island, I can still be safe."

"The people who are after you could see through that," Milo adds.

Traitor.

"You're going to side with them? Knowing how important this is to me?"

"I'm sorry, Wren. No one here wants to see you get hurt." His eyes are soft and my heart skips a beat at the sadness that pours through me with his look.

"Then we'll make provisions around that. What I'm suggesting would allow me to be on my own and attend classes without an escort. It'll further protect me off island so I can come with you. So please stop trying to keep me locked away like a porcelain doll."

Gideon sighs. "Very well. Let's give it a shot at least. It'll provide some extra security. Milo, you should help Wren and Savannah gather ingredients and the right spell for this."

Milo nods. "I'll start now."

I smile. "Thanks, Milo. I'll meet up with you in a bit."

He heads for the door, then halts and looks over his shoulder, nodding once before leaving.

Jesse steps forward. "This little shindig isn't going off without a bang. I'm adding an illusion enchantment to the item. It will help keep others from sensing her power. For all intents and purposes, she'll look like an ordinary mage."

Aww. I'm touched.

"Excellent suggestion, Jesse." Gideon leans back in his chair, seeming more relaxed than just a moment ago.

"I'll go get started then."

"I will handle Anderson's suspension." Soren starts for the door.

"No. I'll do it." Gideon stands from his desk.

I slap my thighs with my hands. "I guess I'll go

meet up with Milo and Savannah. Thanks for every-thing, guys. I really appreciate you agreeing to this option."

Because if they rejected my idea, I would've raised hell.

Gideon and Soren nod. I softly smile as I walk toward the door.

meet up with him and Second. Thanks for everything, guys. I really appreciate you sticking to this plan.

CHAPTER TWENTY-ONE

I'm a little disappointed that Milo isn't in the library when I enter. I find Savannah scurrying about with a large stack of books, moving shelf to shelf and slipping them back into their spots. She glances at me as I step through the door. A few students, books filling their arms, move out of my way toward the exit as I walk to my favorite table. A couple of first-year students from my herbology class look up from their reading at a table nearby. They pop in their ear buds and return to their studies. I cast them a brief glance and continue on.

"Just missed Milo. He's off to see what he can do about the ingredients for the spell we found."

"Oh?" I wait for her to appear around the edge of the bookshelves before continuing. As soon as her violet eyes settle on me, I ask, "You guys did all the work without me?"

She looks at me intently. "I already had an idea of what spell to use. I found it while going through the old books in the back. Thought I'd pick up a spell for my sister, but a warding spell stuck out to me." She shrugs. "Are you really that upset?"

I slump forward on the table, using my bent right arm to prop up my head. "No. Just sort of feel useless."

"Well, it will take a week to prepare. Maybe you can help Milo gather the ingredients? Some of the things we need will require the headmaster's approval as they're high-level items. Maybe you could get a list of those from Milo and get permission while he's gathering the rest?"

"That's a good idea." I nod, sitting up. "What spell did you find?"

"It's an enchanted charm. Milo is picking one out for you. Once we have that, we can apply the spell. As an added measure, Jesse's ready to infuse some of his illusion magic to it." She pauses and holds up a finger. "Actually, we may need help from Soren and Gideon as well." She takes a seat. "Maybe you can let them know?"

I smile. "Oh, now you're asking too much of me." I fake feeling faint, playing it up until Savannah laughs.

"Dramatic much?" Her words bubble out between chuckles.

I drop the act instantly and shrug. "Maybe."

We both crack into a peel of laughter, the sound way too loud for the library as it echoes horribly off the walls.

Savannah takes a breath. "Now, as I was saying… you'll need to wear the charm all the time. Otherwise, it won't work."

I nod. "Sounds simple enough."

"Maybe. I dunno…" she narrows her eyes on me. "That may be too much work for you."

"Hardy har, har. You're a riot." I sit back in my seat and cross my arms over my chest as though I have a bad attitude.

She shakes her head. "Jesse is rubbing off on you, I see."

"Eh, hasn't been much rubbing, but he's trying."

"Pervert."

"Thank you." I laugh.

"Speaking of men," she smiles and bobs her eyebrows, "who's taking you to the Halloween dance?"

Shoot. I had forgotten all about that. It's in a couple days. Honestly, I forced it out of my mind. Dances are something I don't really know how to do. The formal get-togethers, that is, not the action. I love dancing.

Going to a formal dance though? The idea is daunting. I clear my throat. "Um… I don't know. Probably just meet up with them there."

She wiggles in closer. "Do you have your costume yet?"

"I don't. But I'm sure I'll figure it out."

"Well, if you need one, I have a few. It's a masquerade, so it should be pretty easy to find anything to match the theme."

I nod. "Thanks."

She sits back and studies me with a quirked eyebrow. "Interesting."

"What?" A pinch forms in the center of my forehead.

"You're nervous." She states it as a simple non-judgmental fact.

It's true, though.

"Why?"

I shrug. "Didn't really get the chance to go to many formals before my parents… well, you know."

She nods. "Indeed, I do."

I sigh as the silence settles between us and Savannah continues to study me. Her gaze seems to go in and out of focus and I shake my head. "Stop that."

"I don't know what you're talking about." She smiles like a Cheshire cat.

I giggle. "You're horrible."

She shrugs. "I think you'll do just fine. But, if you want to have some help getting ready, just let me know. We'll have you looking like the belle of the ball before I'm done with you."

"Since you put it that way..." I shake my head and laugh.

She chuckles. "All right, all right. I'll go easy on you. But trust me when I say you're going to be gorgeous!"

"That isn't helping."

I spent a good chunk of the last six years of my life learning to fall under the radar. Attention was never a good thing when it came to the trolls. And being the "belle of the ball" or "gorgeous" would bring attention to me. A sense of anxiety quakes through me.

"Hey, relax. You'll see." She covers my hands with hers. "I'll take care of you, and if anyone dares to make the night anything less than simply amazing for you, I'll kick their ass."

I laugh at that. It's good to be a friend of Savannah, The Spunky One.

"Thanks, I'll hold you to that."

"Oh, it will happen. Mark my words. So, still wanna go?"

I stare into her beautiful violet eyes and take in a hint of hope and eagerness.

I sigh. "Yes. Definitely, since you put it so delicately."

"Hey," she pulls at her collar once as she leans back in her seat. "I got your back."

After the recent, tension-filled events, this was just the thing I needed. I'm still a bit reserved when it comes to showing up in a crowded area all done up, but hey, Savannah has a good point.

But she won't be doing the ass-kicking. I will.

CHAPTER TWENTY-TWO

Tonight is the night of the Halloween Dance. I'm already dreading the crowd I'll have to face. Interacting with large groups has never been my thing.

I trudge into my room, exhausted from the day's training and classes. Desperate for a shower and a nap. But as soon as I make it to my bed, I'm taken aback by a long black dress. A note sits on top. I grab the card and it reads: *Wear this tonight.*

I smile to myself. Soren is something else. He and I haven't had much time together since he got back from his travels. I bet this is from him.

I had hoped that we would've had some time between classes or maybe before or after school, but he's been busy. Not being able to hold him in my arms or share with him my day's trials make me miss him, but since he'll be at the masquerade, I'm excited and a little anxious to see him.

I stare at the dress, taking in its mermaid shape and plunging neckline and realizing that I have no idea what I'm doing. How do you even get into this thing?

One person might know, but I need to shower first. I'm not going to a dance smelling sweaty and nasty. Trolls smell like a walk in a park compared to me right now. And that says something. Take my word for it.

With that, I hop into the shower, taking the time to shave everything I need to, and paying a little extra attention to my wild red hair by putting extra conditioner in it. My hair is frizzy from being kept in some sort of bun, ponytail, or some semblance of both for the whole week.

Once I'm fresh and changed into some lose-fitting clothing, I grab the dress and head out the door.

I race through the halls and around the corners with their twists and turns until I reach the House of Kraken. The girl that answers the door could be Milo's twin. Right down to the glasses. Though, she has freckles, and her long hair is piled up on her head in a messy bun. I smile, blushing a little from staring at her. "I'm here to see Savannah."

She nods and holds the door open wider. I quickly make my way to Savannah's room. Her door is propped open. She calls out from the other side of the room. "Come in, Wren."

This girl will never stop amazing me.

I step in and find her at her vanity all set up for a makeover. My eyes go wide at the lavish display of tools and various shades of eye shadow, blush, foundation and lipstick laid out on the surface.

"Uh…"

"Stop that, come on. We need to begin!" She waves me over with quick circular motions of her hand. As I approach, she takes the dress and gently lays it out on the bed. "Sit!"

"Yes ma'am." I giggle.

"That's right!"

As she begins running a brush through my hair, it feels… weird. The fuss with making my appearance such a priority is outside of everything I've known. I don't dare complain though. Savannah is taking time out of her day to help me, and I appreciate the effort. Besides, it feels good to pamper myself a little, and the looks on my men's faces when they see me tonight will be priceless. However, at some point, I'm gonna have to learn how to do this myself.

"This is a rite of passage," Savannah says. "Today, you become a woman."

I snort. "As opposed to being a girl before now?"

I admit that I'm inexperienced with most of this stuff, but come on… give me *some* credit.

"No. Okay, so *woman* was a poor choice of word."

"Just a bit." I squint my eyes and hold up my finger and thumb with just a small space between them.

She chuckles. "How about a lady?"

I think about that for a moment and nod. "Sounds right."

She giggles and shakes her head. "All right, deal."

Never mind this is closer to the normalcy I've been looking for. Sure, not every woman wears makeup, but this is a normal school thing, right?

Right.

Once my hair is up in curlers, I turn my head from side to side and look at myself in the mirror. I laugh at my reflection. Savannah joins in and we busy ourselves for a few moments by making funny faces at each other.

Savannah quickly turns me and the chair to face her as she holds a bottle of foundation in her hand. She dabs a spongy wedge into the mixture and starts to apply the substance to my face in smooth, even strokes. "So, where did the dress come from?"

"I don't know for sure." I close my eyes as she moves around them, applying makeup. "I think it's from Soren."

A wistful sigh leaves Savannah's lips. "You have surrounded yourself with some fine specimens of the opposite sex, my friend."

"Is that weird?" This whole time I've never thought about it, it just feels right to me. I wouldn't choose between them if my life depended on it. Still, I wonder...

"Though it's not as common as it used to be, it's a thing in the world of mages. Most of those that still prefer multiple partners don't advertise it. Especially among humans."

Maybe that explains it. Not sticking with just one guy is in my blood. It feels deeper than that though.

Much, much deeper.

"I didn't know that, about mages and relationships."

"Of course, you didn't." Savannah moves to a different item on the vanity's surface. It's a large wand with a tiny brush at the end of it. She dips it into some dark shadow then uses her fingers to turn my face toward hers and keeps it at an upright angle. "How could you after living in the woods?"

"Thanks for the reminder." It comes off sarcastically.

Her apologetic eyes settle on mine, but her lips turn up at the corners in a slight, barely noticeable move. She strokes the powder across my eyelids and in minutes she's finished. "It's not like the trolls offer Mage Relationships 101. That's something that's taught through families. Generation to generation. It's passed down information."

"Fair point." I shrug a shoulder.

A comfortable silence falls between us as she applies the mascara and liner to my eyes and a healthy, vibrant shade of red to my lips. She quickly undoes the curlers from my hair and styles my hair with my back to the mirror.

"Can't peek. It's a surprise."

"If you say so." A giggle bounces between my words.

With a few tugs and tossing my hair over my shoulder, she spins me around.

"What do you think?"

I gape, my mouth hanging open so wide that a dragon could fly into it.

This is... me? Really?

I mean, this is Blackbriar. It could be an enchanted mirror I'm looking into, but I doubt Savannah is the type to mislead me like that. Leaning forward, I study my brown eyes that stand out against the shadowy lids, almost darker than normal. The browns are deeper. My lips look fuller, and the lipstick color compliments the color in my hair covering my left shoulder, perfectly pouring down the front of me in spirals. A pin made of gold and encrusted with a white gem is clipped to the side of my head.

"Wow." It comes out breathless.

"I thought you'd like it. Now," she claps her hands, startling me from my mesmerizing reflection, "let's get you dressed."

I slip into it, and it seems a bit tight, but as Savannah zips up the back, it hugs my curves perfectly. My breasts even look stunning in this dress as they swell ever so delicately through the opening in the front.

My transformation is beyond amazing. I've never felt so gorgeous in my entire life.

"Now the finishing touch..." Savannah drops a mask in front of my face and helps me situate it before tying it behind my head. She stands back, observing her masterpiece. Clasping her hands in front of her heart, she smiles dreamingly. "Perfection!"

I blush. "Thank you."

She waves it off. "Think nothing of it. I had plenty of natural beauty to work with."

I smile. My cheeks warm and I feel this funny sensation in my chest and stomach. I'm so unaccustomed to compliments. It feels awkward, almost.

With a dramatic bow, she turns and gets herself ready in record time. I imagine getting all done up gets easier and quicker with practice.

Her costume is a simple yet elegant amethyst-colored dress, in an eye-catching crushed velvet material, with long sleeves and a silver cloak. She lifts the hood over her head and adjusts the mask that covers half her face. The mask's design is silver and purple roses, which make her violet eyes stand out even more.

She leaves her beautiful dark brown hair down, cascading over her shoulders. Little rivers of purple sneak through, completing the look.

Striking a pose, she smiles. "What do you think?"

"I hate how beautiful you are." I laugh. "You're going to knock some lucky guys dead on their feet."

She giggles. "Well, what are we waiting for then? Let's go break some hearts."

We lock arms and head for the celebration. As we leave Savannah's room, I catch some of the stares people give us. I want to believe that they're all for Savannah, but it's really nice to see eyes connect with mine and lips parted into O's.

I chuckle.

Break some hearts, indeed.

CHAPTER TWENTY-THREE

I enter the crowded arena and gasp at the room's magical transformation. It's all made to look like a creepy orchard with scary faced Jack-o-lanterns hanging from the trees. More of the carved gourds are scattered along the floor which is coated in a thick fog-like smoke. A star-filled sky spreads above me, with a full moon wearing a creepy grin. Bats float in and out of view as the scent of spices, roasted meats, and baked goods waft toward me. Music, mingled with high-pitched strings, screams, deep wallowing laughs, and creaking wood fills the air.

"Whoa."

"You got that right," Savannah says from my side. She smiles wide and moves deeper into the arena. I lose sight of her among the roaming figures of masked students. I spy her handsome mentor from our initiate trainings, and I can't help but break into a large grin. I'm truly happy for her. Especially with the way his face breaks into a huge smile, which lights up his blue eyes, upon her approach.

There is so much adoration in his eyes, I'm nearly giddy for my friend. She deserves a slice of happiness, and I hope she gets a big piece of that tonight. Such an unusual feeling for me to experience, but I love it.

The music seems to come from everywhere, moving closer toward me and then fading away into eerie echoes, like the ebb and flow of the ocean waves surrounding this island.

I catch pot-bellied gnomes near some of the decorations, entangling themselves in shimmery black webbing and accidentally toppling over a couple of Jack-o-lanterns.

To say that I'm in awe is an understatement. Blackbriar really knows how to go all out for holidays. I'm glad I came.

I notice Milo and Jesse huddled together in a darkened corner. My heart swells at the sight of them sipping drinks and chatting it up. It warms me inside and out that they get along so well. They're dashingly handsome in their suits and masks.

I make my way toward them. As I move, their

attention turns to me and their eyes hungrily take in my form. Milo's mouth parts slightly in awe. Jesse smiles in that devilish way of his. Both reactions stretch my lips, and I really do feel like the belle of the ball with their well-received attention.

As I stop in front of them, Milo gulps.

I chuckle. I could probably get used to this.

"You are simply divine," Jesse says. "A true goddess."

"You look…" Milo licks his lips as he stammers. "Beautiful."

I giggle. "Thanks, boys."

"Here comes the party-pooper." Jesse speaks from over the rim of his cup as he brings it to his mouth, giving a slight nod over my shoulder.

I turn to face Soren. He hesitates in his steps, moving slower as his eyes take in my form, drinking me in like I'm a tall drink of water and he's a dehydrated man. His gaze finally comes to rest on my ample cleavage. He doesn't look so bad himself in his straight black suit that compliments my dress right down to the black beaded details of our masks.

I knew he bought me the dress.

"Wow, Wren. You look…" he sucks in a deep breath, huffing it out, "You look amazingly gorgeous."

"Thanks to you." I gesture to myself. "You've got good taste."

He cocks his head slightly to the side as a flash of confusion passes through his eyes. "What do you mean?"

"The dress is from you, isn't it?" Maybe I was wrong, and it's simply a coincidence we're dressed alike?

"I didn't buy that dress for you. But I sure wish I had." He takes another long look at me.

I blush, but I'm confused at the same time. If he didn't buy this dress for me, then who did?

"I bought the dress for you," a woman's voice speaks from behind me just over my left shoulder.

I spin around and see Aunt Patricia standing in front of me, looking ravishing herself with her silvery-white hair piled at the top of her head like an updo a Greek goddess would have worn. A silver mask with blends of purple and gold seed beads cover her eyes. It complements her high-collared golden satin, form-fitting dress with a sequined purple belt that cinches at her waist. Purple gems dangle at her neckline from a barely visible chain. Her dress is much more conservative than mine, but it suits her beautifully.

Rich and regal.

"Oh, there wasn't a signature on the note, so I just—"

"Worry not, my dear. That's not the point of the gift." She smiles, but with the shadows thick in the room, it's hard to tell if it reaches her eyes. "May I borrow you for a moment?"

Her gaze flits between my men and back to me.

A pinch instantly forms in the center of my forehead, and I'm immediately happy the expression is hidden by my mask. I wonder what she wants to say that she has to pull me away to say it. "Sure."

She steps off to the side, moving a few paces over near an empty table. I know better than to refuse to follow her. As soon as we are out of earshot of my men, she faces me. Her eyes take in the details of my hair, mask, and then my dress.

She seems to scrutinize every detail of my appearance, and I don't like it one bit. It's intrusive versus the complimentary way my men looked at me. Their gazes were at least appreciative of my appearance. Whereas, my aunt's seems... demeaning. I wonder why she bought the dress if she doesn't approve of how it looks? Then again, I may be looking at this all wrong. It's difficult to read my aunt. Even Savannah couldn't read her fully, but even she said she wasn't sure what that meant.

"You favor your mother. Did you know that?"

Her question strikes me as odd. I don't know whether to take that as a good or bad thing. Her voice seems emotionless... big surprise there. And with everything I've observed up to now, it's hard to know her intentions. In any case, I decide to just take it as a fact she intended to share with me. "No, I didn't know that."

"You have your father's eyes, of course."

I give an awkward half-smile. She confuses me by her words not coinciding with her actions. But maybe this is her attempt at opening up to me? She did buy this gorgeous dress. I'm sure it costs ten times more than anything I've ever worn. "Thank you for the dress, Aunt Patricia."

She levels her brown eyes on me as the corners of her lips pull into a grin. "You are very welcome. I did not want you to miss out on something like this. Especially since you have missed out on so much in your life."

Wow. I do believe that smile is purely genuine. Huh... I hope this is a glimpse into that softer interior she keeps guarded so well, but with how little she shows of it, I can't be sure.

She's an enigma, for certain.

However, I feel in my gut there was more behind

the gesture that she wanted to convey, but she doesn't say anything else. Perhaps she didn't feel like this was the place or time. Although I still feel a little awkward, I can at least give her credit for trying. Maybe that impenetrable wall is being chipped away, little by little. "I appreciate that."

She nods. "Think nothing of it. Enjoy yourself for the evening. You have earned it."

I smile. "I will."

"Go on, now." She shoos me away with an elegant wave of her hand.

I nod and turn around, heading back toward my men. All the while I'm making my way back to them, I consider the fact that perhaps I've been mistaken in assuming there was something wrong between us. We have two different personality types, there are going to be bumps in the road as we try to reconnect. I shouldn't let that discourage me. The dress appears to be lavishly expensive. Her gift is a contradiction to the way she acts around me most of the time. Once or twice I've seen her let her guard down, and she did so again tonight, but they are outnumbered by the amount of times she seems less than loving toward me. When she hides behind her wall, I almost feel like she dislikes me with the way she responds to me.

My aunt is guarded and distant. Her demeanor

tonight further proved it, but it also gave me a deeper glimpse into who she is. She did something generous for me without question and without being asked. I saw a little more of that fracturing wall chip away.

Milo was right, we just needed to give it a little more time.

Jesse steps forward, distracting me from my thoughts with the way he moves toward me. I smile. He holds out his warm hand toward me. "Time to dance, my goddess."

I chuckle and take his arm.

He leads me through the trees, into a small meadow-like scene, bordered by old farmhouse fencing sections. Haybales and scarecrows stand guard among more Jack-o-lanterns. The fog is less dense here, and more of my fellow students are coupled up, dancing away to a slower, more gothic-like tune. It's eerie, beautiful, and magical all at the same time.

Simply enchanting.

Jesse spins me once in front of him, then settles his right hand on my left hip. He pulls me close, placing my right hand on his right shoulder as he presses his body against mine, making my magic zing. He smiles happily and I'm mesmerized.

"Bout time I get a little bit of worshiping in, don't ya think?" he winks.

"Careful, my head may explode from over-inflation."

He shrugs. "Can't have that now, can we?" His voice is deep, low, and makes my toes curl in the heels I'm wearing. Pressure builds between my legs and I bite the corner of my lower lip.

"No. We can't. The cleanup would be horrendous."

"Though your pretty bits would fit with the décor."

I smack him and laugh. My belly bounces against his hard abs and it's a thought that brings delicious images to my mind. My fingers trail the valleys between his muscles as he rides me through climax over and over again.

I shake my head to clear the image from my mind and bring me back to reality.

He chuckles, and I get the distinct impression he knew exactly what I was thinking. He brings his mouth to my ear and furthers the dirty thoughts crossing my mind. "Imagine the things that are running through my mind right now."

"Oh yeah? What's that?" I'm playing a dangerous game of cat and mouse right now, and I don't care who sees.

"I want to take you to your room, remove that dress with my teeth, and let my fingers roam over every inch of your body until you beg for me to stop."

Oh.

My knees nearly give out on me because of the image that plays through my mind with his little prompt. Need pulls at my navel as pressure builds even more between my legs. A sigh whispers from my mouth of giving into what it would feel like to have my legs wrapped around him and my fingers tangled in his hair.

"Look at that." He pulls away to look at me then gets close again. "Let me warn you though…" he whispers in my ear again. "The real thing will blow all those images out of the water."

"You're horrible," I mutter, but there's no conviction in the words. They barely come out as it is.

He chuckles. "How about more *sobering* topics?"

I nervously tap his shoulder with my fingers, in time with the music. "I think that would be best for now."

He shrugs. "Okay, well… I've learned some interesting things about shadow wolves."

"And?" My heart jumps a beat. This is what I need to know.

"They are largely tribal in nature and shift into ethereal forms, leaving their physical bodies behind which are guarded by other trusted tribe members."

"Interesting. So, the ones we killed, do they die physically?"

"In a way, yes."

"In what way?"

"I haven't learned that part, yet. But it's not good from what I gather."

"I would imagine not."

"They're the magical essence of their souls. They can take and give physical damage, as we've figured out already."

"The hard way." My eyes blur out of focus as that fight quickly replays through my mind. I shake the images from my mind. I don't want to let something like that memory tarnish the one I'm making tonight.

"You know?" He dips me back and slowly pulls me back up. "I'd make a great shadow wolf."

I quirk an eyebrow, even though I'm not sure it can be seen with the mask on. "Why?"

"Reasons." He winks. "But that's all I could find. Nothing on Jackson Cane. No one in my house has even heard of him."

I nod. "That's okay, we'll keep digging. I'm grateful for your efforts."

He chuckles. "You still don't get it, do you?"

I cock my head to the side and level my eyes on his steely blue ones. "Get what?"

He shakes his head. "Oh, you sexy vixen, you. You'll certainly undo me in ways you'll never understand."

I chuckle. "That sounds horrible."

"Quite the contrary. I'm looking forward to it." A delightful glint flashes in his eyes.

We share in a laugh as he spins me in circles along the dance floor. I feel light on my feet being pressed into him. My magic pulses through me in delicious ways. The sensation is so common that it feels strange when I don't experience it, which happens only when my men aren't around me.

Before long, the song is over, and he walks me back toward our group.

"She's quite light on her feet." Jesse takes his place next to Milo. "Well, what are you waiting for? I've warmed her up for you and everything."

I laugh. "It's okay. We don't have to dance if you don't want to."

"I want to." Milo snaps his head toward me.

"Oh. Well," I hold out my hand to him, "should we teach the others how it's done?"

He can't take his eyes off me, and he hesitates before he takes my hand and tucks it into the crook of his arm. My magic chills me, causing goosebumps to raise over the surface of my exposed skin, and I delight in the feel of it all as we arrive on the dance floor.

Milo is more gentlemanly than Jesse by a long shot. He keeps a solid two inches at least between us, and he gently rests his hand on my hip. He's so formal and proper. I wonder if I'm not corrupting him—or maybe it's Jesse and Soren corrupting me and that's rubbing off on my interactions with Milo—by wanting to kiss him every time I see him. Of course, his eyes never leave some part of me. If they do, it's a quick glance away, and his eyes are back on me.

"You're looking pretty dashing tonight. You clean up well."

He smiles, eyes never wavering from mine. "And words can't compare to your beauty. They all seem too simple and fall short of what stands before me now."

Be still my heart.

Milo just took my breath away.

I smile and step in closer to him, resting my head on his shoulder. "Never change, Milo."

I feel a peck on the side of my head as we sway from side-to-side, not really dancing, but that doesn't bother me. I can feel the drumming of his heartbeats, and his chest rises and falls in fluid motion. I find solace and comfort in the feel of his arms around me.

For the most part, we're content to be like this. No talking. Just simply being.

Before long, much to my dismay, our song is over. We slowly make our way back to the others. Gideon is there now. And it's the first time he's seen me tonight. He forces himself to look away with a quick turn of his head, but it's not for very long. I can tell it's difficult for him. He can't compliment me. Not here, in front of everyone. I know when he has a chance to get me alone, he's going to do far more than just say how beautiful I am.

"Headmaster Storm." I incline my head toward him and smile in greeting.

He clears his throat. "Miss Blackwood."

"Good to see you."

He nods. "Always a pleasure. If you don't mind, I must continue on my rounds."

He starts to walk away and winks. I giggle to myself. "Until next time."

I watch him walk off until he blends in with the moving shadowy forms of masquerade revelers, and I settle my gaze on Soren. His amber eyes focus on me, and light dances in them with all the things he wants to say but he refrains. He's not open with his feelings. Especially in front of others. But I can see emotion in the way he looks at me. I smile reassuringly.

He steps closer, and I angle my head to look him in the eyes. "Wanna dance too?"

He leans forward, lowering his mouth to my ear. "I don't dance."

I fake a pout. "Meanie."

"Put that lip away. I mean it."

"Or what?" I'm teasing him, goading him, daring him even.

He growls as his hands rest on my hips and give a good squeeze. "Don't make me spank you."

"Oh. Promise?" I giggle as he pulls away and shakes his head.

"Dammit, woman."

"Suit yourself." I shrug and take a stance next to him.

He slips an arm along the small of my back, fingers pressing into my side, urging me closer to him. He leans in close, and says, "I've missed you."

I bite the corner of my lower lip as the words he said carries so much more meaning than he's speaking. I meet his gaze as warmth pools between my legs and through my veins. I push down the delicious images in my mind and chuckle. "You're the insatiable one."

"Stay with me tonight." His voice makes me want

to moan with the delightful tingles that rush through me. The desire hidden within them is toe-curling.

I slip an arm around his waist. Meeting his gaze, I wink. "I'll think about it."

But really, he should know it's going to happen. I need the release, and I haven't spent much time with him recently. He should be shown just how much I've missed him too.

CHAPTER TWENTY-FOUR

Training with Soren this evening was... pleasantly delightful. I think of all the delicious ways he sent me into climax last night, and again tonight. If I could, I'd spend the entire day wrapped up in him, between his sheets.

Sad to say, that's not going to happen.

I work a towel through my hair, breathing in the woodsy scent of the shampoo. Once I finish, I pull out a pair of pajamas.

A knock raps at the door and I stare at it with my eyebrows knitted together. It's unusual for someone to visit my room at this time of night, especially when most students are already in their beds and asleep.

I put my money on Jesse, showing up at my door late at night is something I imagine him doing.

Still, I approach the door and open it, wearing nothing but a towel to cover my body.

I look wide eyed at Milo as he takes in my towel-wrapped form, and I think I'm pushing him to implode. He seems to recover slightly, standing a bit taller and adding an air of confidence in his posture. His lips quirk at the corners and his eyes once again take in my mostly naked body.

His darkened eyes reach mine as I smile knowingly at him.

"Hey, Milo."

"I think I've found something."

I open the door wider and gesture for him to come in. He steps inside and immediately goes to my desk. I close the door and head over as well, wondering what's so important that he needs to see me at this late hour.

Though, if I'm being totally honest, I don't mind one bit. I barely get to see him, and this is Milo. My sexy nerd.

He places a sheet of thin, black cloth on the surface of my desk and pulls out the note we found at the facility in Arizona. It's the one that still pisses me off to this day, but I know we will find my father and bring him to safety. I hold onto that hope, especially during times when it seems like I will never see him again.

Milo uses a piece of white chalk to draw a transmutation circle onto the cloth. As he fills in spaces with various runes, I realize that this particular transmutation circle is intended for the revelation of something. The *ansuz* rune, which looks like a crooked "F" is prominent throughout the circle. It invokes insight and truth. I also catch a glimpse of *kenaz*, which looks like a simple arrow pointing to the left, and that one draws on the power of revealing things.

From there, he lays the letter in the center. Instantly, the runes spark and bleed into the cloth, changing it from its original ink-black color to a milky, greyish color. The note gleams with magic and pops out in a 3-D fashion.

I lean in close, drawn in by the magic happening.

"Do you remember when we learned in rune class that they can be used to decode and to unlock things?" Milo's voice reaches my ears, and I vaguely feel myself nod.

"It took me a little longer than I thought it would, but I was messing around with a project of mine and stumbled across this. Your father left you a clue in the letter he sent you before as well. Anyway, I believe the same principle applies here."

"You did all this?" I'm in awe at just how smart and resourceful Milo is. It really shouldn't surprise me. Yet, he manages to keep doing it.

He nods. "I hope you don't mind."

"Not at all." I wrap my arms around him. "Thanks so much."

He pulls away and points to the display of magic. "Watch."

The letters scramble and spread. Some disappear while others appear until a new message appears.

I gasp.

"How did he do this?" I look at Milo.

He runs a hand through his hair as he shrugs. "Your guess is as good as mine."

I watch as the message becomes clearer and the glow of magic disappears.

I pick up the letter, holding it in my hand as the words barely register.

Little Bird, I have no time to explain. Order is after me. I have to stay ahead of them. If they catch me, they will discover my link to the meteorite and to you. Stay safe. I will come to you when I can. I love and miss you dearly.

"This doesn't make sense. I feel like there should be more, but there's not. If my father had time to leave this, did he plan his escape?" I tap my finger on my lip.

"One thing is for sure... the Order is behind every-thing." I hand the letter over to Milo.

He takes it and his eyes rapidly shift over the words. He nods and huffs out a contemplative sigh. "What do you think is really going on?"

"I don't know for sure, but I do think it's going to be a late night.

"Going to tell the others?" His words follow me as I move to the bed and grab my clothes and rush into the bathroom.

Before I close the door, I say, "Yup."

I toss the towel to the floor and quickly slip on the clothes and exit the bathroom as fast as I can. I walk up to him and press my mouth to his. "Thank you. For everything."

He clears his throat and shoves his glasses up his nose. "Anything for you."

"Let's go." I wait for him to gather the letter and cloth and then we head out the door.

The House of Phoenix is quiet as we move down the hall together, careful with our steps and even the breaths we take. We halt at a corner when we hear the fall of footsteps—either someone patrolling or someone else up past curfew. I whisper to keep my voice from traveling to any listening ears that shouldn't be involved in this conversation. "We should find a way to track my father. Bring that up as well when we get there."

"I agree," Milo whispers back. He picks up on everything.

I grin at my sexy nerd. "Okay, let's hurry before they fall deeply asleep."

"Good idea."

We sneak out into the main halls. Our feet whisper along the floor as we pass statues, paintings, and gnomes rushing in and out of sight. I barely catch their blurring figures as they disappear into a small tunnel or around a corner. Not another soul is in sight, and that's good. Being caught in the halls after curfew would put a very sour twist on tonight's rendezvous.

CHAPTER TWENTY-FIVE

I t took a while to get Jesse up and out of bed. I damn near had to break into his room before he finally responded to the soft tapping on his door. Soren was less than thrilled on his sleep being disrupted, but with a short explanation of everything going on, he became alert. Together, we all rushed to Gideon's office.

On the way to the headmaster's office I realize we'll have a difficult time if he isn't there. "What if Gideon is in his apartment? What then?"

Soren glances at me. "He likes to work late. He'll be there. Trust me."

"When does the man sleep?" My voice hitches slightly higher as I strain to keep my voice just barely above a whisper.

Soren shrugs. "Usually when everyone else does." He frowns. "Just never as long as the rest of us."

Gideon *was* working late, thank goodness. At least we didn't have to wake him up too. He doesn't strike me as a man that enjoys having what little sleep he may get disrupted. He has an enormous amount of things on his plate.

Although, him opening a door, revealing his shirtless torso sounds like a wonderful way to find out for sure...

But not tonight.

"What's going on?" His eyes are narrowed on each of us with a hint of concern.

"Milo found something," Soren says, beating me to the punch. I snap my mouth shut and cast him a short glare.

"What's that?" Gideon yawns, covering his mouth with his elbow.

We move toward his desk and stand around it as Milo unfurls the black cloth and pulls out the letter. He repeats the ritual. "It disappears after fifteen minutes. I don't know why, but it may be so the message isn't discovered by the wrong people."

"Smart man," Soren says.

"Mm-hmm." Gideon rubs the stubble along his chin and fights back another yawn. The whites of his eyes are pink and glossy from a lack of sleep. He shifts his eyes to me and smiles warmly. I return the gesture, if not apologetically. He's a busy man as a headmaster, and even busier with helping me.

Poor man needs a vacation. And a week's worth of sleep.

As the magic works through the letter, Gideon shifts in his seat. "How did you discover this?"

Milo shrugs. "I like to research and tinker around a bit."

Gideon's eyes widen. "Perhaps we should give you a designated area devoted to your research instead of having it done in your room. This way if any mishaps occur, we're not replacing furniture. I would like to maintain access to the room and aid when I can."

Milo's eyes widen and lighten with joy while his lips stretch damn near ear-to-ear. "Yes, sir. That would be amazing."

Just like a kid on Christmas. I can't help but giggle. Gideon found a new buddy. Or maybe it's Milo.

Both. Definitely both.

Gideon nods to himself, and for the most part, he remains quiet and reflective as the soft glow of magic illuminates the letter.

Once the letter is completely revealed, he picks it

up and scans the words. He passes it to Jesse, who reads it and then hands it to Soren.

"So, it's official." Soren passes the letter back to Gideon. "The Order is after him."

"You mean, the Order definitely exists?" Although my words came out sounding like a question, it doesn't change the fact. The Order is not a myth or conspiracy. Now, I need to find out what they want from my dad and why he's on the run.

Soren meets my gaze and nods.

Gideon turns away slightly and rubs his eyes. "We've both known for some time. We just never had proof of their existence beyond circumstantial evidence. It's a magusari's purpose to figure everything out."

"Wait." I hold up a hand in front of me. "You and Soren are magusari?"

The magusari are elite mage warriors chosen to maintain peace within the world. Comprised of assassins, soldiers, and official heads of government, the group works to keep the balance of the world in check and rectify any fluctuations within that balance.

But that may be the bedtime story version. However, from what I know of them, they're not ones to be trifled with. And now that I know the Order truly exists, the magusari must be the yin to their yang.

I cock my head to the side, looking at Gideon and Soren in a whole new light and with much more respect.

"Yes. But it's not widely known." Soren rubs his face. "It's a fact that stays in this room." He looks at me, Jesse, and Milo individually. "Got it?"

We nod in agreement.

"Not my story to tell." Milo covers his mouth with a fist as he yawns.

"Indeed," Jesse says. I turn my attention to him as he stands way too casually. Like hearing of members of the magusari being so close is news he hears everyday. "Though, I may capitalize on this fact at some point. Just saying."

And there's the Jesse I know and love. I shake my head. He's poking the bear just to get a rise out of him.

Soren growls.

"This doesn't look good, Wren." Gideon's voice pulls my attention back to him. "If we manage to find him, it's likely we'll pay hell to clear his name. Remember what you've learned of the Order. They are everywhere and have their hands in every aspect of political office. They won't be easily defeated."

"I understand."

He holds up his hands palms out. "Full disclosure, I have to warn you that we may never recover your father."

I shake my head. "Not an option." I move to my perch on the windowsill. My eyes take in the sleeping island and I sigh. "We can track him, can't we?" I face the group. "With magic, I mean."

"Yes. There are many ways this can be done, but none are foolproof. Your father may be constantly on the move, which makes it difficult, if not impossible."

My shoulders slump as I lean into the window. "Go figure."

"I'm just trying to manage your expectations." Gideon's voice is softer.

I understand he's trying to help and not allow me to get my hopes up, but finding my father has been my driving force recently. I reject the idea that it's impossible until every avenue has been exhausted. "I won't give up until there's no other option available to me. I need to find him."

"With that being said," he continues, and I meet his gaze, curious to know what he is going to add, "I may have a way to help. But it will take time to narrow a position and determine a routine, if he has one."

I nod, standing from the window. "Tell me."

I move toward the desk as Soren shifts, crossing

his arms over his chest. Jesse rests his left ankle on his right knee and leans his head on his right fist, elbow digging into the arm of the chair. Milo sits forward, tenting his fingers, resting his elbows on his knees.

"It's a spell that is taxing on the individual. Perhaps, we can all pitch in and help. It will take much more than me. It's possible that this is the true way Deacon found you. It's bothered me since his motivation to bring you here wasn't clear, nor typical."

"Typical?" I ask.

He frowns. "We scout, just like with human sports. We go and observe, blending in and watching. That's how it's supposed to happen."

I let out a sigh. "Why am I not surprised? I doubt that's the only lie he's told."

"You mean he wasn't honest?" Jesse adds sleepily from his seat. "Say it isn't so."

I narrow my eyes at him. He winks at me. I sigh and shake my head, returning my attention to the headmaster.

"Regardless, the spell is dangerous to do alone. But with others…" Gideon pauses to mull something over. He nods to himself, apparently satisfied. "We may just have enough to get to Michael quicker."

"Professor Lawrence said he used a machine. Granted, his moral compass didn't point north." I cross my arms over my chest and shift my weight from left to right, feeling restless. I'm getting tired, and I want to figure this out before going to bed or I will be useless tomorrow. With or without sleep.

Soren leans forward, propping his weight on his arms and lifting himself over the top of Gideon's desk to put his face directly in front of Gideon's. "I know what you are thinking, and I don't like it."

Gideon sighs. "Of course, you don't."

"You're suggesting... You think she can handle it?" Soren nods toward me.

I scoff. "I'm standing right here, you know. And I can handle it... whatever it is."

Soren stands up slowly, eyes never leaving mine. "Don't be foolish."

I quirk an eyebrow. "You're mistaken if you think I won't do whatever it takes to find my father. And I'll be damned if *you* are going to stop me."

"Wren... Don't." Soren's voice is full of warning.

I open my mouth as Milo stands up and holds his hands out toward me and Soren. "We're all tired. We don't need to be at each other's throats. Both of you check your egos so we can get a plan set."

We both stare coldly at him. He drops his hands with a sigh. "Fine, yell at me if you need to. I'm not going anywhere."

I hesitate. My anger instantly dissolves and is replaced by shame. I soften my look, embarrassed. "Never, Milo."

"He's right." Soren pinches his nose. "Wren, I apologize. You *have* shown you're capable of handling yourself. I just…"

I wait for him to finish but he doesn't. He instead meets my gaze and everything I need to know is in his eyes. I'm overcome with the emotion behind his beautiful amber stare.

Well, now I feel even more like an ass.

He just wants to protect me and keep me safe. Honorable, for sure, but not necessary. I'll be damned if I didn't just cheapen that fact with my attitude.

"I'm sorry." The word is awkward in my mouth, but I feel guilty for letting my lack of sleep get the better of me. Soren nods, full of acceptance.

A knock raps at the door, startling us. We all exchange questioning glances.

Soren moves toward the door, a light flare of magic swirling at his fingertips. He answers it, and Savannah steps in. "Oh… family pow-wow?"

"Sort of," I say.

"Am I interrupting?" She approaches us as Soren closes the door.

Gideon stands from his seat. "Not at all. You have an update?"

She smiles widely. "The spell is ready."

"Good." He lowers his sleepy eyes to his desk. "First thing tomorrow, apply it. We'll all need to focus on resting and not over-exerting ourselves for the next three days. At the end of that rest period, meet me here at seven in the evening. Don't be late. I'll reach out to Lady Alene for help as well."

"What are we doing?" Savannah asks.

"You too," Gideon says. "I'll fill you in later. I'm dead on my feet."

"You look it," she adds.

He nods in agreement. "Goodnight, everyone."

We take turns uttering our goodnights and filing out the door. By the time I make it to my bed, I fall on it and close my eyes. I don't bother with getting under the covers or undressed. I'm drained of all of my energy. I need sleep.

CHAPTER TWENTY-SIX

Savannah is on the floor on all fours, drawing a large, intricate transmutation circle with Milo's help. The circle takes up the majority of the cleared polished wooden floor of the secret room inside Gideon's office. Only about two feet of space is free from the chalk drawings, around the outer edges of the room. A slightly smaller circle is drawn inside the larger one, and within that is a square that touches the inner circle. A triangle fills the square. The circle is an amazing sight to see. Made even better by the fact that my best friend and one of my favorite men are working so hard to help me.

Both Savannah and Milo are focused. They never once look up from drawing. It's fascinating to watch them work on something so intricate.

Gideon and Soren stand off to the side in what appears to be some type of meditative stance. It's interesting to watch them with their eyes closed and arms in front of them, their palms facing the floor with fingers splayed out and their index fingers touching, forming a triangle. I wonder if Jesse and I should be doing the same, versus standing against the wall. But I know better than to interrupt such meticulous preparations.

Once the circle is complete, Milo draws the runes, careful to not smudge the lines of the circles. A crease appears in between his eyebrows as he focuses intently on each design.

Jesse leans into me, bumping my shoulder with his. He has his feet crossed at the ankle, and his arms are folded across his chest. I quirk an eyebrow at his casual way of bringing my attention to him. It worked, and I see that he's completely relaxed. Just going with the flow.

"You ready for this?" He keeps his voice low as to not distract the others while they're working. I appreciate that. The only sounds are the soft whispers of breathing and the scraping of chalk along the floor. A loud and sudden voice may screw something up, and I really don't want to know what would happen at that point. We'd probably have to erase the whole thing and start over.

We've been waiting for what seems like hours. But it may just be my nerves making me feel like time has slowed to an agonizing crawl versus the actual time that's passed. Either way, I let out a deep breath as I try to tamp down my impatience.

I shrug as I lean into him a little more. "As ready as I'll ever be."

Savannah grabs the iron bowl filled with the herbal mixture specifically gathered for this spell. She sets it in the center of the circle and carefully steps out of the chalk image, making sure her feet don't settle on or near any of the lines.

With a nod to herself, she dusts her hands with a clap. "That's it. Are we ready?" She turns her attention to the rest of us.

"Just a moment." Milo stares at the circle and examines each rune, studying the drawings and symbols on the pages of the book that's barely left his hands this entire time. I assume he's double checking the book against what is drawn. "Oh… that's it."

He grabs the chalk and rushes to correct the rune that wasn't drawn correctly. Once finished, he steps back and gives the whole thing another once over before nodding to himself and snapping the book shut. "Done."

"Are you sure?" I ask, giving him a questioning look, hoping it looks like I'm just joking with him. I quirk the corner of my lips for good measure.

He sets his beautiful brown eyes on me and raises his shoulders. "Well, you're not going to grow an extra arm now. So, yeah."

I gape, eyes wide and mouth hanging open. "A what?"

He chuckles. "Relax, I fixed the issue. You're going to be fine."

Gideon and Soren remove themselves from their stances. Gideon stretches his neck and Soren shakes out his hands.

"I would've loved to see you with an extra arm." Jesse winks as he joins Savannah and Milo at the circle. Soren and Gideon are next.

After a moment of glaring at Jesse and taking a deep breath to clear my head, I follow suit. My nerves are a mess of anxious excitement. I want this so badly. To be under the radar. Because if any more people find out what I can do…

Well, it won't be a good thing, that's for sure. Not everyone is as accepting as my team is.

"Oh, we almost forgot the pendant." Savannah rushes to her bag and pulls out a pretty black and silver pendant, setting it inside the iron cauldron. She sets her violet eyes on me. "I've got a chain we can put it on later."

I nod appreciatively. "Thank you."

Milo sits on his knees at the border of a circle. "Everyone needs to spread out. Pick a spot."

We move silently, shuffling our feet along the polished wood floor as we pick a spot around the circle to stand.

Milo crouches down and places his hands on his thighs. "Now, get down like me."

We do. I rest my hands on my thighs and take another calming breath. My magic pulses even more, and I wonder if the meteorite truly is sentient, if it's also glad we're doing this. It feels right. So... maybe?

"Place your hands like so..." Milo forms an "L" shape with both of his hands, placing the top of his index finger and side of his thumb along the chalk outline of the outer circle. He leaves a small space between his thumbs. The shape resembles a broken "W" to me.

I look up and see him nod at Savannah. She nods back. "Our intention should be safety, protection, and invisibility to dangers. Close your eyes and focus on that. Be careful not to put too much energy into the circle. Just a trickle should do."

I close my eyes, following Savannah's directions. Over the course of the first semester, I've learned to control my power, to limit the amount of energy I put into my spells. To prevent a mishap like the tree in my first runes class. Today is no different. Savannah has figured out what words to use to help me. So, I imagine a faucet dripping energy instead of a gush of water. Each drop represents what it means to me to be safe, protected, and invisible to dangers.

Drip… drip… drip.

Deep breath in.

Drip… drip… drip.

Deep breath out.

Drip… drip… drip.

I repeat the process until a light flickers to life behind my eyes, and I can't help but open them to see the circle glowing with a light blue aura. As my vision focuses, I realize it's not just an aura, but tiny flames dancing along the edges of the circle, flowing through each line of the transmutation circle. The runes spark and burn with white flames, and the cauldron starts to smoke.

I smile to myself.

Man, I *love* magic.

Everyone else sits up on their knees and watches as the illuminated circle does what it does best… Magic.

I follow suit.

"Now we join hands." Savannah lifts her arms, palms out, and touches Milo's left hand and Gideon's right. Gideon connects with Soren, who connects with me, and I connect with Jesse. The circle is complete as Jesse's left hand connects with Milo's right hand.

"It's up to you now, Jesse." Savannah sets her violet eyes on him.

He closes his eyes, lips pressed into a thin line of concentration. Energy flows around us like wind. It lifts my and Savannah's hair, weaving through in a cool rush of magic.

The flames along the circle increase, but don't emit any heat. I smile at how good and right this all feels, and I cherish the feeling like none other.

Through the light, the cauldron fades into nothing, disappearing as though it was never really there.

I frown.

Did it not work? Was all this effort for nothing? Nobody else seems bothered by this.

It dawns on me that this was the point. It's the illusion that it's not there. Further protection to keep me safe from those who are after my power. Safe from those who would accuse me of being dark. A shadow mage.

It will act as a shield to my meteorite.

And just like that, my smile is back. Wider this time.

The flames disappear, leaving the cauldron in the center of the floor and the circle nothing but charred dust.

We drop our hands back to our laps.

Milo heaves a heavy sigh. His shoulders slump as his face eases into an expression of relief. "That's it."

"The spell is complete." Savannah smiles as she stands from her spot on the floor. She steps through the black ash and reaches into the cauldron, carefully pulling out the beautiful black pendant and brings it to me. She embellishes the motion with a regal bow that makes me giggle. "For you, my friend."

I pluck it out of her hand. "Thank you so much. That's very kind of you."

I stand and take the sleek black stone, shiny and reflective almost like a mirror. Veins of silver and gold run throughout the surface. A band of silver with runes etched in a border decorates the top.

"And here is your chain." Savannah's voice pulls me from my admiration of the stone. She's holding out a chain to me. "Go on, put it on."

I take the chain and slide it through the clasp attached to the silver band, and then clip it behind my head. The stone dangles just between my breasts.

"You'll want to hide that under your shirt," Soren says.

I nod and tuck it in. As soon as it touches my skin, a burning sensation ripples through my chest. It's not painful but irritating like a sunburn. Soon, the burning turns icy cold, tingling with a slight numbness. And then… nothing.

"How do you feel?" Gideon's voice is pitched a little higher with worry.

I meet his gaze and smile. "Great."

"How's it working so far, Headmaster?" Savannah asks.

Gideon's face becomes a stony expression of concentration as he focuses on me. It's almost as if he can see right through me. Within moments, he sighs. "I can't sense anything."

"Good." She smiles. "It worked."

I take in each and every single face of my men and the resolve in their faces, each of them promising to defend me. And my friend, Savannah, the hope in her eyes and the smile on her face tells me that she is willing to see this through. It took time, preparation, and devotion to do something like this for me. I smile, with a look of appreciation at all of the members of my team, my family. "You guys will never know how much this means to me."

"Well," Jesse says, "I mean, we have an *idea*."

"No, really." I shake my head. "It means the world to me. Maybe a little more."

"We'll do anything to help keep you safe, Wren." Milo's words are full of love and truth. "Don't you understand that yet?"

I nod my head in agreement. "Yeah. I guess I do."

One thing becomes clearer with each passing day. Nothing will harm me. Not with my men. Even the firecracker Savannah has been proving herself to be a staunch ally and good friend. And I'll never allow anything to happen to any of them. Ever.

I'm really starting to adore them all very deeply.

CHAPTER TWENTY-SEVEN

After a wave of his hand, and the cleanup of all the ashes is magically done, Gideon announces that it's time to train.

"That's my cue," Savannah says, coming in for a hug.

I wrap my arms tightly around her and whisper, "Thanks again."

She pulls away and winks.

With a quick goodbye to everyone else, she leaves to get ready for her day. Jesse and Milo grab their stuff and file toward me. Milo shoves his glasses up on his nose. "See ya later?"

"Definitely."

Jesse shoves Milo. "Sappy nerd."

To my surprise, Milo chuckles. He runs a hand

through his hair and shoves the other into his pocket. "Yeah, yeah. You're the pot here, in this scenario, you know."

Jesse shrugs it off and faces me. "Kick some ass today, hmm." He places a hand on my arm, just above my elbow.

I quirk an eyebrow. "Sure. I'll do that."

"You'd better. I just might have to spank you later if you don't." He winks.

I playfully shove him away. "Get to class."

"Aye, aye, Captain." He smiles as he saunters off.

I shake my head while I turn to face Gideon and Soren. They stare at me with looks of amusement, and I suddenly feel like I was caught stealing a cookie from the kitchen. Heat burns through my cheeks. "What?"

"Captain?" Gideon asks.

I shrug. "I can't control what that man says. You should know that by now."

"Kick ass?" Soren's eyebrows lift high on his head. "This, I have to see."

"Then I suggest you hang around. You just might enjoy the show." I stand with my head held high, a smile tugging on my lips despite how much I try to fight it.

Gideon and Soren break out in belly shaking laughter. That isn't the response I was aiming for.

I give them a dirty look, wounded pride and all. "Hey! What's so damn funny?"

"Nothing." Soren gasps out the word between bouts of laughter.

Soren, I would expect to be an ass. But Gideon?

They can laugh all they want, but it's time for me to wipe those smirks off their faces. I engulf my palm with heat and light, cradling a medium-sized fireball. I send it flying toward their feet while they lean against each other gasping for breath. As soon as the fireball crashes near their toes, they stumble backward a few steps—that sobered them up quickly.

Game on.

They stare at me with wide eyes. Soren's anger ignites as his nostrils flare and his eyes level on me. I cross my arms and shrug. "Still wanna laugh?"

Gideon's expression turns pensive, narrowing his eyes on me as though he's trying to figure something out. He snaps his fingers and pats Soren on the arm with the back of his hand. "Watch out. I've got this."

Oh really? This should be fun.

Soren moves out of the way as Gideon waves his hands through the air, moving them in wide arcs and then out in front of him in opposite directions.

The room shifts. The four walls sink, and medieval stone curtain walls rise to replace them. The ceiling folds away to reveal a bright blue sky with light fluffy white clouds and a bright yellow sun shining its warmth down on us. Even a few birds I don't recognize fly overhead.

I'm in awe at the sight. But it's not over yet.

The floor shuffles itself from the wood planks to reveal patches of grass, dirt, and gravel. In front of me, stuffed wooden dummies with red painted smiling faces and targets on their torsos pop up from the ground and stand in rows deeper than I can see. The first row of dummies holds only ten across. They each hold wooden weapons and shields.

I shift my gaze to Gideon. He smirks at me.

"What are you doing?" I ask.

"You are actually doing this. Not me." He nods toward the dummies. "Think fast."

The first row of dummies rattle a bit in reaction to Gideon's magic. They come to life and lurch forward in a swift charge.

They're quick. But I'm *faster*.

I conjure fire in both of my hands. As soon as they are close enough for me to disintegrate them, I release a torrent of flames. The smell of burnt wood fills the air, and black smoke rises into the sky, but they don't stop charging.

Damn it.

Okay, so it's going to take a lot more than fire to take them down.

They're close enough for me to feel the heat pour off them, making sweat bead along my forehead. With some quick thinking, I take down the first two with a front kick and a round house kick. The other eight surround me.

I toss strikes of lightning at another two, shattering them and sending splinters and pieces of cloth and straw stuffing into the air.

Four down, six more to go.

For this round, anyway.

I lower to the ground and kick out another one. It crashes to the ground, lying still as though it never held life. I continue with the spin, raising to my feet and punching the next one, kicking my leg behind me to knock another back. It falls over and the flames instantly douse. I—wait...

I double take the dummy on the ground, and I almost can't believe what I see. The face on it went from a smile to a frown.

I giggle. Cute.

I quickly turn around and block an incoming wooden sword attack with my left arm. I grunt in response to the strike, but thankfully it's only wood. I punch the face of the burning dummy, knocking it back a few feet. It, and the remaining four others surround me, pointing their sword tips at my throat. A much more delicate body part than my arm.

I'm surrounded.

Digging deep into my magic, I let it cover my skin in burning flames with little pink electric currents sparking along my arms.

I send a side kick to my right, punch to my left, and spin. I take out the dummy in front of me by double punching it in the chest while electricity sparks from my fists, and a thunderous boom ricochets throughout the room. A gaping, burning hole is left in the center. I spin to face the two behind me, ducking and dodging their wooden swords. Sliding under them, I push out powerful electrical arcs, shattering their stands. My slide ends and I quickly hop to my feet to face the last one. A ball of burning white light forms in my right hand.

Holding the ball up for a pitch, the face on the dummy shifts to a worried expression, with its mouth in the shape of an "O". My lips quirk as I toss the ball into its face. It hits, exploding the head on contact.

The first ten are down. I move to face down the next ten when a hand claps my shoulder.

I spin, ready to take on whoever is interrupting me in my zone.

Gideon's blue-green eyes meet mine, and I drop my guard.

"Sorry."

He smiles lovingly at me. "Stand back and let me show you how it's done."

I scoff. "Yes, Headmaster Storm."

He quirks an eyebrow as he levels his gaze on me. There's a seriousness to them.

I stick out my tongue.

He laughs and shakes his head as he approaches the charging second row, while I join Soren at his side.

"Hey." I bump him with my elbow.

He shifts his eyes to mine without turning his head. "You did good. But you should watch how pros work."

"Asshole."

"Love you too."

I shake my head and turn my attention to Gideon. He's already dismantled four of the dummies. And I missed it.

Dang it.

I kick myself. That would've been really cool to watch.

He moves with such fluidity and speed, he's almost a blur. He controls himself, using magic only when necessary to incapacitate his foes, rather than coming out with it at first. He punches, kicks, and uses the dummies against themselves to take them out.

In moments—mere seconds, really—Gideon has defeated all ten dummies. He spins on his heels and approaches us. He sets his eyes on Soren. "Your turn."

Gideon leans against the wall, crossing his arms over his chest as he leans into me. "Well, what did you think?"

I don't look away from Soren as I answer. "Impressive."

"Thank you."

His shoulder brushes against mine as he shifts his weight from one foot to the other, and my skin is ignited. I suck in a breath and break away from Soren's fighting to cast a glance at Gideon. His face is relatively stoic, but there's a slight upward curve of his lips and a glistening in his eyes that tells me he most definitely knows what his touch does to me.

I take a slow, steady breath out and return to watching Soren. He burns everything in his path. He uses his magic coupled with brute force. A slightly different tactic than mine, but it still works. He manages to make it look beautiful as he moves brutally with sharp turns and quick jabs and kicks.

For the last dummy, he jumps into the air, performing a spinning kick, knocking the head off with an astounding amount of force. With a loud bang, the stuffed ball hits the stone wall on the other side of the room.

I count the remaining rows and see that there are thirty dummies left.

He turns to face us and waves us over.

Gideon chuckles. "Time to play."

"What?" I stare bewildered at the back of his head as he joins Soren.

He stops mid-way and speaks over his shoulder. "Let's go, Wren."

I take the first step as the remaining three rows charge forward. I smile to myself.

Oh, this is going to be fun.

I run to close the space and start taking out dummies left and right as Soren and Gideon do the same.

We work together to destroy the forces attacking us. Soren and Gideon move with each other as though they know each step they are going to take next, and I try to keep up. It's beautiful, amazing, and the feel of sparring with them is *addicting*.

"Stop!" Gideon's voice booms through the room and everything around us freezes like a still frame of a movie, only this is 3-D like none other. I look around and take in the attacks that are in mid-strike and some of the magic is frozen in the air.

"Whoa-ho-ho!" I prop my hands on my hips, unable to stop smiling at how cool this is.

Gideon chuckles. "Take off your conduit."

I snap my head toward him. "What? Why?"

Soren steps forward. A flash of concern crosses through his eyes that makes a lump form in my throat.

Gideon gives me an affirming nod. "Trust me. You'll be safe here."

I take in the depth of his blue-green eyes. There's so much trust and faith in me brewing within them. My fingers slightly tremble as I slip off the cuff. He holds out his hand for it. I press it into his palm. With a nod to himself, he tucks it into his pocket.

He faces the frozen scene in front of us.

"Use your magic. Control it instead of letting it control you."

"Okay."

I trust he knows what he's doing. However, I still feel vulnerable without my conduit. I don't understand the purpose of this exercise, because I doubt if I'm ever really going to use my powers without a conduit.

Not outside of this room, anyway. After all, no one else can know what I can do.

"Resume." Gideon's voice is stern with a level of calm that I wish I had.

All at once, everything comes to life, and it's like the battle never paused.

I use balls of light, magic, and lightning to take out dummy after dummy, and I move quickly through them. Surprisingly, it's a lot easier to use my magic conduit-free, and I'm not sure if that's a good or bad thing. Still, I move through the onslaught of wooden, stuffed foes as if I'm slicing a hot knife through butter.

And it feels *powerful*.

I feel strong, capable, unstoppable.

Before long, I notice I'm the only one fighting. But I'm able to keep up with that little distraction, as I continue taking down the obstacles standing in my way.

And once the last dummy has fallen, I stand up straighter and face Soren and Gideon who are staring at me with wide eyes and full of emotions I can only guess at. I'm not sure if I've shown them too much or impressed them, or… hell, maybe I scared them.

The smoking heaps of burning dummies cover the entire length of the scene. I take it all in, then I look at my hands with an eerie calm. I don't feel dark. I don't feel out of control. I feel… almost whole.

Gideon snaps his fingers and the room starts to

change to its normal shape. He and Soren turn and walk toward the door. I follow them, not wanting to be swallowed by the room, if that is even possible.

Once we are through the door, Gideon makes his way to his high-back chair behind his desk. Soren takes the chair on the left, in front of the desk, while I sit in the empty one to the right.

It's an intense moment of silence. It's uncomfortable as I flash back to that moment in the woods after I disintegrated the lamia that had stalked the little boy and girl. Before I remembered the meteorite and the power it gifted me. My heart flutters in my chest as anxiety takes over. I start to feel like I made a mistake as Gideon pulls my wrist cuff out of his pocket and hands it to me. His fingers brush along the skin of my wrist as I pull my hand away and I close my eyes against the erotic sensation.

Such a small thing with such a big impact.

"Thanks." I put my conduit back on and silently vow to never take it off again unless I absolutely have to.

Soren shifts in his seat. "That was…"

"Incredible." Gideon finishes the sentence.

I rapidly switch my gaze between the two of them and I'm honestly at a loss. "Really?"

Gideon looks at me with discerning eyes. "I

wondered what the differences would be in your performance with and without the conduit. How do you feel?"

I sit a little straighter in my seat. "Amazing."

He sits back in his seat. "Soren, thoughts?"

Soren leans forward, tenting his fingers and resting them on his mouth, setting his elbows on his knees, like he's deep in thought. "It appears she's able to use and manipulate her power better without the conduit."

"Where did you get the conduit?" Gideon looks at me intently.

"Um… Professor Lawrence. Sort of." A pinch forms in my forehead. I rub my temples to ward off a small throbbing sensation.

"Interesting. Why sort of?"

I shake my head. "I picked it out from a small collection he had."

Gideon nods.

"I wonder if every conduit is going to be the same way." Soren leans back in his seat. "Or, if the meteorite has something to do with the difference."

"Either way, we can work with this." Gideon sits forward. "We need to figure out what the difference is between using your magic with a conduit and without. We need to train until your magic comes to you as easily as it does without the conduit."

"You mean the conduit is dampening her magic? Like it's somehow blocking some of her power?" A pinch forms between Soren's eyebrows, his lips form a straight line and his eyes become unfocused as he puzzles through figuring out the differences in my abilities.

Gideon shrugs as he shakes his head. "I'm not sure yet." He taps a finger on his chin. "We still have some time. We can take turns sparring with her, taking things step-by-step. Feeling this out as we go."

Soren nods. "I agree."

"Okay." I stand from the chair. "Let's do this." I move toward Gideon's magical closet.

"You've created a monster." Soren's voice is full of humor as he speaks from behind me.

"We both have," Gideon says.

An hour into our training, I've sparred with Gideon and Soren separately and together. I trained with the conduit on. And that confused me.

"Why have me practice without my conduit in the first place? Especially since I have to use it now?"

Gideon wipes sweat from his brow. "Because, I was curious what the difference would be. Obviously, you can't do that outside of this room. So, our goal is to get you as proficient with magic with a conduit as you are without."

I nod. "Makes sense, I suppose."

Sort of.

I trust Gideon won't make me do anything that would bring harm to me. I'm safe with him. I suppose this is just another step in understanding my power, my gift from the meteorite I've fused with. Gideon is not one to share all of his secrets or give all the answers. I've learned this much about him. His goal is to simply guide us to the answers and help us figure those out. This is likely one of those cases.

"You've grown so much up to this point." Soren's compliment pulls my attention to him. "You're even handling yourself well against Gideon and me. I think we should up the ante a bit and add the other two in."

"Jesse and Milo?" I ask.

He nods.

"I agree," Gideon says. "That will allow us to work as a team as well. I'll schedule it."

I think about how much fun it is to spar with Gideon and Soren together and wonder what adding Jesse and Milo into the mix will mean.

I can't wait to find out.

"For future training sessions," Gideon says, "focus

on the feeling you had earlier when you used magic without your conduit. Let's see if we can hone that more."

I give Gideon an understanding nod.

"I'm impressed." Soren bends forward, stretching his fingertips to the ground. "You gave us a good run for our money."

"But you were taking it easy on me." I level my gaze on him.

He shrugs. "Prove it."

"The demonstration with the dummies." I gesture toward the other end of the room.

He narrows his eyes on me, lifting an index finger and thumb, holding them close together. "Maybe just a little."

I chuckle. "You are so lucky you're cute."

I have to admit that there is something about sparring with him, especially with Gideon added to the mix, that energizes me and puts me in a light-mannered mood.

He quirks an eyebrow. "Careful, I know where you sleep."

"So scared." I make a good show at trembling.

Gideon chuckles. "All right. You need to go shower and get ready for your classes." He points to Soren. "You have a class in a bit as well, don't you?"

Soren gives Gideon a little nod.

Gideon turns on his heels and heads for the door. "Let's go."

Soren and I pick at each other, poking our sides with our fingers and chuckling together as we leave the room which rapidly changes back into a closet again.

After a quick goodbye, I rush to my room for a shower. I'm going to be late to class, and I hate that.

CHAPTER TWENTY-EIGHT

W inter is so beautiful on this island.

It's cold. But beautiful.

Jesse and I walk side-by-side through one of the gardens as the sun is setting, taking the last of its warmth for the day. The constellations start to take shape, and fog leaves my mouth with every breath. Deep purple clouds, darkening with the oncoming night, move in from the north.

We walk down a white stone path, gleaming with the last light of the day. Every crossroad in the path is guarded by statues of winterwolves, krakens, dragons, and phoenixes. Evergreen bushes, as high as my waist, line the paths like hedges.

It's quiet, peaceful, and it feels good to have some time with Jesse.

"Hmm… snow." Jesse barely murmurs the words, and I look at him to see if he actually spoke or if it's my imagination.

"What?"

He points toward the clouds. "Purple means snow."

"Oh." I chuckle. "Is the weather really what's weighing on your mind?"

He shrugs as though he doesn't want to share his thoughts.

I nudge him. He plays it up, pretending to almost fall into the hedges. I laugh. "Seriously, what's up?"

I glance up at the clouds and notice they are quickly moving in. An icy breeze picks up, blowing through me. I shiver and breathe in deep Jesse's intoxicating scent. It's like a mixture of spice and cedar with a slightly sweet undertone but not flowery.

"Cold?" He stops and slips off his winter cloak, draping it over my shoulders. "Better?"

I give him a little nod. "Don't avoid the question."

"No, the weather is not what's on my mind." There is a slight shake in his words, and I want to ask him about that, but he turns his attention to the sky.

He stops me with a firm but gentle hold on my arm. He steps in front of me and looks deep into my eyes with his steely blues. "When I'm around you, I can think clearly. Somehow, you still my racing thoughts, ease the chaos within my mind. You even manage to soothe the worries within me." He shakes his head and lets his hand drop to his side. "You ground me in ways no one else can."

I smile at him and start to open my mouth, but he places a finger over my lips. Huffing, I arch an eyebrow.

"I've wanted to share this with you for a while now, but I didn't know how to phrase it. And I want to say thank you." He removes his finger.

Oh, now I can talk.

"Here I thought it was all fun and games with you."

He chuckles under his breath. "There's a lot more than meets the eye with me."

"No kidding."

"Exactly."

I laugh slightly under my breath, not wanting to disrupt the peace or the mood. But I do wonder, what worries him? He's always seemed like a carefree guy, always looking at the lighter side of things and never taking anything seriously. Although, now that I think of it, there have been a few times when I've seen a serious Jesse come through. The first time was when I first learned about Anderson, right after he stole some of my energy.

I don't care what he said about it. He stole it. Thank you very much.

However, if he's opening up to me, maybe he can shine some light on that part.

"Does what worries you have anything to do with zacars?"

His eyes darken a bit and he huffs out a breath of air through his nose. "Let's continue walking."

"Okay…" I try to come up with a way to get him talking. I don't want him to shut down now. "I only ask partly because of what you just said—which is very sweet, by the way—but also because of your initial reaction to Anderson when we first came here for the trials. Was there more behind reacting the way you did?" I look at him and watch as his features become contorted. Almost as though what I'm bringing up is putting him through incredible pain.

I grab his hand and pull him to a stop. I make him face me. "I'm sorry. I can tell whatever it is that's bothering you really cuts deep." I slide my arms around him and rest my head on his firm chest. His strong arms wrap around me and he rests his head on mine.

His body shudders as his arms wrap tighter around me.

"Whatever it is, we can work through it together.

I'm here for you, Jesse. I'm not going anywhere. Whatever demons are haunting you, I will fight them by your side."

"You will?" He asks, voice soft, almost a whisper.

"I promise."

He pulls away and leads me to a bench. We sit huddled together and he takes a moment to breathe in deep. The pain of whatever he's struggling with ripples off him, covering me in a way that makes me certain we're bonded in a special way. I'm overcome with the need to cry. It breaks my heart deeply to see him hurting like this.

"My childhood was amazing."

Oh. Well, that's not where I thought we were starting, but okay.

"And then it wasn't."

I nod, grabbing his hand and giving it a squeeze.

"A zacar had fallen in love with my mother. She turned down all of his advances, but he eventually grew obsessed with her. We saw him sneaking around the house sometimes, late at night. My dad placed wards, but it wasn't good enough."

"He found a way through?"

Jesse shakes his head. "No. He found a way around it altogether."

I furrow my eyebrows. "How did he do that?"

"By following my mother."

"Oh, Jesse…"

"Just wait, there's more." He sniffs and his knee starts to bounce nervously. "A stranger apparently watched the whole thing happen. The asshole cornered my mom. The stranger tried to step in and stop it, but it was too late. The zacar fed off of my mom. Took too much of her energy and it drove her crazy."

I cover my mouth and gasp. "That must have been so horrible." I lean in closer to him. My own experience was severely unpleasant. I can't imagine what his mom went through to have so much of her essence sucked out of her that it left her brain shattered.

"Eventually, we had to have my mom locked up in some looney bin because the damn soul sucker didn't stop when he was supposed to." He shakes his head and squeezes his eyes shut. A single tear trickles down his cheek. I reach up and wipe it away with my finger. "My dad was never the same. He became a work-a-holic and kept himself distant. I was forced to take care of my brothers until they were old enough to fend for themselves."

I wrap my arms around him. "That's so horrible. No one should have to live through that."

He shakes his head and squeezes me to him. "I came here so I could make a better life and provide for them."

"Where are they now?"

"At home, with a shell of what used to be our father, and here I am, stuck at school."

"Can anything be done to help your mom? Maybe Savannah has something that hasn't been tried yet?"

"Trust when I say, if there was anything that could be done, I would've tried it. And I've tried everything I could think of. She's just lost..." His voice cracks. He takes a few deep breaths to calm himself. "She's broken, and I don't know if she'll ever be whole again."

"I'm so very sorry."

"You wanna know what's worse?" He looks down at me. I shake my head, unsure of what to say. "The zacar got away with it because it was a," he holds two fingers up and pumps them up and down for air quotes, 'secret meeting' between him and my mom. According to him."

"What about the stranger?" I ask.

Jesse shakes his head. His pain slowly leaking into anger. "His word against the zacar's."

"I wish I knew what to say other than sorry."

"I'm going to avenge my mom. As soon as I find out where the bastard zacar is, I'm going to kill him."

I stand up and face him, ignoring the questioning look in his eyes. "I refuse to let you give up on a cure. I'll help you find a way to help your mom and brothers. There has to be something out there that will heal your mom, and I'll help you track the dirty bastard down and deal with him."

His eyebrows scrunch up as he looks up at me. "You would really do that? For me?"

I cock my head to the side. "Why wouldn't I?"

"It's a dirty secret my family treats with shameful remorse. It's not talked about. In fact, we're ignored. They cover up the real story with some idiotic excuse. There's a handful of them, and they just pull one out that seems best fit for the given situation."

"It's not a dirty secret, Jesse. It's a tragedy. A horrible one."

He snorts. "Well, at least you took it better than I thought you would."

"How did you think I was going to take it? You're talking to a girl who was enslaved by trolls and had to sleep on the ground for several years. I know what it feels like to have your entire world turned upside down because of someone's evil actions. You shouldn't have been swept under the rug... you should've been helped."

I offer him my hand. He takes it and brings my knuckles to his lips. He leaves a chilly kiss on them and takes in a deep breath. "I don't know why I thought you'd take it a lot worse than this."

"You're incredibly unobservant." I shake my head and pull him to his feet. "Thank you for sharing your story with me, even though it was horribly painful."

He wraps his arm around my shoulder. "You're stuck with me now, you know that, right?"

I chuckle. "Fine by me." I slip my arm around his waist. "Tell me about your brothers. What are they like?"

Jesse chuckles. "Annoying buggers. They're incredibly strong-willed, kind, and have the biggest hearts of anyone I've ever met. They are twelve-year-old twins. Samuel and Elijah."

I smile. Good big brother. "They sound adorable."

"You say that now. Damn me for caring so much. But wait until you meet them. You'll change your tune quickly. They put itching powder in my body soap. Hung a giant mechanical spider in my room and chased me with it." He chuckles. "Just you wait."

"You want me to meet your brothers?" I ask, my lips stretching into an even bigger smile.

He shrugs. "Why not?"

"I dunno. Just surprised… in a good way."

"The surprises are going to keep coming. Starting with going back to my room, drinking something warm, and creating some friction."

I chuckle. My Jesse is back in full force. "Now you're talking."

CHAPTER TWENTY-NINE

The warmth in Jesse's room is simply magical as it seeps into my frozen toes and works its way up my body, chasing the icy cold away. Jesse takes his cloak and hangs it on the other side of his door on a hook.

With the flick of a wrist, a fire ignites in the small fireplace at the opposite wall of his bed. I watch Jesse move, drinking him in with a new sense of admiration. He did a huge thing tonight, opening up about his heart-wrenching past. And I don't want to cheapen it by bringing it up anymore. I intend to stand by my promise to him, but even more than that, I trust in him completely.

He kicks off his shoes and sets them by the wall on the other side of his bathroom. I take mine off and put them by the wall as well. He tosses a few pillows to the floor from his bed and grabs a blanket. Laying the blanket on the floor, arranging the pillows around the thick comforter, he makes a comfy spot for cuddling. He sits on the ground and then pats a spot next to him. I chuckle and join him.

He adjusts the pillow behind me then slides his hand into mine and leans in close. "Thank you for tonight."

I look at him. His eyes are focused on the fire. But they seem less burdened than before, and it feels good to know he trusted me enough to tell me his story.

"I should be thanking you. It takes a great deal of trust to open up like that. I appreciate it."

He meets my gaze, and the depth within his steely blue eyes takes my breath away.

There are no words to fill the peaceful contentment enveloping us. Even the pops and cracks of the wood in the fireplace barely whisper through the silence. His eyes shift to my lips and I wait for him to kiss me, holding my breath as my heart rams against my ribs.

"I don't have to pretend with you, do I?"

I shake my head, a soft smile on my lips. "Never."

He twists toward me and tucks a strand of hair behind my ears and slides his hand behind my neck, pulling me close. His mouth collides with mine and I nearly melt into him.

His tongue explores the inside of my mouth and he gently rakes his teeth along my lower lip.

A moan escapes from my lips and he hesitates, pulling away slightly. I meet his gaze as he searches mine for something I can only guess at.

"Do you want to stop?"

"I would prefer not." I press my lips to his and that seems to be the only encouragement he needs.

Without breaking from the kiss, he climbs to his knees, sliding a hand around my waist and lifting me enough to lay me on the floor. I giggle between our locked lips, and tingles ripple through me as he chuckles at my thrill.

As soon as my back is on the floor, his mouth moves to my neck, sending delicious warmth through me. Pressure builds between my legs and I don't want it to stop.

His hand lifts the seam of my shirt up, his thumb brushing against my side as my shirt rides up. His mouth returns to mine for a deep, long, passionate kiss. Pulling away, he pulls me up and lifts my shirt over my head, just before I catch the gleeful look in his eyes and that damn near sends me over the edge.

I grab his shirt, undoing the few buttons at the top

and lift it over his head, marveling at his beautifully sculpted abs and pecs. A patch of dark hair rests in the center of his chest, and I bite the corner of my bottom lip in anticipation of his rock-hard body pressed against mine.

Jesse catches my staring eyes and smirks at me. "Like what you see?" His voice is low and gravelly, making my heart flutter in my chest.

I nod. "Very much so."

He chuckles as he pushes me back to the floor, using a hand to unsnap my bra and tosses it to the other end of the room. I honestly don't care where it lands. I'll find it later.

Jesse's eyes take in the form of my breasts and groans. "Woman, you truly are a piece of art." He licks his lips as he lowers himself to my breast, taking in a nipple and sucking with thrilling flicks of his tongue, edging me closer and closer to an orgasm.

And the real fun hasn't even begun yet.

I gasp and run my fingers through his dark hair.

He moves to the next and sends me into even greater heights. Just when I think I'm going to lose all my sense of control, he returns to my mouth, sliding his hands down my sides, slipping a thumb under the waistband of my skirt and tights. He runs a hand along the outside of my thigh, and moves to the inside, inching closer to the sweet spot. He runs his fingers along my sensitive folds, and I moan again.

He chuckles. "You're certainly excited, aren't you?"

I smack him on the shoulder. "Don't be an ass."

"Oh, now you're going to pay for that."

In one, smooth move, my skirt and tights are pulled to my ankles. He slips the skirt off and tosses it away, not paying attention to where it lands. He does the same to my tights and spreads my legs wide, setting his eyes on me with that devilish grin of his.

"I warn you, I won't stop. Not until you scream my name."

I start to mouth a witty come back as he dives right in. But all sense of thought and logic fly out the window as his mouth works its way around my clit and I gasp, clenching my legs together. "Oh my…"

He wiggles one arm over my thigh and wedges a shoulder against my other. A finger dips into me, curling as he massages me into a screaming orgasm.

I can't form words much less his name, and I don't know if I want to. This is absolutely mind blowing.

My climax starts to fade, and he kisses the insides of my thighs, moving up to leave one on my belly, between my breasts, along my neck, and nibbles on my ear.

I fumble with his pants. He grabs my hands, one at

a time, and pins them to either side of my head. "Now, now… I told you I wasn't going to stop until you screamed my name."

I pant. "Do you have any idea how hard it is to think when you are doing such amazingly orgasmic things to me, much less talk?"

He seems to think about it. "Good point. But you're still talking."

"Jesse, if you do not get inside me now, I'll hurt you."

He chuckles. "Temper, temper. There's a process here, love. Allow a man to do his thing."

I roll my eyes and stick my tongue out at him. He smiles as he returns to his sweet, delicious kisses between my thighs.

Time after time, I melt into a screaming orgasm. On the last wave, I shout, "Jesse, please. You're killing me!"

He pops his head up and uses the blanket to wipe off his face. "Well now. I do believe that was you screaming my name. He climbs up on his knees and shrugs. "I mean, close enough."

I chuckle as I pant for breath and have no strength or desire to move.

But as he starts to undo his pants, I watch as the tip

of his erection pokes free and I bite my lip. This man is hung. He's freaking huge.

I lick my lips, aching to be filled with every magnificent inch of him.

He leans in over me and rests his tip at my entrance. His eyes take in mine and he pushes the tip in just a little. It's enough to nearly send me into another release, and I wonder just how many ways this man is going to undo me in one night.

He smiles, a devious glint to his eyes. I smile at him and shake my head. "You're enjoying this—"

He plunges into me, filling me with his entire length. I claw at his side as my eyes roll back and my toes curl. His mouth on my neck sends me into over-drive. As he slowly slides out, I moan again.

He growls. "You do things to me when you do that, woman."

"Good," I mutter, slurring it in a way that makes me sound drugged. Perhaps I am. His moves are damn sure that good.

He chuckles as he slowly slides into me again, filling me in every way possible. His breath pours along my neck with each thrust. The pace is a different stroke from when he was sending me to new heights with his tongue. But this is just as delicious, if not more so, as that was. The buildup is slower, allowing me to savor every second of him filling me.

I lift my legs, allowing him to sink deeper into me, and with his groan my climax peaks. He rides me through the sheer length of it, gripping my thighs as he keeps rhythm with the pulsating his thrusts send through me.

"Roll over." I demand and he looks at me with a questioning gaze.

He must have seen something he likes as he smiles. "Yes, Captain."

He slides out of me and lays on the floor. I straddle him. "Now, it's *my* turn."

"Do your worst."

"Oh, I intend to turn you into a puddle."

He smiles.

I slide him inside me, rolling over the tip of his still massive erection. He clenches his eyes closed and digs the tips of his fingers into my hips. He tries to buck into me, but I clench tight and lift up.

"Uh-uh. I'm in control now."

He chuckles. "Very well."

He doesn't let go of my hips but relaxes into the blanket covering the floor. I ease him, inch by inch, second by second, and he sucks on his bottom lip as he digs his head into the floor, angling into the motion.

But I don't take it easy on him.

As soon as his entire length is in me, I grind against him, bracing myself on his deliciously hard pecs. And I won't stop until he's screaming *my* name.

At some point, we make it to his mattress, destroying the perfectly smooth flat sheet. We continue our love making until light pours into the room from the window. Then, and only then, do we lay wrapped in each other's arms, legs woven together, with my head resting on his chest. The steady beat of his heart lulls me to sleep while his hand rubs along my back.

The last thought that passes through my mind before sleep fully claims me is how each of my men give me something different. Each of them, in their own special ways, make me feel safe, protected, strong, and unstoppable. Jesse makes me feel simply adored and coveted. I can laugh and feel free with him.

I can't see my life without any of them. And I know I will do anything for them.

CHAPTER THIRTY

I wake in response to Jesse's gentle coaxing. I peel my eyes open and set them on his beautiful face. His hair is wet. Drops of water drip from the ends of his shoulder-length curls.

"What time is it?" I mumble, sitting up and pulling the sheet over me to cover my still naked body.

"We slept all day." He smiles. "Wore you out."

I grin, chuckling under my breath. "We wore each other out."

"It's time to get ready. We're going to be late."

I narrow my eyes on him. "For what?"

"Finding your dad."

My eyes widen, and I'm suddenly more awake than I was a few seconds ago. Before I was told about finding my dad. I had lost all track of time and responsibilities with Jesse. I smile as I rush to his bathroom to shower.

I hop in and out of the warm spray of water, in record time. I make sure to spend a few extra precious seconds on cleaning my tender bits. I'm sore. Once I'm out, I gather my clothes, throwing them on haphazardly. Once my shoes are on, I rush to Jesse. Kissing him on the cheek, I rush to the door.

"See you there, I'm going to go change."

I don't wait for a response before I'm out the door and rushing through the halls to my room.

Once I'm there, feeling the clock ticking against me, I throw on a fresh set of underwear, plain jeans, and a t-shirt before rushing out the door again.

By the time I make it into Gideon's office, I'm sweaty and out of breath. Everyone looks at me with concern and questioning eyes. I take a moment to catch my breath enough to push out, "Sorry I'm late."

"Just on time," Gideon says. "We're actually going to meet Lady Alene elsewhere."

I pant a few more times before my breathing slows and returns to normal, along with my racing heart. "Oh."

Gideon takes his gaze and sets it on each one of us. He nods and moves toward the door. "Follow me."

We each file out of the door and follow him back

toward the front of the castle, to a secret door hidden beneath the stairs. It opens to a long, downward sloping hallway, deep into the belly of the castle. The sounds of the ocean waves reach my ears, and it's colder down here. Nearly frigid.

We move along the sewers, which I recognize from my fourth trial. It's hard to get a grasp of which way we're going. We're making so many twist and turns, I think we've even changed direction from North to South a few times.

But before long, we arrive at what seems like a simple wall with an arched design in it made of brick. It just looks like a dead end to me.

Gideon rests his hand on it and mutters to himself. I can't make out any of the words. Once he removes his hand, the bricks start to shift, twisting and folding in on one another from the middle of the wall, toward the sides of the arch. On the other side is a large opening bathed in thick black shadows.

"This is a secret location within the castle. Only Lady Alene and I know how to get in." Gideon turns to face us. "This room is safeguarded that way. Please, step in."

"Why does it need to be safeguarded?" I step in, my voice bouncing off the walls.

"Because of the room's purpose." Soren's voice

follows mine and echoes just as much. It's eerie. Almost like there are more than just one of us.

"You've been here before?" I face Soren's shadowy form.

"A few times."

Huh. Okay then.

As soon as Gideon steps inside, the torches lining the walls in this circular chamber light up with a deep purple flame. Once inside of the lit room, I start to feel strange. In the center of the rounded room there appears to be a large stone orb inlayed into the floor, but it's hard to tell with the color of light being cast by the torches.

Within moments, the flames turn blue, then red, and finally white. They chase away the shadows, which bleed back into the rock walls.

"This is the *impigritas* room. Once used to monitor energy fluctuations." Gideon approaches the stone orb in the center of the room. It's not inlayed into the stone like I thought it was, but sits in a cut-out for it, and the rock just... floats. "For this purpose, it'll be used to locate Wren's father."

Lady Alene appears in the room, standing off to the side. She gestures toward the orb. "Go ahead and take a look."

Gideon joins my side, brushing the back of his

fingers against mine. I turn my attention to him. "We will join hands first, all of us. Once I give the word, I want you to use this," he holds out a needle, "to prick your finger and sprinkle a few drops of blood on the letters." He nods to Milo.

Milo pulls out the letters from my father and sets them on top of the orb.

"It will, unfortunately," Gideon adds, "destroy the letters. But for the sake of finding your father, it is a small sacrifice."

"I understand." Though, my heart isn't in it. Those were the only things I had of my father's.

"We must be clear when we chant *Michael Blackwood*. It's imperative that our thoughts not derail into other things. This will take a great amount of concentration, and it will exhaust every one of us. Some, perhaps, more than others."

He waits a few moments before taking my hand. I use the cue to grab hold of Jesse's hand, who takes Soren's, and then Milo is joined in with Soren and Gideon. Lady Alene remains standing guard, our living statue and patroness, overseeing our safety.

The orb raises as we stand around it. Runes that I hadn't noticed before, glow in a ring around the orb. Gideon hands me the needle. I prick my finger, pressing under the puncture to push the blood out.

Following Gideon's instructions, I let a few drops of blood drip onto the letters before returning to the circle and holding hands.

One by one, we join in chanting my father's name. Our voices rise slowly, careful to enunciate each syllable clearly.

The letters start to smoke then quickly catch fire. The flames burn them to ashes in a matter of moments. If I had blinked, I would've missed it.

The orb starts to spin, glowing with a bright blue and purple aura until shapes start to take form over the surface in bright gold. As I watch, the shapes take the form of a map.

Sweat beads on my forehead, but I don't break focus.

Once a pink blip appears on the orb, just above the state of Colorado, our chanting ceases. The blip disappears and pops up in Wyoming, only to disappear and re-appear over yet another state.

What is he doing?

"Focus on the pink dot that keeps moving," Gideon instructs.

We do, and the map zooms in, following the shape of my father running. Shadowy wisps of smoke that barely resemble people chase after him.

"Who's chasing him?" I ask, nervously. "Is it the Order or shadow wolves?"

"Hard to tell," Gideon says. "Keep your focus."

I nod and do as he says.

Until one thing catches my attention.

The pink blip is starting to dim the more it moves. He must be zapping all his remaining strength trying to stay ahead of whoever is chasing him.

"Come on…" Gideon says. "Find a place… hunker down."

I realize he's not literally speaking to my father, but more to himself. Sort of a silent wish to my father to let us get a lock on him.

But it's no use. My father keeps moving. And I know he can't keep up at that rate forever.

As we watch the blips, my father appears over Colorado again, then Arizona, California, Kansas… I can't make sense of it.

"It's a pattern." Milo's voice pulls my attention to him for a brief second. "He's visiting the same places but in a different order. If we can watch long enough, I can see when the original pattern emerges. When that happens, we can gauge where he's going to be. It's going to take more than just this one time to figure it out."

"If we can figure it out," Gideon adds. "So can the

Order and the shadow wolves if they are not acting on the Order's behalf."

"We just need to find the pattern before they do." I refuse to give up. Not now.

Probably not ever.

"She's right." Gideon squeezes my hand. "We'll get him to safety before they find him. We break the chase and he can go into hiding for a time. We'll have to keep the map up for the best chance, but we don't have enough power to do it."

"Can we not take turns?" Jesse asks.

"To continuously stand here will not only drain us, but it may draw attention."

Speaking of attention, the air took on a static feel, turning hot and sticky.

"I think…" Milo pauses and struggles to maintain focus. "I can come up with a list of possible patterns and we can match them up with the map in intervals. That's the best I can do."

"Gideon," Soren says. "We need a break."

Gideon nods and takes a step back, releasing my and Milo's hands. I watch as the lights on the map flicker and fade, leaving nothing but the smooth surface of the stone.

I bite the corner of my bottom lip, wringing my fingers to stretch them. I ease the ache in my shoulders by rolling my head back and forth and from side-to-side.

"What are we going to do if we can't get a location on Michael?" Soren's words brings my attention to his face, tense with exhaustion.

"It's possible he doesn't want to be caught because the rumors are true," Jesse adds.

I snap my attention to him, glaring daggers, wishing I really could shoot them from my eyes. But that's not realistic. "That's bullshit. He wouldn't reach out to me if that were the case, especially knowing I'm here at Blackbriar."

"But even you have to admit, you don't know for sure," Milo adds. "His movements were very erratic."

"But you said there was a possible pattern," I point out.

"True."

"So maybe he's hoping we're looking for him and this is the best he can give us."

Gideon steps forward. "That is a great possibility, and I hope that's true. But we have to manage our expectations here. Until we know for sure, we need to assume the worst."

"Oh, you're damn right I'm going to find out." I point to my chest. "I'm not giving up on my father. I refuse to do that until we are out of all other options."

"We'll come back in a week." Gideon faces us and looks to Lady Alene for confirmation. She nods. "Any sooner, and we could seriously injure ourselves. Once a week is pushing our limits as it is."

We take turns nodding and mumbling our responses. That really did knock the life out of me. I'm exhausted. I could sleep the whole night away, even though I should be well rested from sleeping all day.

"Milo," Gideon says, "let me know if you think you've nailed a pattern."

"I will." He adjusts his glasses and sniffs.

I smile. Even exhausted and irritated, he knows how to bring a smile to my face with something so simple as adjusting his glasses.

Gideon excuses us and I wave goodbye to Lady Alene. By the time I make it to my room, I'm dragging my feet. I crash onto my bed and don't care that I'm fully dressed.

CHAPTER THIRTY-ONE

I square my shoulders and stretch my neck, waiting for the next attack to be thrown at me.

My men and I are training with the practice dummies and shadow wolves. This time, the dummies wear stronger armor and number a small army. There are *easily* a dozen, if not more, shadow wolves.

The room is set up to look like the desert mountains of Arizona, with stiff terrain and large cypress trees. The insane slopes keep making my feet slip as I dodge and move through attack after attack. And the heat of the room feels like a dry sauna. I'm coated in sweat. My shirt sticks to my skin, and my yoga pants are starting to rub the inside of my thighs raw.

My men stand behind me as I lead the attack.

"Dodge to the left," Soren instructs to avoid the

launching shadow wolf aimed at sinking its teeth into some vital part of my body. I swiftly execute the move.

"Roll to the right." Milo's voice reaches me just before the downward strike of a metal practice sword hits the top of my head. I perform the move, and once I'm back on my feet I shoot him a glare.

"A little faster than that next time."

He shrugs apologetically.

"I thought you guys were joining me?"

Gideon points behind me. "Look out!"

I turn in time to see another wolf charging along with a dummy. I side kick the wolf square in the center of his forehead and spin to elbow the dummy in the throat while I simultaneously grip the dummy's arm with the sword and ram my knee into the torso.

I face my men again, panting and wiping at a strand of hair that's stuck to my face. "Well?"

"Can't let her have all the fun, can we?" Jesse smirks, stepping forward to join me.

Midnight blue magic courses over his hands, traveling up his arms like flickering flames. It's mesmerizing.

I smile. "Thank you."

"Don't thank me yet." His focus sits directly in front of us where a group of dummies stand behind a row of salivating shadow wolves waiting for the silent command to attack.

The command is given, and the wolves snap at the air and charge.

Jesse and I sink into our battle stances, ready to take on our foes. White light covers my hands as I call on my magic. Within seconds, the wolves cross a massive space of land that lies between us, moving at incredible speeds. Faster than the ones we fought back at the facility.

Jesse releases his magic and it blasts the creatures closest to us. They stumble and fall, whimpering. One by one, they sink to the ground and dissolve into dust. I conjure a large ball of light, closing my eyes against the brightness and pushing it out in front of me. It soars through the air and explodes above the rest of the wolves, dissolving them into nothing.

"That's my girl." The adoration in Jesse's voice is clear, and I can't help but smile.

"You haven't seen anything yet." I make the unexpected move of charging forward. My fire magic burns along my arms, coating my skin in warmth. Sizzling past the trees as I aim for the first few dummies in my path. Once I'm within range, I slide to a stop on the side of my thigh. I hold my arms out in front of me and release a torrent of flames, cooking my foes from the inside out.

The metal of the dummies' armor glow orange, dinting and melting as they fall to the ground.

"Wren, come back." Soren's voice echoes to me.

I furrow my eyebrows as I look over my shoulder. He's shaking his head and pacing before he heads over to join Jesse. With a slap of Soren's hand on Jesse's shoulder, together they make a beeline for me. A snap of wood catches my attention. I look into the shadows of forest in the direction the sound came from.

I suck in a deep breath and hold it.

Dozens of glowing red eyes appear in the moving shadows of the trees around me. Deadly growls rumble toward me, and I realize the fatal mistake I just made. I had literally run into a den of wolves. And they aren't looking too kindly on my trespassing, as a matter of fact, they're looking pretty pissed off at my invasion.

Oops.

I slowly and quietly suck in a stabilizing breath and climb to my feet. Knowing full and well if I make sudden movements, it will only aggravate them further and send them howling and gnashing at me. Casting a quick glance over my shoulder, Jesse and Soren are waiting about twenty feet away. I back up slowly, never turning my back to the horde of creatures made of inky shadows and razor-sharp teeth and claws.

Movement within the trees in my periphery catches my attention, pulling my gaze to Gideon moving slowly through the trees, pausing behind them long enough to plan his next move.

I look to the other side and find Milo doing the same.

I smile, picking up on what they are doing.

I continue backing up until I'm standing with Soren and Jesse. "Flanking?"

"Yes." Soren's voice is serious and focused. "Move slowly forward."

Together we take steps forward.

"This is exciting," Jesse says.

I shake my head and stifle the giggle that wants to bubble out of me.

"Stop here," Soren commands. We slow our steps and halt.

"What is it?" I cast a sideways glance toward him.

"Wait for the signal." He nods once, slowly, toward the area of where the majority of the shadow wolves remain hidden, blinking at us with their red glowing eyes.

A blast of light flashes from the right as Gideon launches his attack.

"Now!" Soren charges forward.

Jesse and I run after him as wolves charge from the trees. Magic explodes from the left, on Milo's side, as Soren's arms light up with fire, mine with light, and the midnight smoky blue on Jesse's.

Magic explodes all around us in an array of color and light. Each blow is coupled with whines and high-pitched barks from the shadow wolves falling to the ground. Metallic clinking echoes to me every now and then, letting me know the remaining armored dummies hiding in the trees are also falling to their demise.

Training with my men like this is fun.

I love how we work together, all of us as a team, for one solid purpose. It fills me with joy, and I wish we could do this more often. It's thrilling, powerful, and energizing. The dangerous scenarios that Gideon creates gives us a realistic and practical run-through of what we could face in the outside world.

Soon, the eruptions of magic slows. Soren, Jesse, and I move forward, keeping our eyes peeled for any straggling foes. We pass through the border of trees, crushing fallen leaves and twigs beneath our feet. Milo and Gideon join us. We still look around, keeping our ears trained for the slightest sound.

"Good work," Gideon says.

"It was fun." I smile at him.

He shakes his head as though he isn't sure what to do with me. "It was, yes. But the real thing won't be. You have to take these trainings as serious as the real thing. And for the love of all things in the universe, *never* run into battle like that again."

His blue-green eyes ensnare me with an intensity that makes a lump form in my throat and my heart feel like it sinks into my stomach.

"Sure," I mumble.

"It was very careless to underestimate the enemy like that." Soren's words add a little salt to the wound. And does it ever sting.

Anger starts to burn within me, mixed with the icky feeling of guilt. "I had it. I thought so, at least."

"You thought?" Soren turns toward me, leveling his furious eyes on mine.

Gideon steps forward and places a calming hand on Soren's shoulder. He faces me as Soren stalks off. "Ignore him."

"Gladly." I huff and cross my arms over my chest.

"What I meant to say is disregard his tone. His question is valid."

I turn my glare to Gideon. "What?"

He sighs, holding up his hands and reaching for me, but I step back with a raised eyebrow. He shrugs and drops his hands to his side. "Think about it, Wren."

Dammit, I hate how soft his voice is right now. I feel sick that I reacted so coldly to him. My heart wrenches, and I reluctantly settle a softer gaze on him. After all, I'm still angry.

"What if we hadn't been so close by? Or here at all for that matter?"

"I would handle it the same way I handled the lamia."

It's true. Probably.

"That's not what he means—" Jesse inserts.

I snap my eyes to him. "I know what he means. I get it. I got bold and made a dangerous mistake, but you men never seem to get it through your thick skulls I'm not a porcelain doll. I can and have, handled myself. You all disregard the fact that I lived with trolls for six years of my life. Most of these pampered students at this school wouldn't even survive half of that. At some point you're going to have to give me some credit and faith."

"No one doubts your abilities, Wren."

Oh, Milo. Not you too.

I spin to face him. His arms are crossed over his chest. He lifts a hand to shove his glasses farther up his nose. He shrugs.

Huh. He's standing his ground.

Good for him.

But horrible timing.

I huff a rage-filled breath. "You all want me to what? Sit back and let you protect me, keep me safe and pretty and locked away?"

"No." Soren's voice comes from behind me, startling me nearly out of my skin.

He spins me to face him. The world fills my vision in strips of blurred colors until I'm still, and even then it takes me a moment to refocus. His amber eyes stare deeply into mine. His grip remains on my arms so that I can't stomp away. He's forcing me to hear him out. And I think that irritates me more.

"Only that you need to think of others when you rush into danger like that, especially knowing that you have four men who are completely crazy about you and would sooner die for you than blink an eye. It's not just you out there, and the sooner you realize and understand that we're a team, the more we can face our enemies together."

I... I'm at a loss for words as the truth sinks into me, and I realize that I'm being a touch fool-hardy and unreasonable. I dare not look away from him. And as a million words rush through my mind, of things I want to say, I can't choose the right ones to speak aloud.

For an immeasurable number of heartbeats, I stand there as he waits for me to respond. I can't just say nothing. What good would that do?

"I'm sorry." My apology comes out barely louder than a whisper.

Soren's shoulders slump as he pulls me into his chest, pinning me tightly with his arms. I feel the weight of his worry, but also the strength of his affection. His body trembles slightly, and the strength in his muscles are rock-hard. I feel his heart pounding in his chest.

All of this adds further insult to injury. Way to go Wren. You literally made Soren, of all people, distraught.

Yay, me.

Girlfriend of the year, right here.

I clutch the back of his shirt in my fists and embrace him back. For a long moment I just stand there, feeling like an ass. As I breathe in his scent, I promise myself to be better than this. Promising my men to think before I act.

Because, that's what a team does.

When Soren pulls away, he levels his cooling gaze

on me once more then turns and walks out of the training room. Milo steps up, taking my hand into his, rubbing his thumb over my fingers. "He's right, you know. We care for you deeply."

I nod and wrap my arms around him in a brief hug. He pulls away and follows Soren out.

Jesse steps forward, looking for all the world like everything was okay with his hands in his pockets. He pulls out a hand and uses it to tuck my wild, sweat-covered hair behind my ear. He smiles once then plants a kiss on my forehead. Though he seems calm, I catch the look of concern in his eyes just before he turns to leave the room as well.

I turn to face Gideon. "I'm sorry."

He nods. "You are forgiven. But please, don't do that again. Work with us, not against us."

"Okay."

He approaches me, stopping as our toes meet. He cups my face in his hands and brings his mouth to mine in a gentle, yet swift kiss. It's over before it goes any further. He smiles softly at me once as he walks toward the door.

I join him. "Can we work on that more next time?"

"Of course. It can't be easy relying on yourself and then suddenly being thrown in with a devoted team. I understand that. Soren? Not so much. But give him a chance to see. He's just as stubborn as you are."

"That's the truth." If it's anything I've seen, it's Soren's penchant for being stuck in his ways.

He chuckles. The sound bursts through the murky cloud hanging over me. I smile in response.

That small gesture lets me know things are going to be okay between all of us. I allowed my ego to get the better of me. But next time we train, I'll be better at working with my men.

CHAPTER THIRTY-TWO

A yule log pops and cracks in the fireplace as I stare at the deep green garland draped over the edge of the mantel. Bright red poinsettia flower ornaments dangle from the garland. Gold lights weave around it, creating a peaceful ambience.

I'm not looking forward to this time away from my men. We've gotten so much better at training since that little spat between us. And I feel like I've grown closer to each of them. I'm going to miss them terribly.

Despite how noticeable their absences will be, I'm looking forward to having a break. I've been wanting to look into doing something for myself, so I may even enjoy my time alone. I can explore the island and the castle. Maybe even play with the gnomes. Besides, my aunt will be here for a few days. I wanted to go home with her, but she's going on a business trip. And after that, I'll practically have the entire island to myself.

"Ready?"

Jesse's voice jars me from my thoughts. I turn and face him with a flirty smile. "I was beginning to think you forgot."

"Oh, well," he holds out his arm for me to take, "allow me to start making up for that now."

I giggle while I take his arm and walk with him as he leads me toward his door. "Are you looking forward to going home and seeing your brothers?"

"Going home, I'm looking forward to. Getting off this island for a while, I'm looking forward to. Getting mauled by hormonal boys, not so much."

"Is it really that bad?" I look at Jesse's features that are a mask of calm and peace.

"They're akin to trolls." He settles his serious gaze on me. "I'm going to be refereeing most of the time and hoping they don't destroy the house while I'm home."

"Wow. That's terrible." I shake my head, playing up the hyperbole that Jesse's painting.

He shrugs. "It'll be nice to see the little assholes. I've missed them." He turns his gaze back to me. "Don't tell them I said that."

"Can't have that." I laugh.

"No. They will *never* let me live it down."

"Well, at least tell them I say hi."

He tugs me around a corner and I'm curious what he has planned. "Where are you taking me?"

"To my dungeon." His voice is dark and cartoonish.

I burst out laughing. "Oh no! Not the dungeon. Whatever will I do?"

He pulls me to the side, pressing my back against the wall, sandwiching me with his hard body. He nibbles on my ear and whispers, "Make you scream my name."

He pulls back with a devilish grin and winks.

I'm completely and utterly breathless as he pulls me along by my hand. Once I recover, I take notice of our surroundings. We're nearing the front of the castle.

"Seriously, where are you taking me?"

"If I told you, it wouldn't be a surprise." He's smug. And I absolutely love it.

"Are we going outside?" I didn't bring a coat with me. If that's where we are heading, we're gonna have to backtrack so I can slip on something warm.

"Nope."

Oh.

Sure enough, we pass by the front doors. My mind

goes full tilt into what he has in store for us, and I just can't stop wanting to know more.

"Are we taking a leisurely tour of the castle?" I take in the hall that abruptly ends and turns to the left.

This one is lined by arch-framed windows on one side, giving an enchanting view of the island's western coast. The steep hills beneath the windows are covered with tall trees until the rock becomes too jagged to support them, and the tannish stone glows silver in the moonlight that also reflects off the midnight blue waters. The sky is full of starlight, and the scene almost looks too beautiful to be real.

I pinch myself. Just in case.

"You're getting warmer." He's teasing me, and he knows how bad this is driving me crazy with curiosity.

I smile in spite of myself, because, damn it all if I don't love it.

He gets to me in so many ways.

I playfully groan. "You're killing me!"

"Torturing is the word I think you're looking for." He smiles now, and I love the way his face lights up. "This is more fun than I gave it credit for."

I quirk an eyebrow. "You're purposefully leading me in circles?"

He shrugs. "Maybe I am. Maybe I'm not. I guess you'll just have to keep following me to find out."

I narrow my eyes on him. "Why do I feel like this is an elaborate scheme?"

He feigns insult, though never stalls in dragging me along. "Honestly. Of all the things I've done for you without gratitude or expecting anything in return." He shakes his head. "You think you know someone, then BAM!" He slaps his hands together. "You're given a hefty dose of reality."

I choke back a chuckle as he dramatically waves his hands in the air and bows his head, shaking it back and forth.

I realize he's not going to stop until I prompt him. "Are you done yet?"

He spins on his heels to face me, clutching his hands to his heart. "Wren, how could you think so little of me?"

I chuckle. "All right, all right. I trust you. Next time, bring a friggin' blindfold."

His eyebrows perk up at that. He stands ramrod straight and rests a bent finger over his chin as he turns his gaze to the ceiling of the hall. "Hmm… Now why didn't I think of that."

"Poor planning?" I add sarcastically.

His eyes meet mine and a slight smile pulls on his lips. "Seems like perfect planning so far."

He approaches me slowly, dragging out each movement, taunting me with his approach. His eyes darken and I bite the corner of my lower lip.

"We do have some time left to kill." He looks up and down the hall. "We're alone here."

He licks his lips and I'm instantly turned on fire. I'm frozen in my spot. Not that I wanted to move anyway. He stops when his toes touch mine. He slowly lowers his lips to mine in a sweet, deep kiss that grows deeper and more heated as we become lost to the passion between us.

I'm pushed back until I'm pressed against a wall with his body firmly on mine. He hikes one of my legs around his waist, sliding his hand along my tight-covered thigh. His fingers move under my skirt until he finds the waist band and slides underneath it. His fingers plunge low, flicking my swollen clit with delicious moves.

I moan against his mouth. He presses further, dipping his fingers inside me, curling them as he pulls out, and simultaneously sending me into an orgasm that makes my legs shake and my knees weak. His mouth moves along my neck as I try to keep as quiet as I possibly can.

My orgasm ends, but I don't want to stop. I move a hand to his pants and fumble with the button until it snaps free. I slide the zipper down, stretched to its limits with his erection. I slide my hand down his stomach until my fingers wrap around his hardened cock. It throbs against my touch and Jesse lets out a low groan.

"Damn it, woman. You're going to make me take you right here and now."

I look at him with a smirk. "What's stopping you?"

He growls as his mouth collides with mine, and he bats my hand away. His hands grip my ass as he lifts me up and carries me across the hall to the windowsill. Sitting me down, he looks at me and shrugs with an apologetic look just before my tights are ripped at the crotch with one fluid pull of his hands. Cold air graces the warmth that fills my sensitive mounds only a second before he plunges himself into me.

He thrusts powerfully in and out of me with hungry need. I brace myself against the sides of the window as he rides me harder and harder, filling me with the entirety of his erection. He leans me back as he pumps into me, eyes catching mine, darkened with desire and that sends me over the edge of my climax.

He covers my mouth as my stifled moans whisper through the hall.

Just before I finish, a pinch forms between his eyebrows and he rolls his eyes as he pulls me tighter against him and releases his hot liquid inside me. Only now, his thrusts slow, but don't stop completely. Not just yet.

His cock pulsates in me and it causes me to clench with each throb. He chuckles darkly.

"If you keep doing that, we're going to go at it again."

I smile, a naughty twist in my lips. "I can't help it. It's magnificent."

Sure enough, he grows harder.

He shakes his head with that killer smile of his. "Suit yourself."

He thrusts into me again, holding me upright, bouncing me up and down against him. I angle my hips to feel more of the delightful friction building to a delicious peak.

This time, we climax together.

I'm filled with his liquid, and hunger for more.

I shake the thought from my head. When the hell did I become so lustful?

When Jesse turned me into a sex-crazed woman.

Shame on him.

He kisses me as he sits me back on the sill. He slowly pulls out, and I automatically clench to keep him in me. He chuckles. "I've created a monster."

"Yeah, but you love it."

"Indeed, I do."

Afterward, we continue down the hall until we come to a restroom. I duck into the room and remove what is left of the tights and clean up before rejoining him in the hall. His eyes glance at my now bare legs and he smiles.

I chuckle and shake my head. "Who created the monster in who?"

"Fair question." He holds out his hand for me to take, and when I do, his warmth seeps into me.

Soon, we approach the kitchens of the castle. The smell of delicious, roasted meat and vegetables fills the air and makes my mouth water.

Jesse leads me into the dim kitchen, illumined with candles in a path leading to a small table set for two. I look at Jesse as he smiles proudly.

"A candlelit dinner?" My voice comes out breathless.

"Of course."

As we reach the table, he pulls out my seat for me and I take it with a quick thanks. Once he takes his seat, I set my eyes on the two plates with roasted chicken and steaming potatoes and long, thin green beans.

I take the cloth napkin sitting next to my plate and place it in my lap, grateful for my aunt's unbeknownst crash course in dinner etiquette. Jesse does the same with his napkin and picks up a fork, spearing a chunk of potato and shoving it into his mouth. His manners match my own.

I smile.

"What?" His mouth full of food makes the word come out weird.

"I'm so happy you're you." I dig into my food, no longer worried about how I look when I eat.

"Were you nervous about eating dinner with me?" He quirks an eyebrow as the side of his mouth curves upward.

I shrug. "You could say that."

"Why?" It sounded genuine, curious.

"Because trolls don't have table manners to speak of. My aunt seemed sort of appalled at our first formal dinner together, and I thought you might see me as an animal."

He chuckles, almost choking on another chunk of potato. "Woman, have you not realized I've seen you eat already?"

I pause. Oh. Right.

Duh.

"I didn't think of it. But, you're right."

He points his fork at me. "And don't you forget that."

I chuckle as I dig into the food, happy to be at ease and just simply enjoy myself without pomp and circumstance.

Once dinner is done, he walks me back to my room. As we arrive at my door, I turn and face him. "I wish we didn't have to say goodbye."

"We're not. But I'm touched."

I smack him in his arm. "You're such a smart ass."

He shrugs. "Well, that's a far cry better than a dumb ass."

I giggle. "True."

He kisses me deeply before pulling away. "See you soon."

"Bye." It comes out barely above a whisper.

I turn and walk into my room, unable to hide the smile from my face even if I tried. I'm most definitely going to miss him while he's gone.

CHAPTER THIRTY-THREE

I spend the official first morning on the first day of my winter break at Blackbriar, making myself look presentable for my aunt.

With Savannah also on break with her family back home, I don't have her to rely on for help with makeup, so I decide to go without. I'd probably end up with a horribly outdated 80's look if I attempted it. And *that* I certainly don't want. Especially going to see my aunt.

Satisfied with my messy bun, white button up blouse, and dark khakis, I pull on some silver ballet flats and head out the door. I don't have far to go though. My aunt is meeting me in the common room in the House of Phoenix. From there, we're walking to the kitchens to make and eat lunch together.

As soon as I round the corner, I find her with her back turned to me as she studies one of the many paintings covering nearly every inch of the maroon colored walls. My aunt is dressed in expensive looking tan pants with a tailored white shirt that fits her shape well.

Her hands are in her pockets and her hair is in a perfect braid that nearly reaches her waist. I chew on my lower lip, wringing my fingers as I debate whether or not to change and fix my hair. Just before I turn around, my aunt sees me.

"Wren?" Her voice seems surprised.

Now, how often does *that* happen?

I don't want to say much, if anything at all.

I face my aunt with my eyebrows raised in question. "Yes, Aunt Patricia."

"Did you forget something?"

"No." I shake my head and walk deeper into the room. "I just wanted to double check something real quick. But it's fine."

"Are you sure?" Her brown eyes focus on mine. "I can wait."

I nod. "It's good. I don't want to take up anymore time. I know you have to leave for your business trip in a few hours."

Her shoulders raise a fraction of an inch with the deep breath she takes in through her nose. "Very well. Let's go."

I skip to her side and walk next to her, trying my damnedest to keep up with her long, elegant strides and graceful moves.

It's hopeless.

"How has school been since I've seen you last?" Aunt Patricia keeps her head held high and her back straight as she moves. She doesn't even look at me or cast a glance my way as she speaks.

"It's been good. Classes have been keeping me busy. I'm happy to have a break." I look outside a window as we pass and notice snow is falling, collecting with a light dusting that coats the evergreen bushes and side-walks outside.

The sight makes me grateful for the warmth in the castle instead of the chilly atmosphere of a cave. The trolls usually made me sleep closest to the opening. That thought creates a sharp pinch between my eyebrows. I massage the pressure away with the tips of my fingers.

"Mint and chamomile." My aunt's words pull my attention to her.

"Huh?"

"For headaches."

"Oh. Thank you." I don't have a headache, but I try not to bring up the trolls since it seems to bother her when I do. I play it off and shrug out my shoulders to ease the tension built in them as well.

"Do you get them often?" There's a small hint of concern in her proud, firm voice.

"No. Not really. I'm fine."

"If you insist." She speaks through a sigh and takes a sharp right. The motion makes my steps falter.

She stops and looks at me then. "Child, are you not well? Do you need to go to the infirmary?"

I shake my head. "Foot slipped."

I lied, but she doesn't need to know that.

She glances at my shoes and nods. "Well, pick up your feet a little more when you walk."

"I will."

Soon, we arrive in the kitchens. Instantly my eyes return to the place where just last night, a small table had been set for two, and where Jesse and I spent a beautiful evening together. He left early this morning. I miss him already as memories of the things we did in the hall to each other also creeps through my mind.

I clear my throat.

Aunt Patricia settles her gaze on me with a hitched, perfectly shaped eyebrow. "I'll put on some tea."

I give her an agreeing nod and take a spot at the counter. This counter is a massive island that takes up the whole center of the huge kitchen.

"Will you gather the ingredients for a hearty salad?" My aunt speaks over her shoulder as she fills a kettle with water and places it on the stove.

"Sure." I move to the industrial size refrigerator and pull out a collection of greens, radishes, an onion, and a handful of other vegetables. I take them to the counter and pull out a cutting board and knife, setting them next to my ingredients.

Aunt Patricia digs around for a couple of plates and sets them next to me. She slides the cutting board toward her and begins working on the greens, adding a heaping pile to each plate.

"I apologize for being so distant. As you have probably figured out, I am a very private woman. And after everything that has happened, I always assumed you held some grudges against me."

I look at her intently, watching her expression as she works. She's focused on her cutting, and I wonder where this is coming from. Not that I mind. I mean, at least she's opening up a little.

"It's okay. I understand that it'll take some time for the both of us to get used to the idea of being in each other's life again."

Aunt Patricia glances at me briefly. The look was so quick it's hard to tell what flashed through her eyes before she looked away. She finishes with the greens and takes a group of vegetables to the sink to be rinsed off. "Yes. That is true."

"You don't feel guilty about me staying here during winter break, do you?" I watch her twist to face the counter again, as she works to clear the vegetables from excess dirt and water.

"I didn't have children for a reason. My work is important to me and others. Having a family never has been and never will be part of my plan. Though that changed for me when you came to live with me, until you disappeared, of course."

I nod my head in understanding, even though she can't see it.

She returns to the counter and starts to cut through the freshly cleaned vegetables. "That being said, there is a part of me that does wonder if I should clear my schedule to allow for you to be with me when you need. However, I'm also reminded that you are an adult and capable of taking care of yourself." She pauses in her cutting to look at me. "Do I feel guilty? Not necessarily. Obligation is probably the right word."

Well that's not exactly what I expected to come out,

but okay then. I guess there's more of a hardened interior to her than I thought. "I suppose that makes sense. You shouldn't be expected to drop everything to be there for a grown woman, capable of taking care of herself. Regardless of the circumstance."

She nods, a small hitch in the corners of her lips appears. "Exactly."

She returns to her cutting, and the conversation is relatively dry until we dig into our food.

"I didn't come here just to eat lunch with you."

I meet Aunt Patricia's gaze, and she's wearing an expression I'm sure her face isn't used to making.

"What is it then?" I set my fork to the side and try to discreetly pick my teeth with the tip of my tongue.

"Well, I decided that you deserve to know the truth about what happened to your parents."

I straighten my back and prepare myself for what's to come. "I appreciate that."

She gives me a serious look. "Do not thank me just yet, child. It is not good news."

I cock my head to the side. "Oh."

"Your father was performing unsanctioned magic just before your mother died."

I gasp. "For what?" This doesn't add up at all. Why would my father do such a thing? I don't like where this is going.

Not one little bit.

I don't trust it. My instincts tell me there is something not being said, and this whole confession seems shaky.

"I do not know. I have given myself migraines trying to figure it out. He was always pushing boundaries and causing trouble growing up." She sighs. "Whatever he was doing before he died, it was dangerous work."

I scrunch my eyebrows together. Gideon told me not to share information about my father with her. But if I ask about her assumption, I may get a better picture of what she's thinking. Perhaps I can pick up on something she may not intentionally mean to share. "What makes you think he's dead?"

"He has been missing for over six years, Wren." She shakes her head and takes a sip of her tea. "He is either incredibly skilled at hiding, or he is dead. And your father is not the greatest at hiding anything, much less himself."

I nod slowly, running everything she said over and over in my head. Nothing sticks out to me.

"You do not still cling to the hope that your father is alive, do you?" She doesn't give me a chance to answer before she adds, "That would be tragic and incredibly naïve of you."

My immediate impulse is to snap at her. But a level head needs to prevail here. I can't let her see me get upset or it could clue her in to things she shouldn't know for now. I clear my throat and take a sip of my tea. The liquid warms my throat and provides enough distraction to ease the growing anger within me. "Of course not. I was just curious what you would say."

She levels her eyes to mine and looks at me as though she can see right through me. "If by chance he is alive, he will likely discover that you are as well and reach out to you. But I must insist that you do not respond to him. He is a dangerous man. As unfortunate and painful as my words may be, they are the truth."

So you say. I don't respond. Instead, I listen and observe. Watching her lips hitch as she speaks.

"Whatever he was working on was dangerous. You cannot be caught up in that. It is very likely that his work was the reason the trolls learned of you." She takes a sip of her tea. "Those ridiculous, filthy creatures are known to take human children as slaves. Normally not at the age you were, fourteen seems a bit old for their liking. And they most definitely would not have kept you alive as long as they did under normal circumstances." She pauses and narrows her eyes on me. "You must have done something to prove yourself useful."

"I don't know what it could've been. Not unless you consider being a personal punching bag and form of entertainment useful."

She nods. "If you can remember anything from before you were taken—anything at all about what your father was working on before he disappeared—it may help to resolve the problem and clear his name. I suppose I can do at least that much for him."

"I thought you said he was dangerous." I push my plate away. This conversation is upsetting me, causing my stomach to churn. I'm not hungry anymore.

"He was... perhaps still is, which is why I am cautioning you. But he is still my brother, and I could also be wrong. People can change."

I doubt that.

She takes my plate and empties it into the trash before setting both of them into the sink. When she turns around, she looks at me pensively.

I wonder what she's going to ask. I want to ask what she's thinking about, but this woman is unpredictable at times. I never know if I'm going to say something that will make her clam up again.

"Do me a favor, will you?" she asks.

"Sure." I put on a fake smile. "Anything."

"If you do remember anything, anything at all, come to me first. I will make sure you remain safe and protected. No one will ever get close enough to hurt you ever again."

Well, would you look at that? She actually seems genuine. The moment actually makes me pause.

"I will." I add a nod for good measure.

Honestly? Everything she said to me has been a lot to process, and I want to mull it over with my men. They'll support me in figuring out our next step. No one is here for the moment, but they won't be gone forever. Though I could really use someone to talk to immediately, I can be patient. I have my memory of last night with Jesse to keep me company and help me pass the time.

Aunt Patricia glances at her watch. "I have to go."

She removes herself from the counter and walks around it toward me. She lifts her arms as she approaches, and it takes me a moment to process what she's doing. When she wraps her arms around me, I'm shocked. She pulls away and pats me on the cheek with a smile that doesn't reach her eyes. She looks almost sad. Regretful.

I open my mouth to ask her about that, but she floats through the door into the hall. A short burst of light flashes into the room and I know she's gone through a portal.

That question will have to wait until next time.

After putting the remaining food in the refrigerator, washing the dishes and cups we used, and wiping off the counter, I dust off my hands and head for my room. I need to think. Then I need to plan.

CHAPTER THIRTY-FOUR

S itting around my room day in and day out. Running over everything my aunt said in my head. She mentioned some alarming things about my father, and it's wound me up tight. I don't think I've ever been this upset over anything, ever.

Once I am dressed in some warm training clothes, I head for the training circles. This pent up energy needs to be released. Besides, training has helped ease my nerves and clear my mind before. It's also an excellent way to burn off excess energy.

I return to the first circle Soren and I used when we first began training together. Call it sentimental.

I'm surprised to see targets standing at the far end of my circle. I practice shooting controlled bursts of energy at them before I look at my wrist and briefly entertain the idea of using magic without my conduit. I don't, of course. That would be ridiculously reckless of me.

The entire island may be mostly empty of all staff and students who are lucky enough to have families to go home to for the holiday, but that doesn't mean someone couldn't stumble upon me by chance.

It's a risk I just can't take.

I have enough problems to deal with. Adding another just isn't worth it.

Getting back to work, I practice my dodge rolls and aiming my counter attacks. All the while, I can't get out of my head the possibility that what Aunt Patricia said is true.

But my father *can't* be a criminal. I remember how he enjoyed magic and teaching its basic principles to me. A far cry from casting unsanctioned spells and tinkering with dangerous powers. There's more to the story, and I refuse to accept the accusations against him at face value. I know my father was searching for the meteorite. But for who and why?

I move to a practice dummy that's set up at the end of the targets. Practicing my body shots on it, I work up a sweat. My mind spins, while trying to piece together the puzzle.

The Order was mentioned in Professor

Lawrence's secret room. And with them being after my father, I can't help but wonder if the Order are behind the rumors too. Maybe my father was working for them.

More "why" questions come to me. These questions need answering.

Why would my father work for people like that?

Why does the Order want my meteorite so badly and for what purpose?

I jab, uppercut, punch, and knee the dummy repeatedly until I'm out of breath. Taking a break, focusing on slowing my breathing, I think about the possible answers.

In the end, I don't know. It's all speculation, but I feel as though things are going to get far more complicated before they get better.

I'm growing stronger with each day, honing my power, and learning to use it according to my needs.

As my breathing returns to normal, I create a circuit of physical attacks along with magical ones, bouncing between the two and not stopping until I'm out of breath.

However, the more I train, the more questions I come up with. And with few answers presenting themselves, this session is becoming wrought with confusion and frustration. I desperately need answers.

Without my father, I have no idea where to start looking for them.

A throat loudly clears, and I'm tossed from my thoughts to deal with whoever dared to intrude on my training.

I turn to face Anderson and immediately stiffen, as I give him a deadly stare. I raise my fists and hold them chest high in a fighting stance. If this doesn't scream that he'd better not approach, then I don't know what does.

Ugh! Of all the people staying at Blackbriar during break, he has to be one of them?

I work to control my disgust and anger as I recall Jesse's story about his poor mother. If I'm not careful, I may end up a broken shell like her. After a few moments, I decide to address Anderson. "Don't you have family you should be visiting?"

He shrugs. "I was hoping to have one last go at changing your mind before I left."

"You have got to be kidding me." I angle myself toward a dummy at my left and deliver a hard, right jab into it. I position myself so I can keep him easily in sight. Turning my back on him would be a mistake and one I can't afford to make. Not with how hungry he is for my power. I face him again, and my eyes never waiver from his.

Since the so-called detox that Gideon had him on, the color has returned to his skin and he looks a lot healthier. He edges just a little closer to me, with cautious steps and while keeping eye contact, as if I'm some frightened little animal he needs to pacify.

Well, he's going to find out that I'm more dangerous than he could ever imagine.

"I'm busy training. Leave me alone."

"I can see that." He raises his hands, palms open, to show that he's weaponless. "I could join you. It would be a better session with a partner. You'd like that, wouldn't you?"

"Back the hell off. Now! I want nothing to do with you. The sooner you get that through that thick skull of yours," I jab my fingers at mine. "The better off the both of us will be."

He shakes his head and takes another step forward.

Oh, hell no.

All right. You mess with the bull, best be prepared to get the horns. And this girl is done being fucked with.

My hands instantly fill with magic and I shoot balls of fire at his feet, forcing him to take several steps back.

He stares at the ground and slowly lifts his glaring eyes to mine.

Aww, did I upset the poor guy?

Too bad.

He doesn't retaliate. Instead, he seems to mull something over in his head for a moment. When he throws up his hands and walks off, I know he made the right choice.

I win. Asshole.

Damn straight I do. I gave him more than enough warnings. And today, of all days, I am in no mood to deal with him.

Just before I turn around and start to dig into my training again, a familiar figure jogs toward me.

I smile and run to him.

Soren, you beautiful bastard, you.

I throw my arms around him and he chuckles as he catches me and lifts my feet from the ground in a huge hug. As soon as my feet touch the ground, I pull away. But only a little.

"When did you get back?"

"About five minutes before the show, actually." He levels his gorgeous amber eyes on mine. "Care to explain what that was about?"

"I handled it. That's all there is to say. See? I'm no porcelain doll."

"Wren..." There's a level of warning in his voice, but there's also a hint of worry.

"Seriously, I'm fine. So, don't you dare think about babysitting me."

I'm rewarded with a flirty chuckle. "Never."

"Thought so." I flash a coy smile at him.

"Wanna go get warm?" A flicker of light passes through his eyes.

"Let me shower first, then you're on."

As I lay cuddled on the bed with Soren, our naked bodies glistening from our lovemaking, I let him know about what Aunt Patricia said. Once I'm done, he kisses me on the top of my head.

"What was that for?" I lift my head to look at him.

"To reassure you that everything is going to be okay. From what I've gathered, none of what she has said adds up. There are no hints of unsanctioned magic. If there were, I would've found out about it before now."

I nod against his chest that rises and falls with each breath. His heart beats at a steady pace, as I fight the sleep that pulls at the back of my mind. "So, do you think she was lying to me?"

He shrugs. "Perhaps, or at the very least, she's misinformed. When Gideon gets back, I'll pass along the information to him. We'll see what he wants to do with it, if he thinks it's worth doing anything with at all. Just rest and know we're getting close to finding your father. I know your father will tell you the truth."

"But what if he is dangerous?" I lift up and settle my eyes on his. I'm ensnared in the way he looks at me, and it's hard not to want to smile right now.

"If Gideon believed that was the case, we wouldn't have put as much effort into finding him. And my magusari sources never mentioned your father performing unsanctioned magic. I suggest sticking to what he told you and avoid telling your aunt anything about your father until we know for sure one way or the other."

I lay my head back down and exhale a deep breath of air from my lungs. "You're right. Thank you."

He chuckles. "Whoa. Who are you and what have you done with my woman?"

"Your woman?" I'm smiling big now. The sound of him laying a claim to me is thrilling.

"Duh. Don't like the sharing bit. But as long as you're happy, I'm happy."

"Really?"

He shrugs again. "Gideon and I are already best friends. Milo and Jesse are growing on me. Albeit very, very slowly."

I chuckle. "They are pretty irresistible."

"I wouldn't push it that far." His hand rubs my back.

I close my eyes and relish in the feel for a moment. "What would I do without you?"

"Hmm…" He pauses for a long moment. "Good question."

I tighten my arm around him. "I don't want to know the answer."

"I like that. Good. Let's never try to find out." His voice is soft and tender. With his hand rubbing my back, I'm lulled closer to sleep.

"I promise." I whisper half asleep.

I slip into a blissful sleep wrapped in the warm arms of a man that I'm quickly falling deeply in love with.

CHAPTER THIRTY-FIVE

Three months have passed, and as promised, we have returned to the same room each week until Milo could decipher a pattern to my father's sporadic movements. Though there were some tense moments when we couldn't land a good connection with his essence, we still came back to see if we could narrow down my father's whereabouts.

With Lady Alene quietly looking over the spell from her little corner of the room, the five of us stand around the orb one last time to try to locate my father. This time, the pink little blip appears, and I let out a breath of relief.

We finally found him.

Milo nods in my periphery, pulling my attention to him. "He's revisiting the same patterns. I've nailed. It.

We can project where he's going next... Colorado Springs."

"When?"

"I'm guestimating tomorrow between morning and afternoon."

"What location in Colorado Springs?" Jesse asks. "That's a whole lot of city to cover in such a short window."

"Garden of the Gods National Park." Milo's gaze settles on the map.

Gideon sighs in relief. "Good news."

Soren gives a snort of rebuttal. "Until you consider the presence of humans."

Go figure there would be another hiccup to overcome. I roll my eyes and slouch my shoulders. Why does everything have to come with so many challenges?

Gideon squeezes my hand. I meet his gaze and he smiles reassuringly at me.

Soren continues, claiming my attention again. "It's going to take a lot to get in there unseen, grab her father, and get out of there. If the Order decides to show, that creates another issue. If the shadow wolves have been following him, just add that to the list of problems."

Gideon huffs. "Mortals may have an inkling as to

the mage world, but it's far from being completely known. And we'd like to keep it that way. A magic battle in the middle of a tourist attraction will draw some massively unwanted attention, to say the least."

"Exactly," Soren says.

"But this is the best way to get in there and get my father before it's too late."

"Yes." Gideon breaks from the circle around the map. We follow suit, taking a step back, and I watch as the map fades. "Which means we need a solid plan."

"Once at the location, Soren and I can scout ahead and see if we can pinpoint where exactly my father is located, and any chokeholds or spots where we could possibly be ambushed. As soon as we have a solid understanding of the layout of the area, we come back, and we all go in together."

Gideon beams at me. I've absorbed a lot of tactical knowledge over the last few months in our training sessions as a group. Seeing it being put to use now must be a proud moment.

He should be proud. He's a great teacher.

"We can't portal straight to the location," Soren points out, "with as many people that could be there. It would draw too much attention."

"From our friends in the Order and our extra-special shadow wolf buddies," Jesse adds.

"So," Milo says from his spot on the floor, "that just means we get as close as we can without drawing attention and go in from there. He's going to be deep within the park, where foot traffic is lighter, so the likelihood of people being around is very small. I've drawn up a map of the location. We can go over it just before we leave."

"Excellent idea, Milo." Gideon nods toward him.

"And if we have friends…" I use Jesse's term. It fits. "We can make sure to give them a *warm* welcome."

"A fiery welcome, that is." Jesse sighs. "I do love a good bon fire."

We all share in a chuckle.

Gideon's stern eyes roves over us all. "In any case, I'll cast an illusion over the area so that if and when a fight breaks out, we can do what we need to without passersby stumbling upon us."

"We should also come up with a Plan B." Milo walks forward. "I'll come up with it at the time that it's needed in case any of us becomes compromised by the enemy. The less you all know, the better. Just in case." He gives a nod toward me and there's a flash of worry that crosses his eyes.

"You mean in case they capture and torture one of you to get to me and discover everything we know." I bite the corner of my bottom lip. It wouldn't surprise me if the Order was getting that desperate to go after someone close to me if they couldn't get to me directly. Knowing my men, they would do everything possible to keep me out of harm's way.

Lady Alene steps forward, always remaining an observer each time we have come to the room. Until now. "I can also place a special protection for each of you as well. We can never be too careful."

"That's really gracious of you, Lady," I say.

She smiles softly. "You all hold a special place in my heart. I do not want to see harm come to any of you."

She's so sweet and kind. I'm ever thankful for her being in my life as well. She's like a mother looking over us. That means more to me than words can express.

As the men finalize the plan, I sink into my thoughts. I'm nervous, anxious, excited, and a touch apprehensive. If things go bust this time, I don't know what I'll do. I won't give up, but that doesn't mean I'll be happy with leaving my father out there to fend for himself against whatever's after him.

I'm snapped from my thoughts as I barely register my name being called. As I look up, I notice all eyes focused on me. "What?"

"Tomorrow before sunrise, we'll meet in my office and leave from there."

I give them a small apprehensive smile, while I slightly nod my head. "Sounds like a plan."

Gideon returns my nod, but there's a concerned crease in his forehead. He doesn't address it though. "Let's get as much rest as we can. The time to leave will come faster than we realize."

As we file out of the room, I resolve myself to allowing nothing to separate me from my father again. Not this time. Pity the soul who tries, because I will take out anyone who stands in my way.

CHAPTER THIRTY-SIX

J ust as I pull back the covers on my bed and start to climb in, a knock on my door echoes through my room. I look over my shoulder, in the direction of the door, and wonder what could be going on now.

The knocking starts up again, making my door rattle, and I briefly consider ignoring whoever it is in favor of sleep. It's a fleeting thought that is over just as quickly as it begins. In the end, no one ever visits my door at any hour of night without it being important.

With a sigh of resignation, I cast my bed an apologetic look and shuffle my feet to the door, opening it to Soren. I quirk an eyebrow. "We're supposed to be getting sleep, not naked."

He casts me a reproachful glare and huffs. "Really?"

I shrug casually. "What's up?"

"Gideon's decided that we need to train one final time, cover any last-minute issues before we leave in the morning."

I groan. "I'm so tired."

"We're all tired, Wren. Tomorrow is going to test us in many ways, and you, Jesse, and Milo are not used to losing sleep and facing battles. It will put Gideon and me at ease if we did this."

I roll my eyes and open my door wider. "Since you put it that way, let me get my shoes."

He nods once. I turn for my shoes, slipping them on and making my way back to the door. Before walking through, I cast one last longing gaze at my bed. The door shuts the inviting warmth of my blankets away, and I walk with Soren to Gideon's office.

I fall hard to the floor. The air rushes from my lungs in a forceful grunt. This is the third time tonight that I've had my feet kicked out from underneath me, and it's looking like it's not going to be the last.

This is our last shot at understanding how each of

us move, respond to attacks, and defend each other. To top this whole shindig off, we're all exhausted. The day I've been waiting for will be here in a few short hours. Rescuing my father will be dangerous, and our enemies have already shown themselves to be fierce. So, training in less than ideal conditions will actually benefit us. My focus returns to the session at hand.

As we train, we face an onslaught of different foes. Highly armored dummies unsheathe their swords and shadow wolves snarl as they approach. I even catch a glimpse of magically simulated mages in the mix. Dozens of our attackers move so randomly that it's hard for me to follow and gauge what my enemies will do next.

Gideon's hand appears in front of me. I follow the path of his hand to his arm and eventually to his beautiful blue-green eyes that I swear become more stunning each time I look into them.

I take his hand an allow him to pull me up.

"Are you okay?" His voice holds an edge of concern.

I nod. "Why are they moving so randomly? I can't predict anything that's coming next."

"And you likely won't. That's the point of this exercise."

Gideon rotates on his heels and blasts oncoming

foes as Soren, Milo, and Jesse close in to surround us and create a barrier.

I gape at him. Honestly, that was incredibly impressive for a scenario that appears to be completely random. How did he know that an enemy was sneaking up on him?

"Whoa."

"Ready?" He angles his chin lower and settles his ever-mesmerizing eyes on me.

I smile. "Let's do this."

We continue facing the seemingly never-ending army together. Jesse uses his illusion skills to trip up some of the mages, turning them on each other, reducing each other to ash. He smirks. I give him a nod of approval as I face a dummy. I dodge each of its clever blows and shove both of my fists into its chest. A bright light flashes with the blow. The dummy flies backward, knocking into four of its comrades, taking them down.

Soren whistles. "Damn, that was a good move."

I look toward him, flashing a proud smile as he expertly kicks a shadow wolf mid-leap, tossing it to the side in a lump of shadowy mist like it was nothing but a pillow. He turns to his right, takes out a mage with a blast of fire, and turns around to carry out a deadly blow to the head of a dummy, decapitating it. The headless body falls to the ground in a smoking, lifeless form.

Milo, the clever one, never loses sight of the three foes surrounding him—two shadow wolves and a mage. He works his hands through the air as they start to glow. Magic swirls around him and the earth vibrates, knocking the mage from his feet and forcing the shadow wolves to hunker low to the ground, whimpering.

My word, I could watch these men fight simulations all day long. But to fight with them is beyond amazing. It's a very invigorating experience.

Toss in a bit of teasing and compliments here and there and, ladies and gents, we have fun.

I feel like I'm in tune with them as my focus is reclaimed on the fight ahead of me. I don't even think, blink, or flinch. I simply move. Every motion comes so naturally. I also have more control over my power as I notice the precision of my blasts and the steadiness of my hands. It doesn't quite come as easily as it does without the conduit, but it will soon. With my men's help, I will do this.

We're closer too. These trainings have helped us gain some natural and uncanny ability to move fluidly with each other for a similar cause. And all of us seem to complement each other in different ways.

I face down two more shadow wolves, snarling at me with their razor-sharp teeth and lava-red eyes glaring at me. I smirk. "Come at me." I wave them over with my hand.

They charge. As they get close, one launches into the air while the other goes for my legs. The one still on the ground will reach me first. So, I duck low to the ground, spinning my leg out to trip up the first. The second one flies over me, landing on the ground with a small cloud of dust lifting from his paws. He spins as I deliver a deadly blast of fire to the first one. I shoot a bolt of lightning at him. It lands right between his eyes.

As the two shadow wolves evaporate into nothing, I stand to take out a mage trying to sneak up behind me.

I quirk an eyebrow as Milo beats me to it. I'm astonished at how well he fights. He holds his own, and then some. He's not just a sexy nerd, he's also a talented fighter.

All of my men are capable, talented fighters, and it shows.

Jesse's strength is creating distracting illusions that

cause our enemies to see what he wants them to. Soren's a battle mage, through and through, with calculated tactics and the ability to kill without hesitation if needed. Gideon is the same, though he prefers to viciously disarm his opponents rather than kill them.

And me? I'm out to take down whoever stands in my way. Though I dislike the idea of killing someone again, if there's no other way around it, I will. Because I know that not only are my men's lives at stake, but also my father's. I refuse to let anyone I love die—especially him. We're so close to finally being reunited after so long.

Whatever it takes to protect and keep the ones I love and care for safe, I'll do. To hell with the costs.

My second wind is dwindling fast as I face off with more dummies, shadow wolves, and mages. I see the exhaustion in my men's faces too. "We can't keep up with this much longer. We'll be useless in the morning."

"She's right." Gideon's voice booms over the fray of the ensuing fight. "Let's end this."

I close my eyes and breathe deep. Hoping that I avoid my men with this move, I dig deep into my core, reaching for the power of the meteorite fused within me. The feeling is exhilarating, like a hyper adrenaline rush mixed with a slow burn. I can smell the fallen leaves and fresh dirt, the burnt wood from the heap of defeated dummies, and I can feel the earth reverberate with the pounding footfalls of an approaching horde. Opening my eyes, I move forward, my skin glowing white with magic.

The last of the simulated enemies charge, and once they all surround me, I release the building pressure of my magic begging to break free of my hold. I plant my feet firmly to keep from stumbling and hold my hands steady as I aim the white rush of magic toward the simulations. I see colorful lights dance in my vision as my men's magic join in with mine.

It's beautiful, magical, and deadly.

The burst is over as quick as it begins, consuming the last of the dummies, shadow wolves, and mages. Before a howl or scream can escape their mouths, they're consumed by the combined power blasted at them by me and my men. All that's left is glittering dust floating to the floor.

The world spins as a black rim lines my vision and I fall to my knees. Footsteps pound the ground, rushing toward me. Soren lifts me into his arms and sets me on my feet. After a few moments of regaining my footing and shaking off the exhausting drain my radical move put me through, I weakly smile at my men. "I'm okay."

It comes out weak, and judging by the looks on their faces in response, they all disagree with just how "okay" I am.

"We've pushed too hard tonight," Soren says, keeping me steady.

"Let's get some rest. She should stay with you, and you can keep an eye on her." Gideon's voice comes from directly behind me and I realize he's helping to hold me up.

"I'm fine, really." At least my voice sounds stronger this time. I'm sore, tired, and in need of another shower, but I'm feeling better as each minute passes.

"I think we all need some sleep." Milo stifles a yawn as he stretches his arms above his head.

"I also need my beauty rest." Jesse's remark makes everyone look at him. "What? This level of perfection comes with a price."

I shake my head as a chuckle leaves my lips. Only Jesse.

"All right, everyone off to bed." Gideon walks to the wall with the door, places his hand on the jam. The room begins to shift, shrinking to its unassuming normal closet appearance. We all rush to keep up, making it through before we're swallowed up by the change.

At least, that's what I think about each time we have to exit.

Before long, I'm in Soren's bed, slipping into a dreamless sleep. Tomorrow is the big day.

And I'm banking on things going as planned.

CHAPTER THIRTY-SEVEN

We step out of the portal somewhere near an entrance to a trail head. Behind us is a small circular parking lot. We take a moment to regain our bearings and check to make sure our sudden appearance wasn't seen by anyone. Satisfied that no one had seen us just magically appear out of thin air, we head down the path in a single-file line away from view of the road and parking lot before stopping again.

As we busy ourselves looking over every inch of our surroundings, I force myself to keep my teeth from chattering. This morning is still pretty frigid. I pull my jacket closer around me and step to the right of the trail to allow the runner coming at us to take the left and pass by.

Soren's gaze follows the tall man in sweats and a

hoodie. He narrows his eyes on his back. I glance over my shoulder to see what the fuss is about, but the runner is already gone. I return my gaze to in front of me.

"Why were you looking at that runner?"

Soren looks at me from over his shoulder. "We have to be careful of anyone that we see. They could be informants."

"Oh."

Once we have our bearings, Milo takes the lead, using a watch he enchanted with an alchemical spell to turn it into a device locked on my father's energy. I don't know how he did it, but he did. And the teal glow of magic surrounding the watch keeps us on track, directing us to my father.

Anxiety pulses through me, kicking up the pace of my heart as I realize that with each step I take, the closer I get to him. However, it quickly dawns on me that this area is full of places our enemies can hide.

There are more ways for this to go south. More than we had accounted for. But as long as we stick to the plan and keep our eyes open, we can do this— scout ahead, pinpoint my father's location, and if we run into the enemy, take them down. Today is the day I get my father back, and no one will stand in my way.

Numerous blind spots come to my attention as the

trail we take curves around large rock formations. Huge dropoffs on the left, covered in trees and bushes, are thick enough to hide in. Never mind the high vantage points on some of the larger formations that tower above us. Top it off with the narrow path we are on… we're at a major disadvantage.

"Anyone else get the feeling that we're not alone?" My voice, though quiet, carries through our line.

Jesse, walking casually behind me, places his hands on my shoulders. "Fret not, my dashing beauty. Part of the adventure here is the unknown."

I glare at him from over my shoulder. "I mean there are too many places for them to hide." I gesture at our surroundings before silently pointing out the more obvious spots.

He shrugs. "I still say that is half the fun."

"I agree with Wren," Soren says. "We may have to go to Milo's plan, if they try to ambush us."

Gideon shakes his head. "Not yet."

"Why?" Soren's voice is on edge, and I don't blame him.

I know Gideon said he'd create a veil between us and humans so that any magical battle in the park could be fought without their knowledge, but if those bastard Order goons even try to ambush us when I'm so close to finding my dad, I just may unleash a blast that not even Gideon can contain.

I hope Milo's backup plan is a good one, though I don't know what it is, and for good reason. It'll be our wild card in case things go south. Milo has yet to give me a reason to doubt him, so whatever he has up his sleeve, I'm sure it will help our team.

Gideon holds up a hand as the path widens a little at the base of a curve to the right. He points to Milo's watch. The silence is unnerving, but I suspect it's so we don't give away our plans to the enemy should they be near, listening and watching as I suspect they are.

The rocky wall that leans over the path slightly as it stretches toward the sky makes for a great spot to ambush us. I'm glad we stopped on this side of it.

Gideon nods to me and Soren, and we walk forward. As I pass Milo, I glance at his watch. He nods in the direction ahead and I smile and squeeze the top of his arm. Soren falls in step with me as I approach and stand close to the red stone formation. I angle my head around the corner, raking my gaze over every inch of landscape laid out in front of me. I keep my breaths slow and even and my steps whisper soft. Soren lifts his chin and scans the area with his amber eyes, as if sensing something in the air.

Just on the other side of the path, the land levels

out, filled with a cropping of trees. That's the direction that Milo's watch indicated. If I was keeping someone hostage and intended to trap those coming for my prisoner, I would probably choose a similar setting.

I'm not willing to place my money on this being an easy in-and-out thing. Neither is Soren, as he nods at me in a silent reminder to remain vigilant. I bite the corner of my lower lip as I watch the shadows within the trees. Everything is still. Almost too still.

For the sake of appearance, it's quiet, calm, and deserted.

We rejoin the other men and let them know what we found. Gideon has a pensive expression, as though he is trying to figure out the best course of action. Milo keeps his eyes either on his watch or scoping out the scenery around us.

"We've come too far to turn back now." Jesse stretches out his arms and hamstrings as though he's preparing for a boxing match.

I smile. Smart man. I wouldn't allow us to turn back either. He's on board with this.

Soren looks in the direction of the trees. He frowns and shakes his head. "I'll be right back."

Something during our first time scouting ahead didn't sit well with him, and I watch him head back toward the rocky wall. The sun has risen over the horizon, casting long shadows in various shapes. Whereas, where the light hits, little bits of frost melt and cover the ground. Warmth shines on me, and the chill from earlier is not as deep.

Gideon approaches Milo. "Let me check."

Milo holds out his arm and Gideon studies the watch a moment. With a nod, Milo drops his arm as Gideon looks toward Soren who is making his way back to us.

Gideon faces Soren. "Well?"

"It's like she said. I also couldn't see anything. But I *feel* something."

Gideon huffs a sigh and shakes his head. "The watch is pointing us that way, but it's too easy."

"Shouldn't we take that as a trap?" I ask.

"Yes. We just don't know how much of one to expect." Soren shifts his gaze over everything around us and shakes his head. "Something isn't right."

"I feel that too." I keep my focus on the shadows and the thicker condensed trees where my father is supposed to be. "But we've come too far to turn back now. What else can we do?"

"Reason and logic didn't exactly work out for our benefit the last time." Soren levels his gaze on me.

"Is it possible to draw them out? At least by baiting them we can see what we're dealing with."

Gideon approaches me. "What if they kill your father just as soon as they see you?"

I nod as my mind goes full tilt into what we could do to prevent that. "Jesse can cast an illusion over me so I can dip in and grab my father and get out of there. Once he's safe, we can all take a portal out of here. If something goes wrong, we have Milo's backup plan still in place."

Soren steps forward. "Let's do that but with a small change. Gideon and I will make the first move. That will be a signal to Wren that she and Michael can take a portal out of here. They won't be discovered if everyone is engaged in a fight."

"No." I shake my head. "I can't allow you all to fight without me."

"Do you want your father safe or not?" Soren's beautiful amber eyes settle on mine with intense determination.

"Yes. But, can we figure out a way to do this without me leaving you all behind?" I cross my arms in front of my chest to ward off the chill still clinging to me and to also to send Soren a silent signal that I'm not backing down on this one so easily.

"We don't have time to argue this." Soren pinches his nose.

"Wren…" Gideon's voice pulls my attention to him.

"We'll be fine. Get your father, he can take you a safe distance away. We will find you once the battle is over."

"It's now or never, love," Jesse adds.

I blow out a raspberry. "Fine. I don't like it, but fine."

Gideon nods. Soren sighs. Jesse gives me an affirming look and stands in front of me.

"Be careful," he murmurs and closes his eyes. His hands lift to my shoulders, barely resting on them. A powerful pressure enters them that fades to sharp tingles shooting through my hands and feet. My body becomes heavier, and I wonder if I'll be able to stand once he's done.

Before long, he steps back and I nod.

"Go get him, tiger." Jesse cracks a soft smile.

"Ready or not, here I come."

Taking a deep breath, I step onto the path and start to follow it around the curve.

CHAPTER THIRTY-EIGHT

J ust as I approach the trees, Jackson Cane emerges from their shadows. Wearing a smug smile, he holds his hands out to his side. I stop mid-step and wait, wondering if the spell perhaps didn't work.

"My friends," he says. "Where is that lovely lady of yours?"

"Not your concern." Gideon's voice is stern, and I glance at him as he stands with an air of command.

I shake the need to just stand and observe him for a moment. My father is out here somewhere, and I need to find him before this illusion ends. I step lightly down the dirt path, moving around Jackson and glaring at him. I have to force myself not to hurl a fireball at the back of his head.

"Oh, come now." Jackson feigns some twisted version of disappointment.

Oh, how I would love to give that man the justice he deserves. I don't. But the urge is there. Besides, I can't let emotions get in the way now. My father needs me.

Unseen, I step into the trees and weave through them. Here, shadows move like smoke toward Jackson, making me second-guess the plan to let them fight this on their own. There's a lot of them. But if it's one thing I've learned, it's just how capable my men are, especially in a fight. I still don't like it, but I have to get my father away from these people.

I watch as the figures move around and past me. This isn't good. There are too many of them, and I duck behind a tree to avoid getting bumped into. That would be a very bad thing and ruin all hopes of getting to my father.

After the last shadowy figure passes by, I peek around the tree and see stillness within the shadows and beams of light that shine over the still frozen land. The smell of mud mixed with decaying leaves and wood fills my nose as I suck in a deep breath. I scan the area for a sign of my father.

I find him.

I rush to him as the trees thin and what looks like a

campsite takes up a small open space deep within the woods. He's gagged and tied to the base of a birch. I frown at the sight of his hollow cheeks and thin physical build. A crease appears between his eyebrows as his eyes scan his surroundings and settles on where I'm standing. As the weight of the illusion lifts, his eyes widen and a light of hope shines within them.

"Dad!" I rush to him and rip away his bindings, freeing him from the tree.

He removes the gag. "Wren, what are you—"

A rumble of thunder vibrates the ground and roars through the air. A chill runs down my spine. The fight has started.

Time to go.

I help my father to his feet. "Can you create a portal?"

He nods and tries to stand on his own. He's so weak, it hurts my heart to see him this way.

Movement catches my attention and I narrow my eyes in that direction as a figure approaches us from within the copse of trees.

It's Anderson, and he's joined by a mage whose identity is concealed by robes and a hood. My heart nearly freezes in my chest as I realize the robed mage is probably part of the Order. I reach for my father just as the portal begins to form. The mage lifts his hands and a bolt of black lightning strikes the ground at our feet.

The portal's light fades away as my father stumbles back. I work to catch him from falling over.

"Not leaving so soon, are you?" Anderson's voice sounds overly cocky. More so than usual. And that's saying something.

I seethe with anger as I help my father to the ground on the other side of the tree. Facing Anderson, I glare at him, hoping he realizes that he's overestimating himself if he thinks brute force is going to win me over. "You just can't take no for an answer, can you?"

His eyebrows lift in high arches on his head as he hums. "That ship has sailed. Now I have a new opportunity."

I quirk an eyebrow as I step into my fighting stance. "And I suppose that because we're both here, it's all some big coincidence?"

"No. Not at all." He smiles. Hell, if he wasn't such a douche, he'd be half-way handsome, but his venomous smile just makes the bile in my stomach rise, coating the back of my tongue in bitter acid. "I intend to earn my family's seat."

"A seat?"

"Indeed."

I glance at my father. His rail thin body trembles from either illness or the weather, and I can tell from his dry, cracked lips that he's dehydrated. I can't stand here all day and play Anderson's games. I have to get my father to safety. And some medical help.

"As much fun as this is," I roll my eyes, "I've gotta get going. Have fun with your... whatever." I twist toward my father.

"Oh, you're not going anywhere." Anderson's voice is happy. Too happy.

I turn my attention to him. "Excuse you?"

He smiles and takes a couple steps forward, closing the gap between us. My hands ignite in magic. The battle with my men rages on, and I look toward their direction, silently praying for their safety.

"Yes. I've finally got you where I want you. And turning you and your father in will do just nicely to secure my chair. But first..." he steps even closer.

I fire magic at him and the mage. He stops moving and casts a glance over his shoulder. The mage's hooded head nods once.

"You can't fight me off anymore. I'm going to take more of your power."

"Try it and die."

My father groans. I want to check on him, but turning my attention to him is the exact opening

Anderson needs to take more of what doesn't belong to him.

Hold on, Dad. Please.

I brace for the fight.

The mage is my first target. I don't know who he is or what role he's playing in this, but I don't care. He's on Anderson's side, and so, he must be taken out. I toss a fireball at him and form my magic into a shield, keeping as much distance between me and Anderson as possible.

The mage deflects my fireball. Purple and black smoke-like magic erupts all over his body. My stomach churns in response to the corrupt magic emanating from him. He must be a shadow mage. I've never seen anything like this. My knees buckle, but I regain my composure and fortify my shield.

This is going to hurt.

A lot.

A bolt of black lightning hits the middle of my shield. My feet slide across the dirt as the force pushes against me. Glancing up, I notice Anderson is trying to move in a wide circle around me, trying to be sneaky.

I quirk a smile as my hand fills with white light with pink bolts of lightning sparking through. I make it large enough that it will be difficult if not impossible to dodge, and I toss it toward the mage while instantly twisting toward Anderson and knocking him down with a good blast of fire.

It misses, of course. But I'm not interested in killing Anderson.

Yet.

It was meant to be a warning, to disarm him and make him keep his distance.

Anderson lifts a finger and shakes it at me. "Don't make this harder than it needs to be. I promise to make your experience with me enjoyable until… well, until I hand you over. But you won't know what's happening to you then. Consider it a service."

"A service? From you? That's laughable." I quickly dodge the next bolt of lightning that shoots out toward me. I counter with a blast of white-hot light.

He dodges it easily.

Damn.

Anderson rushes me as another bolt from the shadow mage crashes into the ground, barely missing my feet. The force from the mage's blast sends me flying through the air, causing my shield to collapse and disappear. The world turns end over end until my back slams into a tree. My head crashes against the bark, shattering pieces of it all over my shoulders as dots line my vision with a dark rim. The air is forced from my lungs from the painful blow, and I struggle to reclaim my breath.

I watch as Anderson's cocky grin stretches his lips. He thinks he's won as he approaches. But as I try to move, I can't.

Panic rushes through me as images of Jesse's mother, broken and lost, rush through my mind. There is no damn way this man is taking my power or my mind. Anderson makes his approach, each step is agonizingly slow. He looks over his shoulder at the mage, gives him a nod, and faces me again. He's mere feet from me now, and I know if I don't do something soon, it'll be too late.

My father turns to look at me, as he watches helplessly from the tree behind him, eyes wide and full of horror as he is about to witness his daughter get broken by a zacar. I meet his gaze, fearless, in control, because something inside me *burns*.

My magic churns beneath my skin, soaking into my arms and legs as Anderson closes the few feet left between us. I feel like I'm on fire. My nerves scream at me as sharp tingling sensations pulsate through me. My body erupts in fire and Anderson's steps falter as a look of confusion contorts his features.

My lips pull into a satisfying, devious grin. Anderson's eyes take in mine. I lift a hand and aim it straight at him. I watch as realization dawns on him that I'm about to deliver a death blow, and he starts to dive toward the ground. I release my magic. As his feet leave the ground, my magic slices across his torso.

With a loud thump, he falls to the ground, groaning. He rolls over, and I see a nice gash in his stomach.

"Now, about that plan of yours?" I stand and slowly approach him.

The cowardly worm scoots on his ass to try and escape me. He presses a hand to his bloody wound and screws his face up in concentration, as if trying to gather strength for a counter strike. But it won't do him any good. He's crossed a line and there's no return from where I intend to send him.

The mage shoots magic near my father, obliterating the tree and drawing my attention to him. My father luckily ducked out of the way and is lying flat on the ground. His eyes meet mine with a short nod. I give the mage a deadly glare. "You are going to pay for that."

Anderson uses the distraction to his advantage by jumping up and running away into the trees before I can so much as deliver the blow to end his life.

Slippery snake.

It's just me and the mage now. Fighting magic with magic. Fire with fire. Instead of growing weary, I'm filled with a rush of adrenaline and power. I duck, dive, roll, and shoot in the various ways I've practiced with my men. It comes naturally to me now. I step closer to him with each burst of magic in hopes that the attacks don't get close to my father and seriously hurt him. Explosion after explosion, I remain standing, but just barely. I don't lose focus as fire continues to burn along my skin, sending my magic rippling around me in bright swirls.

The mage takes a step back in response to my power, as if he's never seen anything like it. The mage's attention snaps to the left and right as he spins in place to look behind him and then face me again.

Too bad, there's no one else here to help.

My men are taking care of his friends, and I'm going to take care of him.

The mage's actions become frantic, batting at things that I can't see. I pause, wondering what in the world is going on with him only to realize that I truly don't care. He's tried to kill me and my father. Hell, he even tried to help Anderson get close enough to steal my energy. This monster doesn't deserve an ounce of pity.

Forming a large burning ball of fire in my hands, I steady it in front of my torso. Just as the mage stretches out his glowing hands, I release my magic. It slams into his torso, burning a hole through his mid-section.

As I watch the mage fall to the ground, the fire covering my skin sizzles out. Soren and Gideon suddenly appear at my side.

I face them with a relieved smile and throw my arms around them, thankful they are safe and alive. Once I pull from them, I find Jesse and Milo helping my father to his feet.

"Are you hurt?" Gideon's voice pulls my attention back to him.

"I'm fine."

Soren's jaws clench as he takes in my appearance. I follow his gaze. Burns and gashes cover my arms and legs. Blood stains my clothes, and I'm covered from head to toe in dirt and debris from the surrounding trees.

I dust myself off and inspect myself a little further. Aside from some minor injuries, I'm surprisingly fine.

"Wren." Milo's voice snaps my attention to him as my father's head lulls backward. He's lost consciousness.

I rush to him, finally feeling muscle soreness and the sting of exposed wounds as the adrenaline from battle wears out. "Dad!"

He doesn't respond.

I feel for a pulse. "He's fading. We need to get out of here, now." I face Gideon. With a quick nod, he forms a portal. We pull my father through.

I don't take the time to check out our surroundings as we land on green grass. I help Milo and Jesse with doors as I rush behind Gideon to a room in what I assume is the safehouse. Once my father is on the bed, I step back and watch with bated breath as Gideon and Soren work to stabilize my father.

Jesse cups my shoulder and pulls me toward him. "Come on. Let them work."

I let him guide me out of the room, mostly because I don't have the strength to argue or fight against him.

Please, Dad. Just hold on a little longer. I've finally found you.

CHAPTER THIRTY-NINE

As I sit in the living room of the safehouse, I look at the plain walls that surround a large black stone fireplace. The wood burning in the fireplace, gives off a luminous glow and the faint scent of hickory. The pops and crackles of the flames are the only things I can focus on at the moment. Not the waiting.

Because, as Gideon told me just a moment ago, "Only time will tell."

Jesse's voice intrudes on my brooding. "Drink, Wren."

I take a sip of my almost forgotten potion. My arms scream with the movement and my muscles spasm.

The pain of the battle has set in, as I remember my forced encounter with the trunk of the tree as I slammed into it. A thick purple salve that burns like hell and smells just as bad covers the span of my back. The bits and pieces of bark that had flown around during the mayhem, like shrapnel, feel like little needles lodged in my spine. The nasty salve is supposed to not only help with the small pieces coming out, but also with the mind-numbing pain that's coursing through my entire body with every movement.

"Anderson, that prick." Soren growls the words from his seat to the right of me. "I'll kill him."

"Gotta catch him first," Jesse adds from my left.

"Which is going to be much harder now." Gideon leans forward to set his empty cup on the coffee table that divides the room from the fireplace and the sofa I sit on. He leans back in his chair. "I don't know what seats or chairs he was referring to, but I suspect it has something to do with the Order and their hierarchy. This can't be good. And now we know he is very well aware of Wren and her power."

"He works for the Order." Soren shakes his head. His hands clench into fists over his knees. "His family must be one of the heads."

"Speculation, don't you think?" Jesse asks.

"No." Gideon sits forward, stretching his neck and rolling his shoulders to ease the stiffness in them. "It makes sense, the family name is common, but one that is linked to the Order."

"I thought no one knew who was in the Order?" I ask.

"Exactly. Which is why I said linked." Gideon's eyes drop to my potion. I groan and take another sip. "Anderson's grandfather was a double agent. He was believed to have been killed in action during a mission but has since been sighted near locations suspected to be outposts for the Order. No one could ever get close enough to apprehend him. It's possible he has a high position within the Order. However, his family always appeared to be upstanding members of the community, never stepping out of line. And we don't punish children for the crimes of their fathers. Eventually, sightings of Anderson's grandfather decreased, and over time, the magusari focused efforts on other matters."

"Obviously they want me, but why? Do you think they know about my meteorite?"

A series of shrugs and pondering looks fill the silence that follows my question.

"There's no way to know unless they face you and tell you directly." Gideon sighs and runs his hands over his face. "Unfortunately, that's the best we have."

"Well at least Anderson won't rear his ugly mug at Blackbriar anymore. That should be something."

My men respond to my comment with strange expressions.

"What?"

Gideon clears his throat. "He's still missing, and as long as his whereabouts are unknown, he poses a danger. He's working for the Order, he could be anywhere. If he's not, then there's a possibility he simply tucked his tail between his legs and went into hiding."

"Coward," Soren mumbles.

I agree.

"The magusari will be looking for him." Gideon sits back in his seat, resting his head against the back of his chair.

I shift my gaze to him. A cut over his left eyebrow stands out. I frown as I stare at it. I think back to the battle that they had and wonder how many of their foes were like the one I faced. "Was that mage I fought really a shadow mage?"

"Yes." His eyes take in mine and my heart flutters.

At least that part of me doesn't hurt.

"Impressive that you took him on relatively well by yourself." Soren's voice is full of pride, and though I want to look at him, it hurts too much. "It's extremely dangerous to take one on. And you fought exactly how I would've."

I smile. "Thanks. Though I think he got a good couple of shots in."

"Hey, I helped." Jesse raises his hands above his head and lets them plop back to his lap. He leans in closer to me. "A little."

"Which is why I said, 'relatively'." Soren's annoyance rings through his words as he repeats himself. "Thanks for your help as well."

"Did that hurt?" Jesse asks.

Milo walks in from the hall that leads to my father's makeshift infirmary. His hair is disheveled from the fight, and spots of dirt still cover parts of his face. His pants have gashes in them, revealing bandages. It's easy to see that he's tired, but he decided to help my father before resting himself. And that makes my heart swell. He sighs as he leans an arm over the mantle of the fireplace. Just in time, too. I think Soren would've tackled Jesse, regardless if I sat between them in excruciating pain or not. "No change. We should call in Savannah."

"Soren?" Gideon asks.

"I'll go now."

Jesse wraps an arm around my shoulders, and I wince with the movement. "She'll be safe with us."

Soren huffs a sigh. He nods toward Jesse's arm. "You're hurting her."

Jesse removes his arm gently. "If she drank her potion, it wouldn't hurt so much."

"*She* is sitting right here, and I'm trying." I take another sip, fighting against the agony each movement makes.

"You're lucky your spine didn't break." Jesse shifts in his seat to better face me.

"It probably did." My words come out matter-of-fact.

The weight of everyone's questioning gazes settles on me, and I meet each of them with a brief glance. I sigh, a sharp pain enters my ribs as I tell them how I was thrown against the tree. Their eyes widen as I share how my magic burned through me and then the feeling returned.

I shrug and grimace against the sharp agony of the movement. "If my meteorite didn't repair it, then I'd be toast."

Their expressions darken at that remark.

"But I'm not. And thanks to Jesse's illusion, I took out the mage before he could reduce me to ash."

"Naturally." Jesse smiles. "Bout time I get some credit."

"Hush." Soren's voice is full of warning.

Jesse shrugs, weaving his fingers behind his head and sitting rather smugly. I shake my head slowly, so the movement doesn't hurt. He likes to goad Soren. Death wish doesn't even begin to describe what Jesse's deal is with pushing Soren like that.

Then Soren smiles and I'm dumbfounded.

Well, I'll be.

"Take care of her," he says and sets his eyes on Gideon, Milo, and Jesse.

"You worry too much." I take a sip of the potion and it's even worse cold. "Eek."

"Should've downed it while it was warm." Jesse holds his hand out for the cup. "I'll warm it up. The effects won't be as powerful, but if it'll help you finish it off, so be it. We'll have you repeat a dose in an hour."

Regardless of the pain, I refuse to take in more of the swamp sludge after this. I down the rest and hand the cup to him.

He chuckles as he takes the cup. "That's my girl."

Soren nods once to me. I smile at him and watch as he walks toward the door. The sound of the handle twisting after the door closes lets me know he's gone.

He'll be back soon enough. Just as soon as he tracks down Savannah. She'll come. I have no doubts.

Jesse immediately launches into the tale of how Gideon and Soren handed Jackson Cane his ass. He embellishes his actions in the fight with flourishing motions and as his tale goes on, I laugh, feeling less and less pain.

"Gideon takes out three shadow wolves. At once." He holds up his index fingers on both hands.

Gideon chuckles as his eyes focus on me. I'm finding it hard to focus and I want to know what was put in that potion. Instead, I ask, "So what's the plan now?"

"Now," Gideon says, "We wait. Make sure your father is well, and finish out this school year. Over the summer, Soren and I will continue to train you. I imagine you'll want to spend time with your father as well."

"Very much so." I nod. The motion feels like I'm moving in water. My body feels like it's being pulled toward the back of the couch. I slump against it, breathing in deep the smell of the fire. "What about the Order and Anderson?"

"We'll keep an eye out for them." Gideon's voice sounds farther away despite him sitting less than five feet from me.

Before long, my eyes become heavy. Milo brings me a pillow and blanket from another room in the house. As I lay down, I smile up at him.

"Thanks, Milo."

He nods. "Get some good rest."

My eyes close, and a blissful sleep comes over me.

CHAPTER FORTY

I slowly open my eyes as the last of the fire burns to slightly glowing red embers. The smell of smoke lingers in the air, and there's a slight chill. Sitting up from the couch, I stretch my arms over my head and yawn.

There's no pain. Granted, I'm a little sore. But thankfully, there's no stabbing pain.

I stand from the couch and shake the remnants of sleep from me as I make my way toward the room where my father is. I assume the men are sleeping and Savannah was either in one of the rooms or has gone home. Either way, the rest of the house is whisper quiet.

I step into the room and see that my father's sitting

up in bed, alert, well, and looking younger. His color has returned to his skin and it seems some of his strength has as well. Though he's still thin, a few good rounds of eating out to take care of that.

My eyes blur as my heart beats with joy, and I rush to my father.

"Wren, my little bird. You're so grown up!" He holds his arms out to me.

I lean into him and breathe in deep the familiar scent of my childhood years. "I'm so glad you are okay."

He holds me tighter to him, petting my head and swaying from side to side. "I've missed you so much."

I sniff as the sting of tears nips at my eyes. "I've missed you too."

He squeezes me even tighter then releases his hold on me. A gleam of marvel and happiness shines through his eyes as he looks at me. He barely blinks, almost as if he's afraid that if he does, I'll disappear. I take a seat on the edge of his bed and hold his hand. His deep brown eyes study me as much as I study him, taking in all the changes of his appearance like the grey hair and the salt and pepper stubble covering his cheeks and chin. His dark eyes glimmer in the lights of the room, and it's all I can do just to sit there and smile.

I finally have my father back. And it's better than I thought it would be. My heart soars with happiness and relief.

But a dark cloud fogs my mind, reminding me of the things Aunt Patricia had said. My face relaxes into a frown.

"What's the matter?"

I sigh. I suppose it's better to treat this like a band-aid and get the tougher stuff out of the way. "Aunt Patricia told me you're a criminal."

No sooner did my aunt's name escape my lips did a shadow cross in front of my father's eyes. A pinch forms between his nearly straight eyebrows. He squeezes my hands and commands my attention.

"Whatever they've told you about me, it's not true. I'm not a criminal, and I certainly wouldn't have done something to jeopardize my freedom. Do you believe me?"

Despite his aged face and worn-down posture, I still see the man who raised me, comforted me, and made me happy before my young life was turned upside down. I give him an affirmative nod, letting him know that I do believe him.

He even speaks in the serious tone he would give me when something was so important that I needed to listen and hang on to every word like my life depended on it. Most of those moments were when he first taught me the laws of magic. So, in essence, my life did depend on his words and still does.

I have no reason to disbelieve him. It's the Order that's shown itself to be dangerous and untrustworthy. "I knew you couldn't be a criminal."

He gives my hand a gentle squeeze of reassurance and it works. "You must have a lot of questions. I have a few of my own."

I cock my head to the side and tuck a strand of hair behind my head. "Like what?"

"How was school?" He smiles, and I laugh. "Are you getting good grades? Building on everything that I taught you when you were a child?"

He joins in on my laughing, probably thinking of all the at-home lessons, including the mishaps, that he guided me through as he taught me magic.

"I love being at the academy. I've even made some friends." I grin as I motion in the direction of the living room where the men had been.

He levels his gaze on me. "I've met them. For them to risk this much for you, and me, that shows me they are good men. I'm glad you have found each other. Now, with that said, are you being safe? Do we need to have the talk?"

Another giggle bubbles out of me as I shake my head. "I've got that covered, Dad, but thanks."

"Interesting group." He takes on a pensive expression. "I suppose they're all right."

"Good. I'd hate to disappoint you by hanging out with the riff-raff you disapprove of."

He chuckles. "Your turn."

All my burning questions rush to the forefront of my mind at once. And the most burning question of all is, "Why did you disappear?"

"I didn't have a choice. I hope you understand that. It was go with the Order, or watch you get hurt. They forced me to work on various projects. Each time I failed, I was beaten and tortured, and they promised the same would happen to you. And I just couldn't sit back and let them hurt you. So long as I did what they asked of me, you were safe."

"Why did Deacon Lawrence keep you as a prisoner?"

He shrugs. "Absolute power corrupts absolutely. He got power-hungry and became obsessed with the power the meteor promised. It consumed him and ate him alive, twisting his soul. As soon as his superiors caught on, they increased the detail covering me, as you probably saw."

"That's certainly one way to put it."

"Did he hurt you?" There was a thick edge of anger in his voice.

"Not as much as I hurt him."

He relaxes a little. "Good."

I nod. "Is that why he wanted me? Because of the meteorite?"

He shakes his head. "No. He didn't know you had the last piece until right before I sent you the letter. He figured it out somehow. That's why I warned you."

"You saved my life." I smile warmly. "Thank you."

"No, my darling daughter. You saved mine."

I think about that for a moment and nod. "Yeah, I guess I did." I take a few moments and ask, "Was Mom's death really an accident?"

Tears well up in his eyes as he looks away, staring at a spot on his blanket. "No." His voice cracks. "The Order did it, trying to get me to come with them. They killed her first to send a message. Got me alone and showed me how close they were to doing the same to you. I knew they wouldn't hesitate if I didn't go with them. I just could—"

"Who did Deacon Lawrence work for?" I ask, voice even, though I felt a lump in my throat.

My father's eyes meet mine. "I don't know. I never saw them or spoke to them."

I nod. "Well, I'm glad you're finally safe. Now you can heal, and we can pick up where we left off."

He heaves a sigh. "You need to know something…"

A pinch forms in my forehead. "What?"

"There you are!" Savannah's voice bubbles toward me. I look over my shoulder as she enters the room. She stops on the other side of my dad's bed and lays a hand on his forehead. "How are you feeling, Mr. Blackwood?"

"Better, thanks to you."

She smiles. "My pleasure." She sets her gaze on me. "You, missy, better come see me once you're done catching up with your Dad, okay?"

I smile. "You got it."

"I'm going to let your men know to stop the panicked manhunt. You're safe."

I giggle. "Oh, great. Yes. Please do."

She waves as she turns and leaves the room.

I face my dad again. "What were you going to say?"

He tries to sit up and winces. "It can wait. Sounds like you are needed before the house is reduced to rubble."

I shake my head. "Soren is a beast, I tell you."

He chuckles. "Go. We'll have time to catch up now."

"Promise?" I stare deep into my father's eyes.

His eyes crinkle at the corners as he nods. "Promise."

I stand up and leave the room. My father's right. Now that he's back, I have all the time in the world to catch up with him. And I'm very much looking forward to reconnecting with him.

CHAPTER FORTY-ONE

Fireworks burst in the air, lighting up the warm night sky as the summer celebration for all the graduates comes to a close.

Smiling, I think of everything that's happened to me these past couple of months. I rescued my father and was able to set him up in the safehouse where I visit him every other weekend so we can catch up—I intend to keep my promise. We've all agreed that no one outside our group should know about my father, including Aunt Patricia. She probably still mistakenly believes the propaganda that he fooled around with unsanctioned magic.

Not only do my visits with my father allow me to catch up with him and oversee his healing progress, but it also gives me and my men time to formulate a plan. We still need to clear my dad's name if he's ever going to step out in public again. Also, we haven't forgotten about Anderson.

As the bursts of colors from fireworks come to life and slowly trickle to the ocean water below, I smile in anticipation of my next trip to see my dad. We've actually resumed our popcorn and movie nights, and Savannah was nice enough to visit once or twice and join in.

It's the most normal time I've had since my father disappeared from my life over six years ago, and I'm so grateful to have him back.

I gain one, and I'm losing one.

This was Soren's last year. I shift my gaze to him talking with the other graduates, dressed in long flowing graduation gowns that sparkle with the house emblem on the back. I wonder what he's talking about. He seems happy, proud. He nods and smiles every once in a while, even catching my gaze. I don't know what's in store for our relationship in the future. He keeps side-stepping the topic each time I bring it up. I'm not sure what he has planned, but I know it has to be something big. It's a surprise, probably.

Whatever he has up his sleeve, I know I won't be able to keep him all to myself. He has a duty to the magusari. I wonder how they fit into his plans.

The weekends that I don't spend with my father, I'm enjoying time with my men, or I'm with Savannah. She's the closest thing I have to a sister, and it feels wonderful knowing that she's loyal and willing to help us in our quest. Also, it doesn't escape me that I've put a year behind me. Just three more to go. The progress I've made brings another smile to my face.

Movement catches my eye and I face Milo and Jesse joining me, leaning against the wall of one of the gardens in the vast island.

"Well, well, look what we've found here, Milo." Jesse's hungry eyes take me in. I almost forgot I dressed up in a black pencil skirt and smooth green blouse with black ballet flats. I Figured the occasion called for something that would get me out of a school uniform but was a little more formal than my normal comfortable jeans and a t-shirt.

"You look good," Milo says leaning against the wall on my left.

I bump him with my elbow. "You don't look so bad yourself."

Milo wears a pair of stone wash jeans, a leather belt, and a white t-shirt under a black peacoat.

He chuckles to look down at himself and returns his beautiful brown eyes to me. "Yeah. I guess I look all right."

We chuckle together.

Jesse leans over my shoulder and whispers in my ear. "You look good enough to eat."

Delightful tingles and shivers quake through me, especially at the emphasis of "eat."

"Devil." I smile.

"You like it. Can't deny it now."

I shrug. "Maybe."

"So, going to spend some of the summer with your dad?" Milo shoves his hands into his jacket.

I nod. "Part of it. I'm also training with Soren and Gideon."

"Any idea yet what he has planned for next year?" Milo's gaze finds Soren in the crowd. He snaps his head in an upward nod.

I look over and see Soren walking over and shake my head. "I wish I did."

"Yes, the dark and brooding Soren certainly knows how to keep a secret." Jesse leans against the wall and presses his shoulder gently against mine.

"You say that like you already know."

He shrugs.

I playfully roll my eyes and shrug. "Figures. Well, two can play that game."

He shifts his gaze to me, and his lips quirk up. "Touché."

Soren stops in front of me and holds out his hand. "A word?"

"Maybe..." I take his hand as he groans.

"Dammit, woman. Can I talk to you?" He pulls me away as he grips my hand.

"Not if you rip my arm off." I laugh. "What's the hurry?"

"Maybe I just wanted to spend a little time with you before the night is over and summer hits."

"Uh-huh." Yeah, I totally believe that one. "You're still training me over the summer. Nice try though. So, what do you really want?"

"I told you."

I stare a hole into the back of his head as he continues to drag me across the garden to a bench overlooking the ocean. "Fine. Then tell me what your plans are for next year."

"You won't leave it alone, will you?" He stops and turns my face toward his with a gentle touch of his fingers. He then gives my arm a small tug, pulling me close to his chest.

His eyes take hold of mine and don't let go for several long, beautiful moments. He lowers his lips to mine and says, "You'll just have to wait and see."

With that, he walks off and leaves me to the amazing view alone. I look around and slap my thighs.

"What was the point of bringing me out here?" I shout after him, knowing full and well he won't answer. His form has already blended in with the shadows.

"Hello, Miss Blackwood."

The voice and the rush of my magic send electrifying sensations through me. I turn and face Gideon as he approaches me.

"Let me guess, you're here to fill me in on Soren's little secret."

He shakes his head. "No. Sorry to disappoint." He stops right in front of me and leads me to the bench. We take a seat, and he leans in a little toward me. "I came to have some time with you."

I narrow my eyes on him. "What's really going on? You men been in the punch?"

He shrugs. "Nope."

"I don't get it." I heave a sigh, shaking my head in confusion.

He wraps his fingers around mine, using the back of the bench to hide the small, affectionate gesture. We still can't reveal our relationship. Not yet. "Your first year is behind you. You have three more years until you leave Blackbriar behind. It's going to be two months before Jesse and Milo see you again. And it'll be two long weeks until I get to spend time with you for training."

"Good point." Now that he says it like that, it sounds like forever. And limited. My heart skips a beat at the realization that Blackbriar is temporary. I shove that thought aside to focus on the present.

"You're leaving in the morning, and we all want just a few moments of time with you before the night is over."

I smile and lean into him, resting my head on his shoulder. "That's sweet."

He leans his head on mine and we sit there watching the ocean for a few moments. "This is one of my favorite places on the island."

"I can see why." With a view like this, it's a hard one to beat.

Footsteps approach, and judging by my magic's reaction, it's Jesse and Milo. They stand on either side of the bench. Before long, Soren returns to us with Lady Alene and Savannah.

My family.

I smile at each of them. Savannah rushes in for a hug, and I nearly topple over from the force.

"I'm going to miss your face so much!"

I chuckle. "I'll miss you too."

She pulls back and settles her violet eyes on mine. "You better write to me this time, damn it."

"Okay, okay!" I raise my hands in surrender.

Lady Alene approaches. She holds out her hands toward me and I slip mine into them. "Your growth has been a gift to watch. I look forward to the next school year as we will be working together more often."

"I'm looking forward to it." I smile. And it's true. Having more time with the patron of our academy is beyond amazing. I feel like I hardly had a chance to talk to her beyond an exchange of simple pleasantries.

"We're all here." Soren's voice echoes between us.

I realize I'm standing in the center of a small circle, and everyone around me has joined hands. Magic lights up within their hands and all at once, they quickly raise their hands above their heads, and more fireworks fly into the sky. Beautiful blends of white and red, sparkles of purple and orange, all gliding through the air in a synchronized way that reminds me of fireworks shows I attended as a kid.

I shake my head as I crane my neck to watch the colors burst across the night sky. Tears sting my eyes as I realize they are celebrating their connection to me. They did this for me. My family.

I adore each and every single person surrounding me, thankful for their very presence in my life.

I don't know what I'd do without them. But with them, I'm unstoppable.

Wren, Soren, Gideon, Jesse, and Milo will be back in
The Hex of Blackbriar Academy, coming soon!

Join the exclusive, fans-only Facebook group to get
release news & updates.

Read on for a special note from the author.

Hey, Babe!

Another book is done! Yeah, baby! I'm so happy that you are still with me and you loved the first book so much! I hope you love this next book just the same!

Wren is such a strong woman, and she continues to show us this in this next book as she tries to figure out how to rescue her father and get to know her aunt, who seems a bit too guarded. It was a joy to watch things unfold for Wren as she tries to uncover just what keeps her aunt so guarded and how she takes bits and pieces of information and really tries to digest them into nuggets of facts.

I'm quite proud of our badass.

What are your thoughts on the Aunt Patricia? Do you think she's got some hidden agenda going on or do you believe she's just guarded from whatever troubles happened to her in her past?

What do you think Wren's father's story is? Is he a criminal or is it all a part of the great conspiracy?

Wren's balanced her life quite well, I think, and I hope you are satisfied with the growth between her and Jesse. He's a bit of a horn dog and he knows all the right delicious ways to bring that passion out of Wren. Don't you agree?

His story is gut-wrenching, but his heart is in the right place. I warn you though, tissues!

Swoon!

I especially love how determined Wren is to stand up for what she believes in, but also is willing to accept a bit of constructive criticism from her men. She's learning to be a part of a team, which is new to her after spending years with brutish trolls. Besides, relationships and friendships are still very new for her, but I think she's adjusting quite well. What do you think?

Wren and Savannah's friendship is truly starting to form into besties forever. Savannah is always a nurturing and loving personality, she's that bubbly girl next door who everyone wants to know. And the way she steps up for Wren and her men makes me super happy.

How about you?

So, have you decided on a favorite guy yet? It's such a *hard* (pun intended) decision, I know. But, I'm curious.

What about Anderson's deal? What are your thoughts on him? What do you think is in store for our power team next? Which guy do you think is gonna seal the deal with Wren next?

You'll have to read the next book to find out!

Until next time, babe!

Keep on being your beautiful, badass self.

-Olivia

PS. Amazon won't tell you when the next Dragon Dojo Brotherhood book will come out, but there are several ways you can stay informed.

1) **Soar on over to the Facebook group, Olivia's secret club for cool ladies,** so we can hang out! I designed it *especially* for badass babes like you. Consider this as your invite! We talk about kickass heroines, gorgeous men, our favorite fantasy romances, and... did I mention pictures of *gorgeous men*?

2) **Follow me directly on Amazon**. To do this, **head to my profile** and click the Follow button beneath my picture. That will prompt Amazon to notify you when I release a new book. You'll just need to check your emails.

3) **You can join my mailing list by going to** https://wispvine.com/newsletter/olivia-ash-email-signup/. This lets me slide into your inbox and basically means we become best friends. Yep, I'm pretty sure that's how it works.

Doing one of these or **all three** (for best results) is the best way to make sure you get an update every time a new volume of the *Blackbriar Academy* series is released. Talk to you soon!

ABOUT THE AUTHOR

OLIVIA ASH

Olivia Ash spends her time dreaming up the perfect men to challenge, love, and protect her strong heroines (who actually don't need protecting at all). Her stories are meant to take you on a journey into the world of the characters and make you want to stay there.

Reviews are the best way to show Olivia that you care about her stories and want other people discover them. If you enjoyed this novel, please consider leaving a review at Amazon. Every review helps the author and she appreciates the time you take to write them.